LORD LUCAN: MY STORY

The Lord Lucan Scandal is one of the greatest and most extraordinary mysteries of the twentieth-century. Ever since Lucky Lord Lucan disappeared in 1974 after the murder of his nanny, the world has wondered what happened to Britain's most dashing Peer. Here, in his own hand, is the answer. This is Lord Lucan's personal memoir of his life as the world's most infamous fugitive. It is the story of an Old Etonian Earl on the run; of how a man became a murderer; and how a life-long friendship soured into an enduring hate. Here, for the first time, is the full monstrous account of the life of Lord Lucan. This is his story.

Books by William Coles
Published by The House of Ulverscroft:

THE WELL-TEMPERED CLAVIER

Edited by
WILLIAM COLES

◆

LORD LUCAN: MY STORY

Complete and Unabridged

ULVERSCROFT
Leicester

First published in Great Britain in 2009 by
Legend Press Ltd., London

First Large Print Edition
published 2010
by arrangement with
Legend Press Ltd., London

The moral right of the author has been asserted

This is a work of fiction and all characters, other
than those clearly in the public domain, and place
names, other than those well-established are fictitious
and any resemblance is purely coincidental.

British Library CIP Data

Coles, William.
  Lord Lucan: my story.
  1. Lucan, Richard John Bingham, Earl of, *1934* – – -
Fiction. 2. Missing persons- -England- -Fiction.
3. Biographical fiction. 4. Large type books.
I. Title
823.9′2–dc22

ISBN 978–1–44480–133–0

Published by
F. A. Thorpe (Publishing)
Anstey, Leicestershire

Set by Words & Graphics Ltd.
Anstey, Leicestershire
Printed and bound in Great Britain by
T. J. International Ltd., Padstow, Cornwall

This book is printed on acid-free paper

Dedication

To all those other passengers on this
Ship of Fools who have ventured everything
on a single roll of the dice.
I only hope they fared better than I did.

Editor's Note

The Lord Lucan saga has been one of the greatest and most enduring mysteries of the 20th Century. The very name 'Lord Lucan' has now entered the English language as a byword for the far-fetched and the simply unbelievable. His sudden disappearance in 1974 after the murder of his nanny Sandra Rivett has the fairytale quality of a modern-day Rip Van Winkle. And ever since, the world has been speculating as to his whereabouts. Did he escape to South Africa, to South America, or even to Alaska? Or did he take his own life after realising that his final throw of the dice had — yet again — ended in abject failure?

Here, and in his own hand, is the answer. It is Lord Lucan's personal account of his life as the world's most infamous fugitive.

It is not for me to spoil Lord Lucan's narrative by alluding to the story. But I do think it fair to say that there are a number of anomalies about the text. Sometimes it is difficult to know where reality ends and fantasy begins.

When I was first confronted with the job of

editing this sprawling manuscript, I was tempted to clear up some of the major inconsistencies. But having immersed myself in the project, I realised that these very anomalies have their own charm, as they reveal so much about Lucan's character.

It was also noticeable just how much Lucan's writing style seems to vary. From one chapter to the next, his words can change from bluff to tearfully maudlin. And although Lucan was by no means a writer, his style occasionally has a startling directness and candour.

My editing has largely consisted of clearing up some of Lucan's spelling and grammatical infelicities, as well as putting this hodge-podge of reminiscences into a sort of sequential order. He frequently switches tenses, flip-flopping from present to past, but for the most part I have let these inconsistencies stand. Three quasi-dream sequences, however, have been excised altogether. They were incomprehensible. Should any reader care to have a look at these rambling screeds, or fancies that they might be able to make head or tail of them, I would be happy to supply the details.

For a number of legal reasons, I am unable to reveal the full provenance of the Lucan papers. What I can say, however, is that in

2004, a cache of handwritten documents ended up in the vaults of a leading London solicitors. Two years ago, I was approached with a view to editing these papers. I can only hope that I have done the manuscript justice.

Finally, it should be noted that Lord Lucan levels a number of venomous accusations at his one-time friends, particularly Sir James Goldsmith. I am sure that if the ever-litigious Sir James were still alive today, we would already have been hit with the first libel writ. I was in some doubt as to whether to include these sundry rants against Sir James, but in the end opted to stick with the spirit of the manuscript. I realise that, given his fragile state of mind, Lucan is not a credible witness. But those who seek to defend Sir James must also concede that he was a charlatan of the first order. I am therefore more than happy to leave it to the readers to sort the wheat from the chaff when it comes to weighing up Sir James's many calumnies.

I have included a number of footnotes, the better to clarify and embellish some of the points that Lucan breezily skates over.

But, for the rest of it, this is wholly the work of Lord Lucan. This is his story.

William Coles — Edinburgh, May 2009

1

This is the story of a vile man — and I am that man and I committed a most wicked deed.

There can be no excuses. There are no mitigating circumstances. It was one of the most evil things a man can do.

That events did not turn out as I'd planned is irrelevant. For what I had set out to do, and what I set into motion on that black November night, was an infamous act in its own right.

The cards did indeed fall differently from how I expected. I could never have predicted quite so catastrophic a turn of events. But that is the very nature of events. Things frequently do not turn out as we would like them.

Nevertheless, it was I who conceived the whole of that crazed venture and I who accepts full responsibility for the consequences.

And now that I am in the very twilight of my days, it is time to make full and frank confession of my wasted life. From start to finish, it has been such a waste and there have been so many sins along the way. Most of them venial sins of the flesh.

But there is one sin for which I can never be forgiven.

And I would be the first to admit that.

* * *

Before I embark on my tale, I would like to make two things plain. The first is — and I know this may sound far-fetched — that at the time I believed I had a higher motive. Whatever I did, no matter how appalling, I believed that I was doing for the good of my three children.

You might well say that I was primarily acting out of selfishness and I could not possibly disagree. But, how ever warped it might seem, at the time I truly believed that what I was doing was ultimately for the best for my son George and two daughters Frances and Camilla.

I can almost hear the hollow laughs of disbelief. How on earth does a man plot to kill his estranged wife, leaving his children motherless, yet claim that it's 'for the best'?

It sounds laughable, I know it does. Worse, it sounds utterly self-deluding and pathetic.

But if you are to comprehend anything at all of my life, you must understand that although my judgement may have been twisted beyond measure, at the time I sincerely believed that what I did, I did for the good of my children. All I cared about was them.

They were — and continue to be — the three things that I cherish most dearly in this evil old heart of mine.

And it is, perhaps, a small irony that my whole monstrous plan was conceived so that I could spend more time with my children. As it turned out, I have never laid eyes on them since. I have studied their pictures, I have read their quotes in the newspapers, but I have not seen them, have not kissed their darling cheeks, in over 20 years. To my eternal shame, I have also had to witness how that single dark deed has cast such a hideous shadow over all three of their lives.

That, then, is the first thing you need to understand about my life and my motives. It can never be right to do what I did. But at the time, at least, I thought that ends were justified by means.

The second thing you must realise is the enormity of the price that I have had to pay. I know that this is as nothing compared to the price that Sandra, dear Sandra, had to pay all those years ago, and that while she lies dead in her grave, I at least have been allowed that wonderful miracle of life.

But what a stinking misery of a life it has

been — and, in so far as one can discuss that airy conceit of natural justice, it would be fair to say that I have received my just desserts. Not that what has occurred to me has even been a penny, a scintilla, of the price that Sandra had to pay.

But, it has been a price, an awful price, and to this day I still wonder if it wouldn't have been better if I had done away with myself the moment I realised the whole affair had been botched beyond belief.

I didn't though. Always I waited for the next turn of the card, hoping for something better to turn up. Although it never did. Year after year, things became ever more terrible. In fact, rather than being nicknamed 'Lucky', it sometimes feels as if a more appropriate name might be 'Cursed by God'. That has been my life and what little I have left of it.

I must just say one thing more.

I am very much to blame.

I am the guilty party.

And, as a result, I cannot possibly complain or bleat about the hand that has been dealt me. But — and I pause for a moment on how to write this without sounding full of impious self-pity — it would also be true to say that there has been a man in my life who has not helped matters; a man, that is, who year on year has applied the thumbscrews and who has been making my penance just that little bit more ghastly.

Far be it from me to rail at the odious behaviour of another man towards myself; after all, it was me who all those years ago took the decision to snuff out another human's life and so I certainly cannot complain about the injustices inflicted upon me. But for the past 20 years, it seems as if there has been a malign force in my life, who has sat on my shoulder and who has ensured that, like the Apples of Sodom, every little joy has turned to ashes in my mouth.

The oddity is that, ever since my childhood, I had considered this man to be a friend. A strange, unreliable, unprincipled man, but a friend nonetheless.

He's been described as so many things over the years from a millionaire *bon viveur* to a swashbuckling buccaneer. But for myself I now consider him to be nothing other than the devil incarnate.

The name of this man is Jimmy Goldsmith — and for the best part of 20 years, it has been his especial delight to spend his millions on tormenting me.

I had known for some time that Goldsmith wished me ill.

It was only very recently, however, that I came to understand quite why.

2

My given name is Richard John Bingham — but you will probably know me better as Lucky Lord Lucan, the peer who botched his wife's murder and who disappeared off the face of the earth.

I believe that the story of my crime and my subsequent flight has now become a British legend. In a way, it has become as much a part of British history as that other great mystery that was instigated by my great-great-grandfather, the Charge of the Light Brigade. All my childhood I was brought up on the story of that heroic but insane charge at Balaclava, and could recite that Tennyson poem from the age of six. I can still remember the hair standing up on the nape of my neck as my father rasped to me at my bed-time, 'Half a league, half a league, Half a league onward, All in the valley of Death rode the six hundred!'

Like the 3rd Earl of Lucan, George Bingham, I also contrived to make a historically bad miscalculation — though mine had a far more miserable and pedestrian setting than that of the Crimean War. But then my great-great-grandfather's botch-up was of a scale that's only possible — or indeed conceivable — within the Forces.

What our two moments of infamy have in common is that they have both taken wing. There was something about them that captured the public's imagination and since then they have become part of the very fabric of our nation's collective history.

And what has kept them spinning, and what turned them into daily provender in pubs and kitchens and dinner parties across the land, was not the story itself but the mystery. If there were no mystery, then all the strings of our stories could have been tied up and our tales safely consigned to the history books.

In my great-great-grandfather's case, no-one has the faintest idea what was going through his head when he ordered his cavalry to attack the Russian cannon. Even now, more than a century later, we can still argue the toss, can cite any amount of evidence, but at the end of it all, your guess is as good as mine or the next man's as to what happened on that fateful day in 1854.[1]

And so it is with the murder of poor Sandra Rivett, who at the age of just 29 was hammered to death in the basement of my estranged wife's house in Belgravia. I admit that there is still some mystery as to what happened on that night in 1974.[2]

But — and I write this without any trace of conceit or self-aggrandisement — I am also aware that what has transformed the case from that of a squalid domestic murder into something altogether more electrifying has been not so much Sandra's death as my disappearance. And the disappearance, to boot, of a peer of the realm who had worn the family ermine in the House of Lords.

Were it not for the murder, I think I might have enjoyed the notoriety. At times, it used to seem as if I were the Scarlet Pimpernel — 'We seek him here, we seek him there' — and with that came the delicious knowledge that I was the only man on earth who truly possessed the answer to this conundrum. But, as it is, blameless Sandra is dead, and the knowledge of that has entirely soured any pleasure that I might have taken at becoming, quite literally, a legend in my own lifetime.

So before I begin this story proper, I would like to apologise most profoundly to Sandra's friends and relatives for the hell that I've put them through. I apologise to my wife and to my children. And, not that it's worth a damn, but if I could, I would also apologise to Sandra.

Sandra, I'm sorry.

* ★ *

There have been over 30 books written about Sandra's death and my subsequent disappearance. I have read a number of them, with their far-fetched ideas about what happened on that November night in 1974 and their grandiose theories about what happened to me afterwards. Most of them read like those cliché-ridden penny-dreadfuls I used to wade through, rolling my eyes in disbelief after each page of that drivel.

What irked me most was the utter certainty of the writers, as if there wasn't a trace of doubt in their minds about where I've been holed up since the murder. (Or 'lying doggo' as they always call it. I happened to use the excruciating expression 'lying doggo' in one of the last letters that I ever wrote as Lord Lucan, and since then it has cropped up in every single book about me.) The one consistency among these Lucan authors has been that every man jack of them claims to have tracked me round the world and to be on the very brink of bringing me in.

As far as I know, not a single one of them has even come close.

Along with the books, I believe there have been hundreds, if not thousands, of sightings. I've been spotted in Africa, the Orkneys and even as far afield as the Antarctic, where I've apparently been whiling away my lonely life on top of an ice floe. Most of these sightings have usually ended up in the papers, along with a grainy photo of myself — though, for all their use, they might as well have used the pictures to prove the existence of the Abominable Snowman. So I would now like to put it on record that almost every one of these alleged sightings was without foundation.

Though there was a time, just the once, when I was very nearly undone. So close. So desperately close. And ever since, I've always wondered why she never did turn me in. Maybe, in the end, she did love me. All of that I will come to in due course.

Most of the books about me tend to start with the moment of high drama — that is with Sandra's murder. The authors so love to go into the detail about how Sandra was hit six, seven times over the head with a lead pipe before being bundled up into a US mailbag. After that they describe my drive to the home of dear old Susan Maxwell-Scott, my ever more frantic phone calls, my last scribbled letters. And that's the last they know. To all intents and purposes, that two-hour meeting with Susan was the last time on earth that a human being was publicly prepared to admit to seeing the 7th Earl of Lucan.

And after that — well, for the authors and the journalists, not to mention the general public, my life and my story has been a blank canvas. There was of course the car and the missing boat. But you could paint any picture you wanted. Take your pick: drowned at sea as my scuppered boat sank to the bottom of the Channel; whisked abroad by my cronies at the Clermont Club; or even suicide and being fed to the tigers at John Aspinall's zoo. (I don't know how that last story came about, but of all the far-fetched tales about my disappearance, this one actually bore the closest resemblance to the truth.)

My various biographers have always revelled in the details of my earlier life, or 'back-story' — and what a revoltingly shallow back-story it was too. Page after page of tales about my incorrigible gambling, my furious marital spats and all the rest of that tiresome filth that went to make up the disaster of my life. I can barely bring myself to write another word about it as it was all so unutterably tedious. Do you know that during my entire married life, I always had smoked salmon and lamb chops for lunch? Almost every day, without exception. I was in a rut the size of the Grand Canyon.

But my point, anyway, is that since so

much has already been written about the night of the murder, and so many acres of print have been used to describe my louche, amoral character to the Nth degree, I do not feel any pressing need to recap on facts that are already very much in the public domain.

Later, I may well touch on my marriage, my children and the events of that night. But as to my character, amoral or otherwise, I am quite sure you will be more than capable of judging that for yourself. I do not especially feel the need to flag up any of my more significant character defects before I've even started.

And so to begin. There has been so much speculation about what happened after the evening of Sandra's murder. So many people have tried to fill in the blank canvas of my life. And now I will tell you the truth of it.

3

It speaks volumes about the enfeebled state of my mind at the time that I had actually believed that one of my plans would come off. I had been plotting the murder of my estranged wife Veronica for over a year and I thought I had it planned to the last detail.

It had not even occurred to me to have a back-up plan, some sort of escape pod just in case things started to unravel. Though given my previous form, I think it might have been wise to have had not just a Plan B, but a Plan C, D and E, all the way through to Plan Z. Because, make no mistake, although for a very short time in my life I had been considered 'lucky', the truth was that since my marriage I'd been the kiss of death to any project that came within a mile of me. I had the opposite of the Midas touch; everything that came into my grasp was by some magical alchemy turned into ordure.

I knew this full well, but still I'd always been a gambler and it was in my soul — and even the unluckiest gambler in Christendom always believes that everything will come good on the next throw of the dice.

There was, I believe, one other reason why I had no back-up plan that night, and that was because the consequences of failure were just too awful to contemplate. For on that night, I was a gambler who was betting the farm: not just everything I owned, but my life, my family and my entire reputation.

If it came off, then all well and good, and — or so I naively believed at the time — my problems would be over. Hand in hand, my three children and I would walk together through green fields into that golden sunset.

And if it did not come off . . .

If something went wrong . . .

The consequences were too awful to contemplate.

So the result of all this was that I did not contemplate anything other than that my hellish scheme would come off in its 100 per cent entirety. It was the power of positive thinking. Since I was not even countenancing the possibility of failure, then it could not, could not possibly occur.

But it did happen — in the sort of spectacular fashion that only a Lucan could manage. If it weren't for Sandra's death, it could have come straight out of a West End farce. Of all the various scenarios that might have occurred that night, there had seemed to be but two options: either Veronica was killed

— or she survived. Either one or t'other, just red or black on the roulette wheel. Never once did it occur to me that there might in fact be a third scenario: that my wife would survive, and that it would be the nanny who ended up on the mortuary slab.

As I said, it takes a Lucan to turn a set-back into a disaster of nightmarish proportions. Sandra was lying dead in the cellar; Veronica was screaming blue murder; and I was leaving London for the last time. I have never set foot in that city since. All I knew was that within hours, the entire British police force would be searching for me. Worse, I didn't have a plan.

The one thing that I had catered for was efficiently and permanently to dispose of my wife's body. And now that she was still very much alive — alive and cursing me from the rooftops — I had not the vaguest notion of what to do next.

I remember how my brain galloped through all the possibilities. From one thing to the next, from giving myself up to doing myself in; and then what would happen if I did give myself up? Would I try to deny it all, or would I be the man and make a clean breast of it? You can see, perhaps, that I still had a number of options available to me, and the only thing they had in common was that they all seemed particularly unpleasant.

The friends that I called up that night all said the same thing. Give myself up, they said. Turn myself in. Let the police sort it all out.

But of course they were going to say that — because they all believed me when I'd told them I'd had nothing to do with Sandra's murder. And if I were innocent, then obviously I had nothing to hide, and the best course of action by far was to go to the police.

A perfectly reasonable course of action — if, that is, I'd been innocent.

The truth, though, was that I was in it up to the eyeballs. Giving myself up did not really seem like an option. Can you imagine it? The first hereditary peer in I don't know how many centuries to be convicted of murder? It might even have come to trial by my peers. Then jailed for life and the ignominy of being shunned by my children and friends. Too awful to contemplate.

With hindsight I would have given myself up the very next day. Anything at all, even a full life-term in the Scrubs, would have been preferable to the exquisite agony of my life over the last 20 years. And given the unusual circumstances of the case, I think I might well have been out in ten. Who knows — I might even be on speaking terms with my children: they might have found it in their hearts to forgive me. All these scenarios I have come to contemplate during my infinite hours of soul-searching.

But — as obviously you know — I did not take my chances with the British judicial system. It was not in my nature, and that nature was part formed by my schooling. Of the many things I'd learned at Eton, one of the key lessons of survival had been that simple adage 'Deny, Deny, Deny'. Never own up. Never admit guilt. Lie through your teeth. Just hold your nerve and there's a chance that something better might turn up.

I'd just left Susan Maxwell-Scott's house in Uckfield, Sussex. She'd given me a drink, we'd talked things through and, although she'd offered me a bed for the night, I had left before my resolve weakened. I'd fobbed her off by telling her that I had to get back 'to clear things up'.

But I tell you now, I never had the slightest intention of going back. At the time, anything at all seemed preferable to limply turning myself into a pawn and handing myself in to the police. That would have been craven — throwing in the hand just because I didn't like the look of my cards. At least, for a little while yet, I was still master of my own destiny. And what a destiny it would turn out to be.

Outside it was as dark as the Earl of Hell's waistcoat. I'd been driving for about 30 minutes in that beaten-up Ford Corsair that Michael Stoop had lent me a couple of weeks earlier. The same Corsair in which I'd planned to transport Veronica's dead body to Newhaven dock before dumping her in the Channel. It sounds brutally blunt when I write it like that. But there's never a pretty way to write about murder.

I remember how every instinct in my body was yammering at me to flee — jump into my powerboat, *Charybdis*, and head for the Continent. What I'd do once I'd reached France or Holland, I had no idea. I had no money, no passport, no change of clothes, not a razor, nor even a toothbrush. I had nothing but the clothes I stood up in — grey slacks, still wet from the blood that I'd had to sponge off, a shirt and jumper. I didn't have a hope. Most likely they'd have caught me on the Channel, and if not there I'd have been caught thumbing a lift by the side of the road, or sleeping rough in the woods. Without help, I didn't stand a dog's chance.

For some minutes I'd been driving aimlessly, heading I suppose in a sort of southerly direction for Newhaven where I'd left the boat. But in a sudden moment of clarity, I realised it was pointless: if I were going to try and escape by boat, I might as well give myself up then and there. At least I'd avoid the indignity of being caught on the run after a month living like a vagrant.

It was misty as hell. Even though I was only dawdling, I remember the shock as I nearly ran over a badger by the side of the road. I jinked the wheel as the car slewed to the side, before pulling over at the next layby. I didn't have a clue where I was, somewhere in the wilds of Sussex. What was the point in driving any more when I didn't know where I was heading?

I took four valium tablets to try to calm down and for a while I dozed. It was the first of the nightmares. Real, genuine, scream-out-loud nightmares. They have dogged me now for 20 years. Even in my sleep, I've been unable to escape the demons that torment me.

Some car headlights woke me up. My skull jerked back into the head-rest, and then that sudden, awful realisation as it dawned on me afresh just exactly what had happened. That same feeling you experience after a bad night at the tables, when you wake up and it slowly trickles through that you've lost a year's wages on the single turn of a card. And this was way more than just the ignominy of bankruptcy: that had occurred to any number of peers over the years. No — this was of a different category altogether. This was scandal on a grand scale.

At least the nap, however fitful, had helped sort out my potential courses of action. I could never escape by myself; I certainly, at that stage, didn't want to give myself up to the police; and, therefore, by ineluctable logic, I was left with but the one option. I would throw myself on a friend's mercy and beg for his help.

But who to call?

I had, perhaps, a dozen friends who might have been prepared to help. But I did what I had often done before in times of crisis. I called John Aspinall.

There are several dramatis personae that crop up in my story, some with bit parts and some who were players. But of all these characters, it was John who was the stalwart. He did what he could, while still attempting to stay true to his lights as his gentlemen.

Of all my friends, it was only Aspinall — universally known to his friends as 'Aspers' — who had the deviousness, not to mention the thirst for adventure, to carry it off. More importantly, I knew he could keep a secret. Over the previous decade, I'd lost thousands to him at cards and backgammon, yet he'd never told a soul.

Eventually I found a phonebox in the middle of a Sussex village. I knew his number by heart.

He picked up on the third ring. 'Yes?' It was not a kindly tone of voice — but then Aspers was not a kindly man. In fact, that one word greeting entirely summed up the man's healthy scepticism for every man and every woman who crossed his path. Please don't misunderstand me. Aspers would move mountains for his friends. But for the great unwashed general public, his attitude was always one of indifference bordering on contempt.

I pumped coins into the phone as the pips went.

'Aspers — it's Lucky here. I'm — I'm — ' I paused, not knowing how to continue. 'Aspers, I've done a terrible thing. An awful thing, and — ' I trailed off.

'And you'd like me to help?'

'I — I need time to think,' I said. 'I might want to turn myself into the police later. I probably will turn myself into the police. But I just need time to sort things out in my head. I need to weigh up my options.'

'Right,' he said, all business-like. 'Where are you?'

'Somewhere near Uckfield. I'm parked up in a layby.'

'Does anybody know where you are?'

'I've been with Susan, Susan Maxwell-Scott, for a couple of hours.' I wondered briefly what she was doing at that moment. 'She's a lawyer, so she's not going to lie to the police.'

'True. But Susan won't necessarily tell them right away either. Let me think.' He started to click his tongue against the roof of his mouth. It was a familiar sound that I had heard many times at the gaming tables as John had weighed up the odds of a finesse or a squeeze in a re-doubled grand slam.

The pips went again. I pushed in a few more coppers.

At length he spoke: 'Here's a plan then. Why don't you drop the car off in Newhaven. I'll pick you up. Then you can lie low with me. How does that sound?'

I was lost for words. 'That — that would be perfect. Thank you Aspers. Thank you.'

'By the way, what is it?'

'I'm sorry?'

'What have you done, Johnny? What am I getting myself into? Is it murder?'

'I — I very much fear it is.'

Aspers grunted to himself. 'Be over as quick as I can. See you in about an hour by, let's say, St Michael's, that Medieval church on Newhaven's hill overlooking the Ouse.'

'Thank you.' I was about to hang up, when a quite tangential thought entered my head. It was to be strangely prescient. 'Oh, one more thing Aspers, dear Aspers. Don't tell a soul. Don't tell a single person otherwise I'm undone.'

'I won't.'

'Especially don't tell Jimmy.'

'I won't.'

4

Being involved in a murder gives rise to very similar feelings to that of a bereavement.

In the first few hours afterwards, there is this sort of numbed detachment, as if you can't quite believe that it's happened. It was like I'd felt at my father's death ten years earlier. At first I'd viewed it rationally and thought to myself, 'Daddy's dead'. But then my mind would drift onto other things, I'd think about the title that had just become mine, and then a sort of mental jolt would hit me with the realisation that it wasn't a dream, that it was a reality and that my dear father really had left to join the Great Majority.

And those were so similar to my feelings as I drove through the early morning light to meet Aspinall. My head was like a spinning top. I couldn't believe that things had fouled up so badly. I couldn't believe that it was Sandra, not Veronica, who was dead. And, although it was only hours after the event, I could hardly comprehend that it was me, me, Lord Lucan, who'd had a hand in it. I was a peer on the run. It was going to make the front pages of every newspaper in the land.

Maybe it would be best, easiest, if I were to slot the car into overdrive and slam her into a tree at 100mph.

On I would potter, my mind half-aware of the signposts and the mile-markers along the way. I'd peer out of the open window, my face numb in the spitting rain. And then it would hit me all over again, just as strong as it had the first time. Sandra was dead. I was on the run. The newspapers. First peer in centuries to be tried for murder. Yes, that one fact exercised me greatly.

There are a great many privileges to be had from being a hereditary peer. There's the title and with luck the large inheritance to go with it, and there is also the natural deference that is conferred to people of rank. Even in the Swinging Sixties, just the fact that I had a title meant people mentally genuflected when they were in my presence. Distasteful it may be, but it is nevertheless true.

But if there is a downside — and I admit it's not that much of a downside — a hereditary peer is always very much aware of the weight of history weighing down on his shoulders. For I wasn't just Richard John Bingham, and nor was I just Lord Lucan — no, I was the 7th Earl of Lucan, and everything I did, for better or worse, would reflect not just on my ancestors but also my descendants. From as early as I can remember, I was aware that my every deed would be chalked up against the Lucan name.

Do you know anyone else, apart from royalty, who is judged by the folly of their great-great-grandfather? Not a soul, I'll wager. But for my entire life, I'd always been pigeonholed in the same bracket as the poltroon who'd ordered the Charge of the Light Brigade.

So that morning, along with all the other thoughts whirling through my head, I could hear the anguished knock of my ancestors drumming at the door. In one fell swoop, I had tarnished all their good works and every one of their great reputations. It was quite possible that my one scandal might even eclipse the Charge of the Light Brigade. And even the dotty 3rd Earl managed to redeem himself in the end, eventually becoming the oldest soldier in the British army, dying in 1888 at the age of 93. But with a murder under my belt, there was never going to be the slightest chance of redemption. It would be a blot so massive that it would tarnish not just my good name and that of my ancestors, but also that of my son George and his sons after him. It reminds me of a quote from that fire-breathing Old Testament prophet Jeremiah, 'The fathers have eaten sour grapes, and now the children's teeth are on edge'.

It's a terrible thing for a young man to have hanging over him, but that is the price of being born a blue blood: you inherit not just the grand family name, but also your family's collective history. And even though it was only a few hours since Sandra's death, I still had the wit to realise that I'd royally fouled things up, not just for me, but also for George, my son and heir.

Without even realising how, I'd arrived in Newhaven. I parked in a discreet side-street and for a while I just sat there. I had a few minutes to kill and I started cleaning up the car. There was blood all over the place, on the dashboard, the map box, the steering wheel. There was even blood on the passenger door. Without any proper cleaning materials, it was hopeless. Not only was the Corsair smothered with my prints, but everyone knew I'd borrowed it.

I tucked the keys above the vanity mirror, tapped the wheel for old time's sake, and without a backward glance I left the car and my old life with it. To all intents and purposes, that was my last moment as Lord Lucan. And what a typical way for me to have ended my life as a peer — with, yet again, another great howler of a gaffe. A gaffe of Lucan-esque proportions that could only have been made by someone who was determined to bungle every single thing that he turned his hand to. For although it was quite true that it wouldn't have been worth my time cleaning the car for prints, it would have taken but a moment for me to check the boot.

A simply unbelievable mistake. The sort of blunder that, were it in a detective story, would be deemed too far-fetched to be plausible. But in my case, it was very much a reality. It really happened. It's there in all the history books.

Now I fully concede that my mind was frazzled at the time; I wasn't thinking straight. But still . . . as acts of criminal idiocy go, this one took the biscuit.

For as I'd loped up the hill to St Michael's, I had completely forgotten about a two-foot length of lead piping, my spare bludgeon. I had brought it along as a back-up, just in case the primary murder weapon wasn't up to the job.

And somehow I had contrived to leave this piece of *prima facie* evidence in the boot of the car.

It was to be a couple of days before I remembered, with that pit of the stomach queasiness, where precisely I'd left that damnable piece of piping. Of all my many acts of incompetence, that is the one that still makes me shudder. It was like a bucket of ice water in the face. I was left almost winded by my own stupidity.

And that one act turned out to be my Rubicon. Before then, there might have been a chance of pretending that I'd been in the wrong place at the wrong time — that I really had peeked in through the window to witness the very act of Sandra's murder. It was unlikely, but I'd have had a chance of getting away with it.

But with that second piece of piping in the boot of the car, almost identical to the actual murder weapon even down to the white taping that I had so meticulously wrapped round the handle? Not a hope in hell.

On such small things do our lives turn. If I'd taken just a few seconds to check the boot, I could have dumped that piece of lead piping and my cock-and-bull alibi might have held water — at least for a little while. I might well have given myself up to the police.

As it was, the detectives had soon discovered the 'smoking gun' in the boot of my car and from then on I was irrevocably set on my path as a fugitive.

What a hash; what a foul-up. I know that it's all of apiece with everything else that has occurred in my pathetic life. For when it boiled down to it, despite more than a year's worth of planning, not only was the wrong person killed, but I couldn't even properly dispose of the spare bludgeon.

My ineptitude was of such staggering enormity that it was almost laughable. As the ever pithy John Aspinall was later to remark, 'Maybe, Johnny, you were never especially cut out for this business of murder in the first place.'

5

The man himself was already waiting for me in that battle-scarred Land Rover outside St Michael's, engine ticking over, pumping out great clouds of exhaust into the chill air. This was unusual for Aspinall. Normally he was late for everything, usually at least two or three hours late. The only exception, as I was later to realise, was in times of crisis.

I knocked on the window. He smiled, impish as ever. 'Hop in.' He gestured to the back. 'Probably best not to sit in the front, old cock.'

'Quite right,' I said, clambering into the back and sitting on one of the side benches. It was strewn with straw, bags of feed and God knows what else from his zoo at Howletts. 'Thank you.'

'Not a problem.' He crunched the Land Rover into first gear and we were away.

For the first time in what felt like days, I let out an immense sigh. Quite unconsciously I'd been holding my breath. And now that I had surrendered myself up to John Aspinall, I knew that for a while I could relax.

He was, quite simply, one of the most

extraordinary men I've ever met. In appearance, with his receding blonde hair and those huge sideburns, he looked like some bumpkin gentleman of leisure and he usually capped off the image by driving a filthy Land Rover and wearing pink cords and a ripped coat. He had huge shoulders and often carried himself like a gorilla, hands swinging palm backwards — you'd almost think he was consciously mimicking the alpha-male struts of his great apes. But, you underestimated him at your peril — as many men had learned to their cost. I think it was those ice blue Nordic eyes that gave the game away. After all, he was a man who'd made his fortune from skinning people alive at the gaming tables.

Aspers had had his own casino, of course, the Clermont Club in Mayfair, and that had used to provide him with a steady income. A couple of years earlier, he'd sold the club to Playboy for £350,000, though I believe he'd always regretted it. What he really loved — and what he lived for — was going toe-to-toe with another big-hitter. Not that he was anything like the addict that I was. But there is nothing quite so thrilling as the prospect of losing slightly more than you can afford to lose.

Ever since I'd met him when I was fresh out of Eton, he'd always been lucky. Luck that I could only have dreamed of; luck that actually made a profit. But on top of that, he was utterly nerveless; he had the skill too and was as close as you could get in those days to a genuine professional gambler. When we played backgammon, he'd memorised most of the complex end game variations by rote. His knowledge of horses was encyclopaedic. And when it came to poker, he didn't just know the cards and the probabilities, he knew the men he was up against.

My relationship with Aspers had always been rather peculiar. At first, he'd considered me as just another rich young blue blood ripe for the plucking. And pluck me he most certainly did.

But for some reason that I have never really understood, he took a shine to me — and, for want of a better expression, he became the big brother that I'd never had.

We still gambled, me ever eager to win my money back, but for the most part I think he was just toying with me. I remember one hand from one of our early poker schools. We were playing straight Texas Hold 'Em, which is one of the dozens of bastardised variations of poker. Each player has his own two cards 'in the hole', and you then make up your hand with three of the five communal cards on the table. I had two aces in my hand and there was another ace on the table and one more card yet to come. For the first time that evening, I was coming out swinging. I think I'd wagered a thousand pounds. My two aces were lying face down; I can even remember the pattern on the back of the cards: flowers, a profusion of wild flowers. Only someone like Aspers could have got away with having such a florid deck of cards in a casino.

I was in a head-to-head with Aspers. It was his turn to bet and he made a very simple £20 raise. I was about to throw another ton of money into the pot when Aspers clucked at his mouth and, patiently, almost mournfully, stared at the back of my two cards, before glancing at the pack. And very quietly, he'd said, 'Don't do it, dear boy, I've got you beat.' I'd raised an eyebrow at that. 'Honestly,' he said. 'You can't beat me.'

But I raised him anyway, raised him another grand, just for the hell of it. He simply shook his head and called, and of course he'd got a straight. Although I was too callow to realise it at the time, not only had he warned me off but he could have cleaned me out. Years later, when he eventually came to sell the Clermont, he gave me a small present: a clutch of my old cheques, all the money that I'd lost to him over the years, and every one of them uncashed.

By his own lights, Aspers would have considered himself a gentleman. But that certainly never stopped him from cheating — though I think, I hope, that he stopped short of rooking his friends. As for the bookies though, they were absolutely fair game. I well remember one memorable coup at Wincanton races where he gave the bookies an absolute pasting. I won't bore you with the detail, but at the end of the big race, when the bookmakers realised what he had done to them, he had to race for his life to the limo waiting by the exit gate. He genuinely feared that they were out to lynch him.[3]

Aspers was about ten years older than me and when I'd first known him had been almost rangy looking, though by 1974, when he was nearly 50, he'd been running a bit to flab. As had I, come to that. A couple of years earlier he'd got married again, to a delightful woman, Sally. I never knew her that well, but he always said she was the love of his life.

That then is a brief sketch of the man who was to be my saviour. Without him, I wouldn't have given myself more than a couple of weeks before I'd been cuffed and put behind bars. But with Aspers on my side, I was able to make a fresh start — and for that I will always be grateful. Though I am also aware that it was because of Aspers that

Jimmy Goldsmith arrived on the scene in all his foetid malignity. Not that I'm grumbling, not that I would have the gall to complain. But let's just say that life would have been much the sweeter without Goldsmith's presence.

We'd been driving along for a few minutes in silence, Aspers for once content to leave me with my thoughts. He wasn't normally a man to let a silence linger, but the circumstances were, I suppose, exceptional.

'Going to be a lovely morning,' he said. 'Look at that sky, Johnny, what a gorgeous hue of pinks and crimsons. The sort of morning that Homer had in mind when he was talking about his rosy-fingered dawn. Though come to think of it, Homer was blind, so what the hell he'd know about it, I have no idea. Worth being dragged out of my bed just to see it.'

I peered round the seat and caught a glimpse of the streaked artist's palette on the skyline. 'Wonderful.'

'Animals are going to need feeding when I get back. One of my favourite times of the day feeding the animals — must be something almost primeval about it. Is there anything in life to touch throwing a haunch of meat into the tiger pen? And the gorillas. How I love those gorillas. They've got more true nobility in their hearts than any human I know, and that even includes you Johnny.'

'Yes.' I was non-plussed by the conversation. There was me, a fugitive wanted for murder, and yet Aspers was jabbering on about his zoo at Howletts.

'The neighbours are being a total pain in the neck. They just never stop complaining, never stop, constantly whingeing about the noise and the smell and anything else that could conceivably upset them in their nasty little homes. Do you know what I've started doing to teach them a lesson, Johnny? At night, I go out and howl at the moon. If I keep it up for a full minute, then the wolves join in too.'

'Forgive me, Aspers,' I said. 'But don't you want to know what happened?'

'Not especially,' he said. 'I presumed you'd tell me in your own sweet time.'

'But . . . but if it all goes wrong, you could end up being an accessory.'

'And what of that? Is it immoral? I never came across anyone in whom the moral sense was dominant who was not heartless, cruel, vindictive, log-stupid, and entirely lacking in the smallest sense of humanity. Moral people, as they are termed, are simple beasts. I would sooner have 50 unnatural vices than one unnatural virtue.'

'Oscar Wilde?'

'My one weakness — as you know.'

Yes indeed, it was a slight weakness of Aspers to quote from Oscar Wilde at the very smallest provocation. He must have spent many nights poring over Wilde's quotes and would then use them to spice up his conversation. If ever he were at a loss for something to say, he would always fall back on one of Oscar's pithy apercus.

'Let the cards fall how they may,' he said. 'I will play them to the best of my ability. You're not seriously suggesting that I shirk away from helping out an old friend, just because we're indulging in a spot of illegality? Is that the sort of fair-weather friend you take me for? Not a bit of it, dear Johnny. I'll help in any way I can. And if that means providing you with a hideaway, then provide it I will.'

'You have one?'

'Very much so. Believe it or not, I have been waiting for just this eventuality. Admittedly, I did think that it might be me who would be using it. But for a first time run, there's no-one I'd rather see in there than you.'

'Well — thank you.'

It is difficult to describe my feelings during this utterly surreal conversation. On the one hand, just a few hours earlier I had been involved in the most unbelievably gruesome murder, and on the other, Aspers was chatting away as if he'd done nothing of any more consequence than pick me up from the station.

Aspers hummed to himself for a while, beating his fingers on the wheel. 'I suppose it was Veronica?' he said, matter-of-factly.

'No, not Veronica,' I said. Then for the first time, I made a clean breast of it. 'It was supposed to be Veronica. But there was a foul-up, a bloody awful foul-up, and the nanny got hit. She's dead.'

I could hear Aspers' tongue clicking against the roof of his mouth, but I couldn't see his face. After that, I only ever saw the mask.

'Dear, oh dear,' he said. 'That's terrible.'

'It is. The whole thing has been one ghastly cock-up from start to finish.' I held my hands up to my face. My stained fingers were trembling with delayed shock as the enormity of it sank in. 'The wrong woman's dead. And they want me for murder.'

Aspers was again clicking his tongue. 'Bad. Whenever a man does a thoroughly stupid thing, it is always from the noblest of motives,' he said. More Wilde again, I was sure of it. 'Tell me. What were you going to do with the body?'

'There's my boat moored up at Newhaven.

I was going to drop her in the Solent. Veronica had gone AWOL before. I'd hoped people would think that she'd just bolted again.'

'Possibly, possibly.' Aspers revved the engine as he double D-clutched down into second. Then he shrugged. 'Still, it can't be helped. The sooner we get you hidden away, the better. It will give you some time to, ahh, evaluate all the available options.'

For the rest of the journey, Aspers talked about his zoo, his animals and Sally, who fortuitously had spent the night in London so was none the wiser about Aspers' rescue mission. It was as if once I'd come clean about Sandra's death, Aspers had tucked the information away in that analytical brain of his and continued with business as usual. He was a man who could talk the hind-legs off a donkey, and would think nothing of delivering a two-hour monologue. In full flow, he was unstoppable.

But, as I sat hunched in the back of the Land Rover, elbows on knees, I was more than happy to let him have the floor. I was too shocked and too weary for conversation, and had the traces of a hangover kicking in from all the whisky and vodka and the valium. One picture, in particular, kept flashing through my mind. It was the blood in the house. I'd been shocked at how much blood there had been, and it was spattered everywhere, on the walls, the carpets and even the ceilings. A pool of blood at the foot of the stairs in the basement. And the awful, awful sight of Sandra's tiny body tucked into a US mailbag. Just the thought of it still makes me wince to this day. I can never forgive myself. Dear, dear Sandra, I would give the world to take it all back.

I must have dozed off, because I don't remember how we got into Howletts and never even caught sight of the grand Palladian mansion that Aspers had spent such a fortune restoring. I'd been there a few times over the years, right from when it was nothing but a ramshackle ruin at the time he'd bought it for a song in the fifties. But, by 1974, it was the perfect show-home for a millionaire gambler, with that grand sweeping entrance and four resplendent columns at the front portico. When he'd bought Howletts, I don't think it had been touched in 50 years, and there'd even been talk of pulling the place down, but Aspers had quietly set about the business of restoring its much-faded glories.

Only once was I to witness any of this grandeur during my stay at there. I'd thought at first that Aspers might be spiriting me away to some secret room in the attic of the main house, or a snug priest-hole such as had been used to hide Catholic churchmen. But, as with everything about Aspers, he had every angle covered. That was one of the surprising things about that great lumbering man. To look at him, you wouldn't have had an inkling of his enormous attention to detail. That, I suppose, was why he was always such a successful gambler.

He reversed into a large triple-door garage and cut the engine. 'Stay there a second, while I close the doors. Be annoying for you to be seen in here.'

I peered out of the windscreen at a little strip of blue sky, wanting to snatch every last scrap of freedom, of nature, as if I knew that all too soon it was to be denied me. Aspers wheeled the doors shut, before switching on the lights and opening up the back door. He ushered me out with an extended hand, as if welcoming me to a palace. 'And here we are.'

I'd only just woken up and was still befuddled. 'Here? I'm staying here?'

'Do you like it, old cock?' he said, twinkling that ever-mischievous smile. It was so very typical of Aspers. Even when I was in the direst of straits, he still couldn't resist pulling my tail.

I blinked in the glare of the strip-lights and took the place in. It was a sizeable garage, with a black workbench at one end along with various pumps, pulleys, dead tyres, jacks and other bits of car detritus. The walls were part brick, part whitewashed wood, while up above was a solid slate roof. In the middle were a couple of deep five-foot reception pits so the mechanics could get in underneath the cars, while over on the far side was parked another equally dirty Land Rover.

'It's . . . ' I could think of nothing to stay.

Aspers burst into a great peal of laughter. 'It's a bloody awful place to hide. But it is, nevertheless, a good place to hide a trapdoor. Take a look at this.' He sauntered over to the workbench and started counting the bricks along. 'Haven't been in for a while,' he said. 'From the corner, it's 25 along and six up.'

The brick looked identical to all the others. Not even a hint that it was in any way different. He pressed it as if it were a button. The brick moved forwards a fraction of an inch before springing back. I could hear the faint sound of a click. 'I don't know how this thing works,' he said. 'All I know is that it does work. Took me ages to find the chaps to do it. Two brothers, Mark and Giles, efficient, ingenious, absolutely rock steady. I didn't want a team of them, otherwise they'd have blabbed it round the whole of Kent.'

'And you can trust them?'

'I should hope so,' he laughed. 'Dear Mark is dead, stabbed in the eye in a pub brawl in Romsey, while Giles has gone mad from Black Lion or some other revolting form of syphilis. They put it in about ten years ago. Both of them brilliant engineers. You wouldn't believe the workmanship.'

He led me over to the middle of the garage and walked down the stairs into the reception pit. Its concrete floor was pristine. The few reception pits that I'd ever seen before had been black with oil and grease, but this one looked as if it had been scrubbed down that morning.

The pit itself was about three feet wide and six feet long.

Aspers walked to the end and squatted down on his haunches. 'Come and take a look over here. See if you can spot the join.'

I knelt down beside him and stared about me. The pit's walls looked exactly like any other wall I'd ever seen — red brick and mortar.

'You wouldn't believe it, but you're staring right at the door,' he said as we crouched there knee to knee. 'Your nose is about a foot away from it.'

I squinted more closely — but could still see nothing. Not even a trace of a crack or an opening.

Aspers chuckled. 'When they first built the thing, I spent hours looking for it — and I knew where to look. The joins are completely seamless. And now for the clever bit. The door's so well-balanced that you could open it with your pinkie.'

At that, he held up his little finger and pushed at the seemingly solid brick wall. Although I'd been expecting it, it happened so suddenly that it was like an optical illusion. For just as you see in the movies, a portion of the bricks moved backwards to reveal a small three-foot by four-foot hole of gaping darkness, jagged edges at the side. It was like staring into the abyss.

'There's a switch just here on the right,' he said, giving it a flick to reveal a short flight of concrete steps. 'It's a bit awkward at first, but once you're down the bottom it's fine. Oh, and close the door behind you. Now that my den is being put to good use, it would be as well to take all due precautions.'

With that, Aspers showed surprising agility as he ducked through the doorway and, still bending forwards, walked down the steps. He stood upright at the bottom and beckoned. 'Come on in — the water's warm!'

I poked my head through the trap-door. I'd been expecting it to smell damp, but it was quite dry, although there was that mustiness

45

that you often find in old houses. Stooping low, I walked down a few steps before turning to close the door. It was more than a foot thick and made of solid bricks, pivoting on its edge. It was extraordinary; even though the trap-door must have weighed at least two hundredweight, it glided so easily that it might have been made of gossamer.

'Giles took ages on that trap,' said Aspers. 'I think he put a sort of veneer on the outside to cover up the cracks. See that lever on the back? Just give it a turn to secure the bolts.'

Like everything else about the den, the bolting mechanism was another superb piece of craftsmanship. The bolts slotted home without a sound. I joined Aspers at the bottom of the stairs.

'I hope you feel suitably honoured,' said Aspers. 'Apart from Mark and Giles, you're the only other person who's been down here.'

'Doesn't Sally know?'

'God no! Don't be ridiculous.'

We must have been at least 15 feet below the ground. Aspers led me along a short brick-walled passage before we came to a gunmetal grey door. He opened it, fiddled for the light switch and walked in.

'We've arrived,' he said. 'I hope you like it.'

I goggled in amazement. I suppose I had, at best, been expecting some barren concrete cell with perhaps a bed and a wash-basin. But this was of a different category altogether. It was indeed a bunker — but quite unlike any other bunker you've ever seen or heard of. And the first thing I registered was the books — thousands of them. Long lines of collected works, leather-bound in black and brown, along with a huge selection of modern books. Every single square foot of wall space was lined with books on handsome two-inch thick oak shelves.

'Incredible.'

'Took me weeks to get all those books down here,' he said. 'Had to do it myself. Did it at night while I was in between marriages.'

Gradually, I took in more of Aspers' den. It was a goodly size, way larger than my own office, and on the floor was a made to measure rug, a thick pile of dark swirling crimsons, browns and purples. At one end of the room was a desk and a comfortable leather chair, while in the middle were two classic club armchairs, each with their own foot-rest, side-table and reading lamp. No windows, of course. It was a temple to reading.

Aspers had gone over to the three doors that led off from the main-room. 'Kitchen in here,' he said. 'I'll sort you out with some fresh food later, but the deep-freeze is chock solid, enough to keep you going until the summer. Bathroom and lavatory in the middle, and the last one is your bedroom — compact but as silent as the grave. You won't find a quieter bedroom on earth.'

I gaped, plucking at my moustache, completely at a loss for words.

'It's — it's unbelievable,' I said. 'You're a life-saver.'

'Not a bit of it,' he said. 'Tell you the truth, I've been dying to show this off to someone ever since I first had the place done up.'

'It was a bunker?'

'Think they built it in 1939. Must have been easily big enough for the entire Howletts household and all their staff. When I bought the place it was derelict, like everything else here. I didn't know what to do with it for a while, and then it came to me: the perfect hideaway, my little ace in the hole just in case everything went belly up.'

He stared glassily around the room, eyes flittering over the book-spines but not really taking any of them in.

'Better be getting on,' he said. 'Ought to go up to London to find out the lie of the land for you. I'll try and pop in this evening.'

'Thank you Aspers. Thank you so much.'

'Now now. A little sincerity is a dangerous thing — and a great deal of it is absolutely fatal.' He gave me a cheerful salute as he stood at the door. 'Do make yourself at home.'

I waved goodbye, and stood there motionless, quite taken aback at how the treadmill of the previous 12 hours had suddenly come to a dead stop.

At the time, I thought I might be there for a week or two.

As it turned out, that dark airless, windowless bunker was to be my home for nearly four months. It nearly drove me crazy. In fact, now that I think of it, it did drive me crazy. Stark, staring, yowl-at-the-moon mad.

6

I stared at myself naked in the mirror and for the last time stroked the moustache that had become my trademark.

I knew it had to go but still I prevaricated as if somehow I realised that when the moustache went, that would truly be the last of Lord Lucan.

I'd had it since Eton, and for a time had considered it dashing — though now I think it made me look like a fop. Still, it had been with me for half a lifetime, so it was nearly as much a part of me as my own nose.

Aspers had kept the bathroom well stocked with a cupboard full of razors, shaving creams, badger-hair brushes, toothbrushes, toothpastes and two full shelves of lavatory paper. I worked up a good lather and dabbed it onto my face.

With five quick strokes of the razor the moustache was gone. I splashed on some cold water and patted my face down with a towel. The patch of skin on my upper lip was a tone lighter than the rest of my face, like an echo of the hair that had once bristled there.

I realised I should have done it a long time

ago. It took years off me.

But the job was not nearly done.

I took up a pair of kitchen scissors and methodically started to hack off my hair. Chunk by chunk, curl by curl, my black locks dropped into the sink.

In my prime, I had been quite inordinately proud of my hair. It was thick and full and with not a trace of grey. Every morning, I used to spend ten minutes grooming my crowning glory, rubbing in the Brylcream before brushing it with the two ivory-backed brushes with the family crest. They had been given to me by my father on my 16th birthday.[4]

And now that I was to lose the lot, I didn't feel a trace of emotion. It was just a deed that had to be done, and I had steeled myself to the job, just as the previous evening I had steeled myself to dispose of Veronica's body.

Though I wasn't consciously aware of it, I had already made my decision. My mind was set. From that moment, there was never a chance that I was going to give myself up. No — for better or for worse, I was committing myself to a life on the run.

After 15 minutes, I had hacked off as much hair as I could. I dully registered that I was staring at a stranger. With his crew-cut hair and those black rings under his eyes, he looked like a convict.

I rubbed the shaving foam into my scalp and, little by little, shaved off what remained of my hair. I turned to the left and right before bending forward. There was not a hair left on my head.

I know it's a cliché, but in this case it's true. Not even my mother would have recognised me. The effete dandy that was Lord Lucan was dead, and in his place was this monster, this bald, wild-eyed fugitive who had taken the decision to live the rest of his life outside the law, and to hell with the consequences. I tell you, it gave me a feeling of extraordinary liberation.

It was also strange to feel the texture of my scalp as I traced my fingers over my head. My skin was hyper-sensitive, every nerve-ending ajangle. If I hadn't been able to see it with my own eyes, I would not have believed it was my hand that was touching my own bald head.

The last of the hair was washed down the sink, and, with nothing better to do, I went to bed. As I closed the door behind me, I could have been in my own coffin. The room was as dark as night and so quiet that I fancied I could even hear the sound of my own heartbeat.

I was tired but I couldn't sleep and, when finally I did drop off, it was only to visit a nightmarish land that was infested with cruel, callous brutes, some of them human, some of them not. I'd never experienced anything like it. Dreams that were shocking in their barbarity.

At least they used to shock me. But over the years I've got used to them, for they are merely a continuation of the living nightmare that has become my life.

I was woken by a knock at the door. Aspers was standing silhouetted in the doorway. I sat up in bed, blinking in the light. Aspers gawked at me for a moment.

'God, you look a sight,' he said, before coming a step into the room to look at me closer. 'I suppose it had to go.'

'I think so.'

'Remarkable. I could walk past you in the street and I wouldn't have given you a second glance.'

'Yes,' I said. 'Yes.' I patted at my upper lip and felt my scalp, as if to confirm that it really had all gone. For although I had no hair, it was like some phantom limb, with the lingering sensation that I still had a full crop of hair. I suddenly remembered where Aspers had been that afternoon. 'And the meeting?'

'It went well,' he said. 'But if, as Wilde says, one has a right to judge a man by the effect he has over his friends, then you're a very fine

53

fellow indeed. You probably don't realise what an exceptional group of friends you have. They'd do a lot for you. In fact you should have been there; about as close as you could get to attending your own funeral. I'll tell you all about it when we're on our way.'

'Are we going somewhere?'

He tapped at the side of his cheeks, as if to wake himself up. 'You need to get dressed, old cock. There should be some clothes in the cupboard, probably about your size. We've got things to do — and if it were done when 'tis done, then 'twere well it were done quickly.'

'Right,' I said. Aspers didn't bother to avert his gaze as I got out of bed; he'd always been indifferent to another man's nakedness, as if it were no more worthy of comment than seeing a gorilla in the raw.

He nodded in approval. 'I'll make some tea,' he said, ambling off to the kitchenette. 'We'll drink it on the way.'

There were some clothes in the bedroom's walk-in wardrobe, a few pairs of jeans, some shirts and thick jumpers, a little tight round the stomach, but plenty good enough for me. I was pulling on some paint-spattered work-boots in the library when Aspers came through with two steaming mugs of tea.

He shook his head as he caught sight of me

and laughed. 'That bald head of yours is very disarming,' he said. 'Every time I catch sight of you, I think, 'What's that thug doing down here?' '

'Got a hat?'

'Have a try of this,' he said, tossing me one of the round beanies that he had in his pocket. 'You'll need it. It's going to be cold tonight.'

'Yes?'

'And wet. Very wet. I've got an oil-skin for you.'

Aspers led the way out of the bunker and up the stairs at the end, ducking as he climbed out into the inspection pit. Though the garage doors were almost closed, I could see it was already dark outside, the rain drumming on the roof tiles.

'Into the back with you,' Aspers said, holding open the Land Rover door. 'We'll just get out of Howletts and I'll fill you in.' He gave me a wink. 'And there is much that you need to be filled in on.' He was humming to himself as he opened the garage doors.

Up until then, I don't think I'd realised quite how much Aspers was enjoying this whole escapade. Already in his mind's eye he had dissociated the matter of Sandra's murder from the fact that I was on the run. Almost from start to finish, I think he loved it, as if it were nothing more than the most glorious adventure. I use the word 'almost' advisedly, because there was one incident, one short hair-raising incident during my four month sojourn at Howletts, which really put the wind up him.

I was again sitting on my side-seat at the back of the Land Rover and, although I was thirsting for news, I kept my mouth shut until we were out of the park and onto the main road; Aspers humming all the way, as if he hadn't a care in the world. And come to think of it, he probably didn't. He'd made his bet and he was going to see it through to the end.

Finally, with the windscreen wipers going pell-mell, he turned round and said to me conversationally, 'Would you like to know where we're going?'

'It had occurred to me.'

'Back to Newhaven.'

'Newhaven? Why are we doing that?'

'To make them all think that you've killed yourself. I thought it might take some of the heat off.'

'Can we start at the beginning?'

'But of course.'

He told me all about it, and my heart sank as I learned of the hue and cry in London — front page of all the evening papers; leading every radio bulletin in the country;

and fast becoming a story that was round the world. I don't really know what else I'd expected.

It was a shock, nonetheless, to realise how my tawdry little drama was at that very moment being discussed in every household in the country. In my new incarnation as a fugitive, I had quite failed to appreciate how the nation's editors would be licking their lips with anticipation over a murder that involved a peer of the realm; and, better yet, a peer of the realm on the run. For those first few weeks, there was hardly a day went by when the story wasn't on one of the front pages.

Later on, as I had time aplenty to contemplate all the ramifications of what I'd done, I could see how the mystery of my disappearance had ensured that, even a year later, the story was still making front page news. How different it would have been if I'd given myself up. There would have been a scandal and a trial, and I'd have been jailed, but there would have been none of the mystery, not an inch of leeway for people to go about that delightful business of speculation.

In large part, it was my actions on that rainy night after the murder that helped ensure that the story of Sandra's murder would remain in the public eye for — as it turned out — the rest of my life.

'It's very simple,' said Aspers. 'If we are going to make them think that you killed yourself, we do at least have to provide them with a certain amount of corroborative evidence.'

'You must be right.' I looked down at my feet, which were pumping up and down with nerves.

'You can't just write a suicide note and leave it at that. Well . . . you could just write a suicide note and leave it at that. But it wouldn't be overly plausible. They'd smell a very large rat. If, however, you were to leave just a slight sniff of evidence, a subtle hint, if you were delicately to allude to somehow having done away with yourself, then they might be more likely, ahh, to swallow the bait. Possibly swallow the bait — ' And so Aspers carried on talking — and talking and talking.

'We're going to dump your boat in the Solent. I'll motor out and you follow, then you can open up the stopcocks and down she goes.'

'Yes?'

'No suicide notes. No final phone calls. We just scuttle the ship and leave the detectives to come to their own conclusions. Talking of which, do you remember that 'suicide list' that I used to have at the Clermont? You were definitely on there.'

I grunted. Yet another piece of spectacular bad taste from Aspers, who ten years earlier had drawn up a list of the friends who were most likely to kill themselves.

'I think you were laying odds on me of five to one.'

'That's right!' he chuckled. 'Dear Charles Benson was the favourite at 13–8 on! And I daresay that if we succeed in faking your death that I'll have a few of them calling up to claim their winnings.'

And they did too, as it happened. Aspers chortled to himself for a while. He really did have the blackest sense of humour of anyone I've ever met. Within just a few days of my disappearance, he'd even stuck up at a notice at the Clermont that read, 'If Lord Lucan comes in, will he please ring 999 as someone wants to interview him.'

I kicked at the filthy straw on the back seat. 'They'll know the boat's gone?'

Aspers snorted as he tapped the steering wheel. 'Every bloody constable in the country is looking for you. They've got your photo up in every port and every airport in Britain, if not every port in Europe. They've already been steaming through every one of your private possessions in your flat in Belgravia. Doubtless by tomorrow they'll have started working on Veronica and your friends — so yes, yes, my dear boy, I would have thought that within a day or two they will have ascertained that you kept a boat in Newhaven, and that that said boat has now somehow disappeared.'

'With me on board — '

'Doing the decent thing.'

'Does anybody else know? You haven't told Jimmy?'

'No I haven't told Jimmy — nor anybody else, just as his Lordship commanded,' he said testily. 'Though I may say they all wanted to know if I'd seen you. You should have heard them.'

'Who was there?' I asked.

'Oh, the usual lot — ' and he reeled off a list of names that, I suppose, had made up all the various mile-markers in my life. There were around eight of them, all convened together ostensibly so that they could decide what 'to do' if I ever turned up. But, human nature being what it is, the reason they were so prompt to attend Aspers' ad hoc lunch-party was to find out the gossip. It must have been the juiciest piece of gossip that had come their way in years, and there they were imagining themselves right at the heart of the conspiracy. Oh, how we thirst for a little adventure to brighten up our humdrum lives.

It sounded like a perfectly sublime lunch-party; how I would have loved to have been there. There were all of my oldest friends, a limitless supply of wine, and plenty of good, old-fashioned school dinner food. The more I think of it now, the more it sounds like heaven. If you could plant me anywhere in the world at this moment, that is where I would wish to be. They'd even thoughtfully left a spare place for me, just in case I popped in.

Of those whom I remember hearing attended the luncheon, there was my brother-in-law Bill Shand Kydd, who'd married Veronica's sister; my gambling mentor Stephen Raphael; the banker Daniel Meinertzhagen; Charles Benson, the *Daily Express'* racing correspondent; and of course, Dominic Elwes, dear old Dominic, always the very life and soul of the party, and who regrettably became yet another piece of collateral damage from my shambles of a murder.

I was surprised that Aspers' chief partner in crime, Jimmy Goldsmith, hadn't shown up. It was very unlike him — Goldsmith loved anything that whiffed of intrigue and chicanery.

'Where was Jimmy?' I asked.

'Jimmy was tied up,' he said. 'Knowing

him, he'd probably found some new woman. Jimmy can be happy with any woman as long as he does not love her.'

'Now that must be Wilde. *A Picture of Dorian Gray?*'

Aspers laughed. 'You know me too well. One of my favourites.'

'And what happened during the lunch?'

'We drank champagne and we toasted your good health — whether you happened to be in this world or the next. I'd never seen them all so excited, Dominic in particular, yapping away like some little terrier, and all of them interminably asking what we should do if and when you got in touch.'

'Yes?'

'Not one of them said they were going to turn you in. Said that if a close friend came in covered in blood, the very last thing they'd do was turn them in. You should have heard Dominic, saying stuff like 'It goes against every last instinct of human loyalties and to hell with the law or the common norms of civic behaviour.' As for me, I told them that if you turned up at Howletts I'd do what I could for you. Didn't make any bones about it.'

How utterly glorious it was to hear him say that. All of us like to think that, far from being 'fair-weather', our friends are storm-proofed and will stick with us to the end. We like to think that, but our friendships are rarely tested. Nobody knows whether at the death their friends will still be hanging on in there.

Well, there is not much to envy about my life. But I do happen to know the answer to that particular question. Not that I've seen any of them since, but what I do know is that each and every one of them was an absolute trouper.

Aspers suddenly drummed his fingers on the wheel. 'Oh, but I didn't ask,' he said. 'Did you try anyone else, or was I the first port in the storm?'

'You were the first port.'

'Good, good, always nice to know that I was your first choice, old cock. You should have heard them, gaggling on like a lot of fish-wives, and not entirely complimentary about Veronica either. Funny thing was that at one stage or another, every single one of them came up to me and asked if I'd seen you. But I do so love acting. It is so much more real than life.'

'I'm sure.'

I'd seen Aspers enough times on the opposite side of a poker table to know that he could bluff and double-bluff with the best of them, not to mention dodge, scheme, and dissemble till he was blue in the face. He was a gentleman, but was also capable of the utmost deviousness; in fact often enjoyed being devious just for its own sake. The only person who could match him was Jimmy Goldsmith — but Jimmy was not just devious but utterly unscrupulous with it, and there was no way on God's earth that you could ever have mistaken him for a gentleman. As I told him once to his face; he never forgave me for it.

As we drove on through the rain, Aspers filled me in on a little more about the lunch, but seeing as none of them knew a damn thing about it, it was just a couple of hours of theories and hypotheses. And all of it, I suppose, exactly typical of a million other conversations being carried out over lunch that day. What had gone wrong? Had I done it? Had I the makings of a killer? And — the most pressing point of all — where was I holed up?

Although at the time they knew none of the pertinent details of Sandra's murder, they most definitely knew their man — because there wasn't a person at Aspers' dining table who seriously thought that I'd killed myself. In the words of dear Dominic Elwes, 'He's addicted to gambling — and he wouldn't dream of throwing in his cards.'

This, I suppose, is true, but even gamblers

are not immune to being bowed by the weight of the world. Sometimes it feels as if you're in so deep that, of all the various options, death can seem like a most wonderfully pleasant alternative.

When we pulled into Newhaven, it was pouring as if the very heavens had opened. A good night not to be noticed as you walked down the street with your coat wrapped tight about you. But, on the other hand, no-one but a madman would have ventured out to sea on a night like that. It must have been Force Eight at the very least.

We walked the ten minutes to the seafront in silence. There wasn't a soul on the streets, not a person to see us flit to our boats.

I remember how odd it was to climb on board my old powerboat in the rain — everything so reassuringly familiar, yet everything so incredibly different. To see my old mugs and my whisky bottles all neatly arrayed in the drinks cabinet, my tins of bully beef stacked away in the pantry and a couple of bottles of booze chilling in the fridge. It was just the usual mundane scene that you'd see on a 1,000 boats across the land. But, for me, it was home; and it was to be the last time in my life that I could ever say that of a place.

I'd called her, of all things, *Charybdis*, a

character from *The Odyssey*. Charybdis was a whirlpool who lived close to the six-headed monster, Scylla. And when a Captain sailed past these two horrors, he had to weigh up the risks. On the one hand, he could take the Scylla route, knowing for certain that six of his crew would be eaten alive. Or on the other he could sail past Charybdis. And sometimes the whirlpool was calm, and every tar in the crew would be saved; and sometimes she was in full flood, and the entire ship met with a watery grave. Charybdis, if you like, was the all or nothing option. How very appropriate for a man like myself. I risked the lot. And — as you well know — I got swallowed.

It was odd being back on *Charybdis* that night. Only 24 hours earlier, of course, I'd been expecting — hoping — to be boarding the boat with Veronica's slight body hefted over my shoulder. Such an enormous thing to dispose of a murder victim, but I think I would have approached the deed with far more equanimity than actually scuttling the ship.

It was all about a question of outcomes. If I'd weighted down Veronica's body and tossed her over the side of the ship, that — I'd believed — was going to be the end of my problems.

But as it was, the scuttling of the ship was

only the very beginning of my problems. It was the first slice of a machete as I embarked on a long journey through the thick and impenetrable Amazonian jungle.

Still, even though I had all these night-mares in front of me, I could at least savour the moment. As I cast off, I took a bottle of Bollinger from the fridge and swigged it straight from the bottle.

Aspers, in a much larger boat than *Charybdis* — as befitted a multi-millionaire — was already clear. He flicked on his lights as I followed him out into the open sea.

What a night to go boating — the rain stingingly hard as *Charybdis* drove head on into the great crunching waves. All I could see was Aspers' lights twinkling ahead of me and the occasional foaming white crest of a wave as it thundered over the side of the ship. Sea-water cascading everywhere, swirling through to the galley. If I hadn't been wearing Aspers' oil-skins I'd have been drenched in seconds.

To some, with the keening shriek of the wind and the towering seas, it might have been hell on earth. But, now that I think of it, during these past 20 years since Sandra's death it was probably my happiest moment. Not much of a moment, and not a moment that I was able to share with anyone; but, with

Bollinger in hand and the rolling ocean beneath my feet, I was, for a short time, truly happy.

Ever since my childhood, I've always loved the sea and, since I attained my Majority, have always owned some form of power-boat. Now this is not a time for false modesty — heaven knows I have given you plenty enough reasons to despise me — but I was competent on a boat and knew how to handle one. In fact, I knew the Channel better than Belgravia.

It was also the first time since Sandra's death that I'd been caught up with the thrill of the adventure. I was a fugitive and every last shred of my old life was over. The circumstances, perhaps, were not quite as I would have wished them. It was a disaster, a monumental catastrophe. I'd wanted my wife dead and had instead ended up with Sandra's blood on my hands. But, we must take our adventures as they serve — and that is especially true for Eton-educated Peers who have spent their entire lives on railroad tracks as they follow their destinies all the way through to the family vault.

I don't know if it was the Bollinger that was making me light-headed, or whether it was a reaction to the madness of the previous 24 hours, but I remember hauling back the cape of my oil-skin and revelling in the lash of the rain as it fell on my face. Did I sing? I might have done. One hand on the wheel, I rolled easily as the boat bucked beneath my feet. I poured the Bollinger into my mouth, letting it froth over my cheeks, the taste of the fizz mixed with the salt tang of the sea. My scalp was extraordinarily sensitive to the rain; I could feel every drop as it smacked onto my head and dripped down the nape of my neck.

I was crazy then, whooping out great animal shrieks of . . . I know not what — perhaps a lust for life. It was a time when I was totally in the moment, focused on nothing more than keeping my nose head up as the *Charybdis* was buffeted by the most enormous waves. When Aspers finally stopped, I had half a mind to throw myself into the sea; for certain I knew that my life was going to be all downhill from then on in.

At a guess, I think we must have sailed about ten miles out, though it's difficult to estimate your speed in a storm. I tossed Aspers a line, went down below and started work on the stopcocks with a monkey-wrench. In five minutes, I was walking back through the galley and the water was already fountaining up at my feet.

On a whim, I picked out the last bottle of

Bollinger from the fridge and skipped up back to the wheel. She was already pitching less as the water rolled around in her hull. Aspers, cigar tight between his teeth, eased his boat over until he was alongside.

I took one last look round my old boat and my old life. But I have never been one to prolong my goodbyes. In fact I usually prefer not to say any goodbye at all — which, as it unwittingly turned out, was precisely how I took my final departure from not just my friends but also my own children.

Aspers' boat bumped alongside and I jumped, clinging to the rail for a second as my feet trailed in the sea before clambering up. I untied the rope and went to join Aspers in the wheelhouse, which was snug as anything after my hour in the elements.

Aspers looked out at the *Charybdis*, which was now in its death throes — very low at the stern and with the water cascading in from all sides. The first time that I'd ever seen a ship dying in the water; I watched with an utter sense of detachment.

For his part, Aspers was not so much watching the ship go down as watching me watch my own ship sink. That was him to a 'T', always keeping his eye on the man, rather than the peripheral stuff like the cards on the table. Although it was unusual to see a boat sinking, it was far more rare to watch a man watching his own boat slipping beneath the waves.

And with a final rush *Charybdis* was gone, one moment all but submerged, and with the next she was raked from the side by a sweeping roller and without even a murmur of complaint she did her master one final service by sinking into the sea.

Aspers heeled his boat over, taking the cigar out of his mouth. 'Very prettily done.'

'I brought you a small memento,' I said, bringing out the Bollinger from my oilskin pocket.

'My dear chap,' he said, eyes briefly running over the label. 'Give me the luxuries, and anyone can have the necessaries.'

'Just had a thought. We're not going to be seen by the harbour-master?'

'On a night like tonight? Are you insane?' Aspers crowed. 'Actually — you might want to take the Fifth Amendment on that one.'

Looking back, I suppose I did take the Fifth. We didn't say another word as we puttered back into Newhaven, side by side at the wheel, accepting the bottle in silence.

It was only when we were about a mile out and Aspers switched off the lights that the enormity of what we had done — of what I had done — struck home. I was shivering, part with the cold and part, I'm sure, from the delayed shock.

It was still raining, stormy even, when we finally pulled into the harbour. He took it dead slow, practically a crawl, as we eased past the trawlers and pleasure boats, before nudging into our berth.

I was tying her up before she'd even stopped moving and in under a minute we were walking along the quay, just a couple of old soaks slowly wending their way home.

And again, there was not a soul to be seen — not a soul on the streets, and not a glimpse of a passer-by to catch sight of me as I clambered into the back of the Land Rover.

It had gone perfectly, without a hitch. And for a moment, you know, I might even have believed that the luck was with me and that my life was set for a turn around. But it was not to be. It was just a momentary aberration, a fluke of good fortune, for the abiding trend of my luck was exactly as it had been in every other aspect of my life. I'd be the first to admit that good fortune has occasionally smiled on me — especially in the matter of my birth. But the ultimate trajectory of my life has been nothing other than sheer cataclysmic disaster.

We arrived back at Howletts without mishap, our routine now so well-honed that not a word had to be spoken as Aspers closed the garage doors before I climbed out of the back.

I watched without a quiver as the door slammed shut, sealing us off from the last of the rain. The weather is such a small thing if you have total freedom to come and go whenever you please, but, as I was soon to find out, the very moment that the outdoors is denied you, there's nothing that you yearn for so much as the sun on your face and the wind at your back.

After going over to the work-bench to unlock the trap, Aspers led the way down into my bunker. The silence of that library was in stunning contrast to the thrashing of the rain and the ocean; in fact, it was so quiet that if I closed my eyes I fancied I could hear the sea still lapping at my feet. After the fresh breath of the salt water, the bunker smelt unbelievably fusty.

One thing I do remember, as it was so very typical of Aspers. He walked into the main room and just shrugged off his dripping oil-skin and let it drop to the carpet. He was like my young son, still unaware of the niceties of hanging up your clothes.

'Phew!' Aspers said, rubbing his hands together. 'Do we need something to drink.'

I picked up his oil-skin from the floor and

dumped it in the bathroom along with my own.

He had found a bottle of whisky. We chinked, and like men who have done a fine deed and who have come out the other side, we looked into each other's eyes. With a grunt, Aspers nodded and we each of us subsided into the armchairs.

It was one of the things that I miss most about my old friends — the ability to sit and drink and not to have to say a single word. To dwell in your own thoughts but to have the company of an old comrade. There's not any especial need to talk, but if any idle thought comes up then you can blurt it out at will.

I don't know how long we sat there, my hand occasionally moving up to my skull to pat my hair and then discovering afresh that there was not a hair on my head. A whirl of thoughts galloping through my mind, one after the next after the next, but all of them disjointed. Flashes of Sandra dead in the cellar; and of my sinking ship; and of my ten-year-old daughter Frances peering down the stairs as she saw me for the last time. When you cram so much into the space of 24 hours, it takes a long time to digest.

Aspers leaned over and topped up my glass with Laphroaig. Funny that I should remember the exact drink; I've never tasted the stuff since.

'I don't think there's much more we can do at the moment,' said Aspers. 'But we must be ahead of the game.'

'Thanks to you,' I said. 'Thank you.'

'Not a bit of it.' Aspers laughed wryly, genuinely amused. 'Been dying for something like this to happen all my life. Wouldn't have missed it for the world. One can live for years sometimes without living at all, and then all life comes crowding into one single hour.'

'Well — '

'Honestly,' he said. 'I'm loving it. To live is the rarest thing in the world. Most people exist, that is all. Going out like that tonight. Not something I'd have done in a million years. But it was glorious. Utterly glorious.'

'And — ' I deliberated for a moment, still not clear in my mind what I wanted to say. 'And have you had any thoughts about my future?'

'None whatsoever!' He laughed, whisky slopping over the side of his tumbler as he threw his head back. 'Never done this sort of thing before, so I haven't the faintest clue. Still — don't think there's any great urgency to decide what we have to do next. As far as I'm concerned, you can spend as long as you like here. Become another member of my menagerie if you like.'

'Very kind,' I said, tipping my glass in acknowledgement. 'But that would be an imposition.'

Aspers belched as he stood up. 'I don't know when and I don't know how, but we'll get you out somehow. Best to sleep on these things. Got any idea where you might like to go?'

I shrugged. 'Don't know. As you say, I'll sleep on it.'

Aspers was just at the door when he turned and said, 'Oh — just one thing. There's already talk of the police taking sniffer dogs to your friends' various homes. I'll clean up the garage. But just for the moment, it might be best to stay down here.'

'That might be wise.'

He waved. 'Well — see you on the morrow.'

I heard the thump of the trap-door as I slipped back into the armchair.

Four months — that was what I had just consigned myself to. Four long months — I counted every day of them — incarcerated in that underground bunker. What a hellish place in which to keep a man.

7

Trying to recall my state of mind during my stay in the bunker is an impossibility.

It's like trying to recall why on earth I'd married Veronica 11 years earlier in November 1963. I mean it's obvious that at the time, when I married her, I must have thought it a good idea. But quite why I thought it was such a good idea . . . well I just don't know. I have no recollection of my thoughts, my feelings or even my reasoning. Come to think of it, I'm not even sure it seemed like a particularly good idea at the time.

And it was the same with those nightmarish early weeks in the bunker. There are a few events from two decades ago that I can recall with the utmost clarity, but just why or how I came to take leave of my senses in that bunker . . . it's beyond me.

It might, in part, have been the sheer lack of company. Aspers did the best he could and would try and pop round, but he had other things on his plate — his new wife Sally, for a start, as well as numerous evenings up in London — and so for days at a time, I was locked in this dungeon living the life of a hermit.

Some days, Aspers would pop down for an hour or so. He'd sometimes bring the papers with him just so I could see how bad things were — although of all the worst-case scenarios that I could ever have contemplated, not one of them was ever a patch on the reality.

To put it bluntly, I was the world's most wanted killer. You can forget that there hadn't been a trial or even an inquest. The facts were that Sandra Rivett was dead and Veronica was proclaiming — loudly and repeatedly — that I was the murderer. Besides I was a fugitive. And why else would I be on the run unless I were guilty?

The press was having a field day and who could blame them? The story had everything you could possibly want: murder, and intrigue, and blue bloods and cover-ups.

I wasn't aware of it at the time, but, once somebody's been arrested and charged, the press is very limited in what they can write about a case. It's in order — or so I understand — to avoid prejudicing a jury.

But, if no-one's been arrested . . . then, or so it seems to me, you can write whatever you like. So for those first two months after Sandra's death, it was open season. There was not a single theory that was not dissected in the most forensic detail. Some of them, as you'd expect, proved to be unwittingly accurate, but for the most part it seemed to me as if the hacks were doing nothing more than waltzing off to the pub and saying, 'What shall we write about Lucan today?'

There we go — don't I sound full of self-pity? But that's not what I'm about. Listen — I'm not a writer. But what I am trying to do is give you a little window into my state of mind at the time.

What I remember is how enormously vexed I became as my reputation was traduced and my family name dragged through the mud. Everything that I had ever done was put under the microscope and then given the worst possible spin. Time and again, I had to read about the Charge of the Light Brigade and how the Lucans had turned out yet another bad apple.

Today, I can see that I deserved nothing less. But locked away, gazing at my navel in the bunker, all I can say is that your mind plays tricks with you. It may not have been logical. And given what I'd actually done, it may come across as fantastically self-centred. But I had this huge sense of grievance at seeing my reputation in tatters and yet being unable to do a thing about it.

There — that is the truth of it. Even though I had plotted Veronica's death, I still felt outraged at the incredible amount of hostility — worldwide hostility — that was being directed at me. Day in, day out, I was pilloried in the press, and not a word was said to somehow redress the balance.

It goes without saying that the opportunity to give myself up had long gone. Any chance that I might have had of trying to bluff my way out had gone as soon as the police had discovered Stoop's Ford Corsair in Newhaven.

God it makes me cringe to think of my own stupidity.

For a couple of days after we'd scuttled *Charybdis*, there was still a part of me that was at least contemplating giving myself up. It was at least an option, though a highly unpleasant one.

And then one evening about two or three days after Sandra's death, Aspers had dropped in for a drink. He came round after dinner, which was his favourite time to pop down to my dungeon.

I'd opened a bottle of wine — a really expensive bottle of wine, a Pauillac, I think — in his honour, and, as ever, we were sat in the armchairs surrounded by those magnificent books.

He took a sip of red and smacked his lips with satisfaction. 'When one pays a visit, it is for the purpose of wasting other people's time, not one's own,' he said. 'What a supremely good idea to have laid down some decent wine here. Your good health.'

'And yours.'

Aspers started settling himself into his chair, fiddling with his cuffs and tugging at his trousers, minding me nothing so much as a gorilla before it goes to sleep. 'Went down to Newhaven this afternoon,' he said. 'Police swarming all over the place. They were checking the boats too, dozens of them all along the sea-front as if you were holed up on shore.'

'Good luck to them.'

'I suppose they must have found your car.'

'Probably,' I said. 'Pretty easy to spot the blood inside — '

I paused and looked at Aspers, and my mouth literally dropped open as my own unutterable stupidity suddenly dawned on me.

The moment the penny dropped — the moment when I realised that I'd left that damnable spare bludgeon in the back of the Corsair.

'Ohh!' I said. 'Godfathers!' That was all I could say. My immediate reaction was to bury my face into my hands. I just could not conceive how I had been so monumentally stupid. You, of course, can see that it's much of a muchness with all the other idiotic acts of my life. But for me this act of self-revelation was as stunning as a punch to the solar plexus. To have once considered myself a cool-hand in a crisis when I was capable of such a monumental blunder — what an idiot. What a total idiot. And it took me a full 40 years to realise that.

'What's wrong?' said Aspers.

My face was still buried in my hands as I rubbed my fingertips deep into my scalp. 'I've screwed it.'

'Well tell me!' Even Aspers, a genuine cool hand, sounded alarmed. 'Can they trace you?'

'No,' I said, shaking my head as this dreadful weariness swept over me. 'Nothing to do with that. It's the car. I'd forgotten. I had a spare bludgeon, just in case. Just in case the first one wasn't up to the job. And — ' I took a sip of wine, still staggered at my own folly. 'And I left it in the boot of the Corsair.'

Aspers clicked his tongue against the roof of his mouth, staring over the rim of his glass. He stared at the books, he stared at me, and he took a sip of wine, swirling it in his mouth.

'And the police? They have the original murder weapon?'

'It was left at the scene.'

'So — ' he said. 'So they have two murder weapons, both presumably similar, and one of them has been found in the boot of your getaway vehicle.'

'That would be right.'

'Well — ' He shrugged and smoothed his thinning hair back over his head. 'It would seem to me that you are Fouquet in Le Touquet!' He gave a bark of laughter before draining his glass. 'Certainly simplifies matters. Give yourself up now and it'll be Clink for you. Don't think we've got any option but to get you out of the country.'

I nodded blankly. It is a very humbling thing when your self-image comes crashing down at your own feet. And, along with that, there was also the knowledge that the rest of the world — apart from my eclectic group of friends in the Clermont Club — thought that I was a complete heel too.

There was one last thing though which, to my mind, pushed me over the edge. Getting the picture?

It was my children, my three dear children, George, Frances and Camilla. I would give the world now just to be able to kiss them on the cheek and tell them that I loved them.

But as I sat there for weeks on end in the bunker, I came to appreciate a number of different matters pertaining to the three of them. There was the knowledge of what I was putting them through at that very moment; and the knowledge that I had lumbered them with the sort of infamy that would take a lifetime to live down.

Even a month afterwards, it was still sinking in that I'd made the gamble of my life — and that not only had I lost, but the winner was Veronica. She'd got the money, the house, and, most harrowing of all, she'd got the children.

All these grim thoughts would whirl through my head, but the thing that was to torment me more than anything else was the realisation that, in all probability, I'd never set eyes on my children again. And that, to my mind, is one of the most terrible punishments you can inflict on a parent.

I know that many people might consider me to have been a fairly absentee father, who had precious little interest in his children and who spent his life gambling. I'm not going to argue the point. But what I can say, hand on heart, is that I loved those children to distraction and would have done anything for them. Hell — why do you think I wanted to do away with Veronica in the first place if not for the children? It certainly wasn't for the money, I can tell you. Although, now that I think of it, perhaps the money was a pertinent factor.

Do I contradict myself? Very well then, I contradict myself. I am large. I contain multitudes.[5]

So that hellish bunker, with all those wonderful old books, was the perfect place to contemplate all the things in my life that had now been denied me. Just the simple things. Holding George's hand as we went to the shops to buy the papers. Watching television with Camilla, side by side on the sofa, but not a word spoken. A kiss on Frances' cheek as she lay asleep in bed (for some reason, another beastly relic of being a blue blood, I always preferred to kiss my children when they were asleep. Heaven forfend that they should have been actually awake and conscious of their father's kiss.)

All of it was gone. I suppose there might have been a chance of me meeting up with them, once the whole hullabaloo had died down, but I knew it might be over a decade before that was ever likely to occur. If ever.

If I can be said to have any kind of pipe-dream these past 20 years in exile, it would be the hope that one day I could see my children again. I'd have liked, through

Aspers or the like, to have dropped them a line so that we could have arranged to meet up here. I've thought about it a lot, and several times had come close to penning the letter that would have set the whole scheme in process. But I always funked it at the last. And I'm sure you can see why. I'd put my children through quite enough of an ordeal already — and, or so it seemed, they had found a kind of equilibrium in their lives. They always had the background hum of their dear father's old skeleton rattling away in the cupboard, but — from what I'd read — they seemed happy enough. And having wrecked their lives once already, I was loth in the extreme to once more come trampling into their existence.

But I never did make the call, or write the letter, and so events have indeed turned out just as I'd feared all those years ago in the bunker: I will go to my grave without ever setting eyes on my children again.

These were the things that occupied me during my time in the bunker. But when I was not gazing in all my shallow introspection at my navel, I did actually make time for some reading. Damn all else to do.

I'd read a bit of Dickens when I was at Eton, but hadn't touched him in over 20 years. Given my state of mind, the books were not easy, but I kept at it and for a few blissful hours would occasionally find some release as I was locked in the Victorian worlds of *Nicholas Nickleby* and *Bleak House* and *Great Expectations.*

But the story that struck a chord in my heart was Dickens' *Christmas Carol.* I thought I knew the story well, had seen it several times on television. But all of it was just a pale imitation compared to Dickens' masterpiece. I cried the first time I read it — and this, mind, from someone who'd not shed a tear in over 30 years, not even at the death of his own father.

I'd never quite realised before how it was such a glorious story of redemption. A man who's sunk to the depths, who's merely counting the hours till he goes to his dreary grave — and yet who suddenly finds that magic can happen; that even when all appears to be lost, there is still a chance to make amends.

I can almost hear you tutting and rolling your eyes at how, having planned murder, I was snivelling away at Tiny Tim and the rest of them. But that's how it was.

Later though, after I'd snapped out of my *Christmas Carol* reverie, the true awfulness of my position was like a cold slap in the face. Scrooge had had his ghosts and his slice of

Christmas magic, and that had been more than enough to set him on the path of righteousness.

For me, I knew that I was already long down the road to hell — and that I was now utterly beyond redemption. I was disgraced beyond measure and I would never see my children again.

Mine was not some heart-warming fairytale where I could make atonement and seek redemption. I was beyond hope.

I loved *A Christmas Carol*. And I hated it. But it was the week before Christmas, and I could not stop myself from returning to it.

Empty bottles were strewn all about the kitchen and the library. I'd been drinking alone all day. Aspers had been stuck in London for three or four days for the Christmas parties, and I'd had nothing but my books, my bed and my booze. Did I mention it was December 18? And what a way to be celebrating my 40th birthday.

It was night-time, late-ish, and my hands were trembling as I turned the closing pages of that old leather-bound volume of Dickens' Christmas stories.

For the first time, the utter hopelessness of my position had sunk in. Hope is such an inexplicable quality. In most situations in life there is always some little hope left; some reason to be optimistic; some tiny glimmer of light that shows it's worth continuing the fight.

But as I sat there in that wing-backed arm-chair, with the tears still stinging in my eyes and a vodka bottle dead at my feet, I realised that I was beyond hope. That, even given the very best-case scenario and the most benign fall of the cards, my life was destined to be the most unutterable nightmare.

Such a feeling of despair. My memories of that night come in bleak little flashes. Stumbling through to the kitchen where I grab at a Sabatier carving knife, picking it up by the blade, but unaware of the pain as I gashed my hand.

In the bathroom, blood dripping from my palm, aware that I was looking at a maniac in the mirror, with his angry stubble of hair and those treacherous red eyes. Peeling off my clothes, letting them all fall to the floor as I run myself a deep bath, as hot as I can take it. I wince as I place one foot then the other into the tub, before very deliberately kneeling down. Enveloped by steam.

Imagining myself like some disgraced Roman senator, dispatching myself with honour amid dreams of Olympus and Empire.

I lean over to the basin and snatch up the carving knife. Idly inspect it. Detached, not even especially aware that the Lucan show was finally coming to a close.

Beads of condensation forming on the wicked steel. I sniff once. A tear dripping down my cheek and splashing into the water.

I strop the knife once, twice, up and down the length of my arm, and, casual-like, slash down hard into the veins at my wrist. It was surprisingly easy, took but a moment. I don't even remember any pain, just this feeling of light-headedness as this easy trickle of blood turned the water rosy pink.

A vague recognition that I am in the very act of committing suicide, and this is my butchered arm dripping out my life-blood.

Unconscionable weariness. The knife clattering to the floor. I sink back into the bath, water so deep it almost covers my face. Staring at the lights in the ceiling, dazzling in their brightness. And, my final thoughts, not of Veronica, not of my children, nor honour, nor family — no, just what a pathetic end to such a pathetic life.

★ ★ ★

Of course I didn't die; that's why I'm here now, nearly 20 years later, still clinging on to tell my tale.

The bloody truth of it was that, in the usual vexatious Lucan manner, I'd messed it up.

Didn't do a proper job of killing Veronica; and didn't do a proper job of killing myself either.

If I'd known, if I'd bothered to do my homework, I'd have slashed my veins vertically, elbow to wrist, before subsiding back into my warm-watered grave. Does the job quicker, and — crucially — even if you're saved, it's almost impossible to patch up a vein that's been slashed the length of your arm.

Would to God that I'd done a decent job of it.

8

As I came to, I was in almost complete darkness except for a glowing red light, which would move from side to side before occasionally flaring bright.

My eyes flicker. A roaring headache. A moment to get my bearings: in my bedroom in the bunker.

And in the doorway, silently standing there in black silhouette, was a man. He was so still that he might have been a statue, and all the while doing nothing but stare at me.

'Hello?' I said. Weak as a new-born.

There was no reply. Only the red dot moves about his face. For a second, I thought it was some freak of my imagination.

'Is anyone there?' I said again.

And do you know the first sound to assail my ears? It was a chuckle, a wry chuckle, as he took a puff of his cigar and let the smoke wreathe round his head.

'Deary me,' he said. 'Dear, oh dear, oh dear.'

I may have been enfeebled from loss of blood, but my heart was suddenly clattering in my rib-cage. For I knew the owner of that dry rasp of a voice only too well — and knew, also, of the sort of infamy that he was capable of.

'Jimmy?' I asked. 'Is that you Jimmy?'

'Himself,' he said, and with a flick of his hand he turned on the light. After the darkness, it was dazzling.

I grimaced at the shock, throwing up my hand to shield my face, massaging my temples as I allowed myself to peep through my fingertips.

Jimmy strode into the room. He had this cat-like grace, very fluid movement as he squatted down beside me, all the while twirling this cigar between his chewed fingernails.

He looked at me close-up for the first time, blue eyes but a foot from my own, a smile for ever playing on his lips as if he were about to erupt with laughter. 'My, Lucky,' he said, eyes flickering over my face and scalp. 'Like the new look.'

I shut my eyes as this wave of revulsion flooded over me. Perhaps I'd actually died — because there couldn't have been a more appropriate person to welcome you through the gates of Hell.

Jimmy Goddamn Goldsmith.

And now that my wretched nemesis has finally made his grand entrance to my story, I barely know where to start with him.

I'd known him for over 25 years, ever since our time at Eton. Such a long time ago. But I remember it better than the events that occurred to me last week or even yesterday. Yes, Goldsmith certainly made his mark, befouling the water wherever he went.

He was a shark in the business-world; a bastard in his personal life; and, along with everything else, he screwed every single woman who took his fancy. Goldsmith was incapable of fidelity — he was, after all, the man who coined the phrase, 'When a man marries his mistress, he creates a vacancy.'

Never one to forget a slight, he was quite capable of taking his revenge many years later.

I don't especially know why he took such particular pleasure in tormenting me. You'd have thought that, with all his double-dealings, he'd come across plenty bigger fish to fry.

But, for some reason, I must have hit enough of a nerve to make him want to keep coming back for more. Always, when I thought I'd seen the last of him, he'd come back to dish out a second, and a third, and even a tenth basinful of punishment.

But from whence did it all stem? Was it just some general malignance? Didn't he like the cut of my jib? Or was my title a perpetual reminder of the many festering sores in his life?

Or was there, perhaps, some other catalyst? Quite possibly so . . .

It was at Eton — of course — that we met for the first time. Quite liked the place; I enjoyed it well enough.

Although Goldsmith was a year or two older than me, I'd known all about him within a few weeks of arriving at Eton. The Goldsmiths were an offshoot of the Rothschilds, and he had inherited all the bumptiousness and braggadocio of a boy born into huge wealth — but without having the money to back it up.

Goldsmith was no richer — and no poorer — than most other Etonians, but even as a young teenager he had about him this air of entitlement, as if he were some princeling to whom the rest of the motley Eton crew should pay obeisance. And it wasn't just my nose that he managed to get up; he infuriated masters and boys alike.

He had his admirers, of course, because even at 16 Jimmy had this remarkable chutzpah. Nothing awed him, and nothing frightened him. Even when he was beaten and beaten again by the senior boys in his house library, he always came out smiling

— for ever laughing and with a cruel jibe for anyone that displeased him.

At school, he used to be a runner for one of the big London bookies, William Hill, I think, in Jermyn Street. His job was simply to trundle the bets up to London, and then return back to Eton with any of the winnings. For a man like Goldsmith, it was just too easy for him. He'd started bilking the lower boys out of their money. Told them to go to blazes, and what were they going to do about it?

For this — along with his general air of entitlement and his over-weaning conceit — Goldsmith was given a 'Pop tan', flogged by every prefect in the school, and there must have been well over 30 of them. Strong, beefy chaps, I'm sure, and I hope they laid it on thick.

Although we were in different houses at Eton, we'd come across each other occasionally at the races — where we would coolly eye each other up and perhaps give a nod. For let it be said that I more than knew my place in the pecking order — and the heir to the Earl of Lucan more than trumped some minor branch of a Jewish banking dynasty.

And now we come to one of the most extraordinary events that I have ever witnessed. I've seen many incredible things in my time, but I've never seen anything quite like this.

For I was there, there at Lewes races on the day that a 16-year-old Goldsmith won an absolute mind-blowing fortune. The figures — even in old money — were astronomical. No-one was ever quite sure how much he made when that triple came off, but in today's money I'd say it was close to half-a-million, maybe more.[6]

Of course, I was aware of none of this at the time. I was in my second or third year at Eton, and had gone off to Lewes with a few friends. Didn't I think I was the swell in my brown Trilby and bespoke suit in Prince of Wales check from my London tailors Johns and Pegg.

I didn't know that much about horses, never really been my thing. Racing, for me, was always much more about the party and the place to be seen. As for knowing what to stake my money on, well I'd have a look at the horse, I'd take a look at the form, see which one was looking frisky in the ring, and then I'd stick on my money just like every other mug punter on the course.

That day I'd been losing money all afternoon, but by some complete fluke I'd had a hit. I'd staked £10 to win on Merry Dance, and wouldn't you know it but she'd come in — and with enough of a pay-out to cater for a good night on the tiles in London. The girls cooed, the chaps slapped me on the back, and I smiled and patted my wallet. I may not have learned much from me dear pa, but I did at least know how to win with a good grace. Even at 15, I knew it would have been inappropriate and unseemly to have started hollering about my good fortune.

I was picking my way through the crowds to collect my winnings. A couple of friends had come along too, merely for the pleasure of watching the bookie stump up. Two fellows were in the queue ahead of me, but it was one of the few times in your life when it was a pleasure to queue. Punters who are waiting to collect their winnings do not object in the slightest to queuing.

My friends' good-natured prattle cascaded over my ears. I basked in the late-afternoon sun, wondering where to blow my winnings.

My ears were suddenly being assailed by the most raucous screaming. It was common and uncouth, and sounded like a football rabble.

And through the crowds, being held aloft like some Eastern Pasha, came Jimmy Goldsmith. He had a bottle of champagne in one hand, and with the other was delving into a white Panama hat and hurling out great glittering showers of coins.

You can imagine the furore. Everywhere you looked, punters were scrabbling on the ground, looking like nothing so much as grunting hogs as they grubbed for all Goldsmith's loose change.

Goldsmith would take another swig of champagne, grab a further fistful of coins, and again hurl them into the rabble. The punters shrieking with delight, Goldsmith's bearers singing some ditty, though with all the racket it was impossible to make out any sort of tune.

Total bedlam — and exactly the sort of scene that Goldsmith lived for, with him at centre-stage and the rest of the world just open-mouthed at the extravagance, the cockiness and the sheer damn impudence of the man. I call him a 'man' because he was the most precocious teenager you'd ever meet. He was 16 going on 30.

It was obvious that Goldsmith had had a big win — a really big win — but it was only the next day, after I'd read it all in the gossip columns, that I realised he'd scored the most incredible triple. The final odds were just eye-watering, something like 800 to 1.

I watched dispassionately as Goldsmith's caravan jostled through the crowd. I could see more clearly now, and saw that Goldsmith was sitting on two of his cronies' shoulders, with a great swell of people behind him. By chance, they happened to be coming straight towards me. I stood my ground, heedless of the rabble at my feet, who were clutching up Goldsmith's grubby loot.

'Madness,' said one of the friends at my side. 'Just look at him.'

Goldsmith was red-faced and bawling at the top of his voice. A slight raise of my eyebrows; I shook my head. Such an oik, that's what he was. Such a total oik.

And our eyes met. By now Goldsmith was only a few yards from me. He recognised me in a moment, and suddenly his face was wreathed with this vulpine smile, blue eyes crinkling. For I was there to witness him in his moment of triumph.

'Lucan!' he yelled. I could hear him clear above all the noise. 'Here Lucan! Have some chump-change! Treat yourself!' And with that he grabbed another handful of coins and tossed them in the air, the shillings pattering all about me in a shower of silver rain.

I didn't move, of course I didn't move. I wasn't suddenly going to start rootling for Goldsmith's petty cash. My face must have contorted in disgust as I snorted in derision.

And do you know what I said? Not to

anyone in particular, mind, but just as a sign of my contempt.

I looked him straight in the eye and hissed the words that were — I believe — to make me a marked man: 'Bloody Jew. Vulgar bloody Jew'.

There, you have it — along with everything else, along with causing Sandra Rivett's death and much else besides, I'm also an anti-Semite.

Let me clarify the point. It wasn't that Goldsmith's behaviour was typically Jewish. I've got no especial opinion on Jews either one way or the other. I just wanted to hurt the bastard any way I could.

Goldsmith heard me all right. His face changed in an instant; I've never seen a look go from euphoria to such total rage in under a second. His face went white, mouth pursed tight, while his eyes turned to gimlets.

He stared at me for a second, before giving me one very curt nod. That's all. A small acknowledgement that there was now a debt to be repaid, and that one day, in his own time, he'd fix me. And so he did.

Well, on the back of that historic triple, Goldsmith left Eton at 16 and duly squandered his winnings. But the vast difference between me and Goldsmith was that although we both have lost immense fortunes over the years, he always has had the ability to bounce back and make an even bigger one.

Before I continue with my tale, there is just one other story about Goldsmith, so that you can get the measure of the man. This one story — all true, I promise you — is an especially good indicator of the man.

When boys left Eton, it was customary to present their housemaster with a gift. I think I gave my man a case of port, though books, pictures and bits of silverware were always welcome.

Goldsmith's housemaster was, I think, Nigel Wykes, who was, by all accounts, a brittle man. He was a musician and an aesthete, the total opposite of the boor that was Goldsmith. The pair were for ever at loggerheads — which, given Goldsmith's dilettante ways, was hardly surprising.

It was a few days after his historic triple at Lewes races. Goldsmith had already taken his leave of his housemates, treating them all to dinner before telling them that he did not believe 'a man of such means should still be at school.'

And, just as tradition demanded, his final act at Eton was to take his leave of his housemaster. To Wykes' ecstatic delight, Goldsmith had bought him a collection of

Beethoven's nine symphonies.

Wykes was not a little touched. Had he, perhaps, misjudged the lad? Not one bit of it.

'Oh, but one thing,' said Goldsmith to his smiling housemaster. 'I couldn't just have those records back for a moment could I?'

Poor old Wykes, little realising what was about to befall, passed over the records — and watched aghast as Goldsmith smashed every single one of them on the side of the desk.

Know what I'd have done if I'd been that housemaster? I'd have knocked Goldsmith's teeth right down the back of his damn throat.

Never did do it to him though, and now that I'd like to — love to — it is not altogether possible.

So this then was the man that was squatting beside my bed in the bunker, in his pin-stripe suit and his perennial 'lucky' gold cufflinks. Goldsmith was one of the most superstitious people I've ever met, and for choice would normally wear these large gold cufflinks that he'd once worn during a successful deal. Although I couldn't see them, I knew that Goldsmith was bound to have a number of other superstitious oddments about his person, including a green stone frog that had been given him by Ginette[7] as well as a lump of amber that Aspers had once given him for luck. Of all Goldsmith's bizarre fetishes, I'd have to say that the amber was his favourite; if he wasn't playing with a cigar then out would come the amber.

'Well aren't you going to say hello?' he said. 'I thought you'd be thrilled to see me. Must be ever so lonely down here.' From those words, you might have thought he was bantering, some light-hearted joshing between old friends. But it was nothing of the kind. He was just probing before he turned the knife.

'Hello Jimmy,' I said, weariness covering me like a quilt.

'Let's see how that wrist of yours is getting on,' he said. He took my arm between strong fingers and, with his fat cigar champed tight between his teeth, started unwrapping the white bandage on my wrist. 'Don't know if there's any need for this bandage any more. Suppose it's possible the stitches might burst. That would be unpleasant, wouldn't it?'

The last of the bandage was stripped away to reveal a crusted black gash across my veins. It seemed to have been sewn together by a seven-year-old child. It was the sort of thick, uneven stitching that you'd see in a comic version of Frankenstein's monster.

'Catgut,' said Goldsmith, as he blew a jet of smoke up to the ceiling. 'Best I could do.'

'You did it?'

'Course. Aspers found you bleeding away and didn't know what the hell to do. He'd dragged you out of the bath and tried to stem the flow with a shirt. The only fortuitous thing was that I was staying at Howletts. Otherwise you'd have been a goner.'

'Yes — ' I said, limp as a rag. When I'd tried to kill myself, just a few hours earlier, it had never occurred to me that my position could get any worse.

'One of the oddest things that's ever happened to me. I was just having a brandy in my room when Aspers bursts in, covered in blood, and bawling at me to come and give him a hand. Think we got the cat-gut out of the vet's room, though — ' He looked again at my wrist, wrinkling his nose with distaste. 'We might have used something slightly finer. You could have sewn up a rhino with that.'

I'd have liked to have pulled my wrist away, but just didn't have the strength.

'Still had my dressing gown on, and there's Aspers bustling me out of the house. I wondered what the hell we were doing. At first I thought it might be one of the animals going into labour, but then, of all places, he brings me down to this old garage — and just look at the wonders that I discovered here.'

It was all I could do to look at him, a bullock in a cattle-crush as it turns its terrified eyes on the slaughterman.

'This bunker eh? Isn't it fantastic! Never knew it existed. And then what should I discover in here but the world's most wanted man! Bleeding all over the place like a stuck pig. The carpet's ruined, you know.'

'Where's Aspers? Get me Aspers.'

'Aspers? Don't worry about him. He'll be along soon enough. We've been taking it in shifts to look after you. Anyway, I was most hurt when I realised it was you. Aspers had sworn blind that he hadn't seen hide nor hair of you since you did for the nanny.'

'And then down I come and what do I see but Lucan with no moustache, a bizarre shaven head, and half-a-gallon of blood spattered all over the floor.'

My voice was now a whisper. 'Could you get me Aspers?'

'All in good time,' he said, shifting himself to sit on the end of the bed, as if he were some solicitous relative. The cigar was by now barely more than a two-inch stump. 'Why did I mind so much? It wasn't the lying that I objected to. That's just what Aspers does — he lies to everyone, even his best friends. Know what I think it was, Lucan? He had this most delicious piece of gossip — and yet he thought fit to withhold it from me.'

I turned my head to the wall. Goldsmith

had just downgraded my calamitous misfortune to, as he called it, a delicious piece of gossip. He'd said it just to rile me, of course — and he succeeded. 'Get me Aspers. Please.'

'I keep on telling you,' he said, stroking my hand. 'All in due course. Neither of us knew much about sewing, but I said I'd have a stab.' He cast a judicious eye over my wrist. 'Not the neatest sewing known to man. But it appears to be doing the job. And let's face it, Lucky, your days as a male pin-up are long gone — '

'Get me Aspers.'

'Tell me though, did you murder her? Aspers wouldn't tell.'

'Go to the devil.'

'It's a perfectly civilised question, and I'll thank you to give me a civil answer.'

I looked into those blue eyes again. Malicious beyond belief, and capable of any sort of mischief. 'I had a hand in it, yes.'

'Course you did,' said Goldsmith. 'That's why you're here now. Don't you worry though. Now that Jimmy's on board, Uncle Jimmy will get you out of here.'

He then sat on the end of the bed and picked up a newspaper from the pile on the floor, scanning the front page.

'I daresay,' he said conversationally, 'that you may end up being more famous than your great-great grandfather. That would take some doing, wouldn't it Lucky? The papers are obsessed by it! Take a look at this from *The Sun*, 'Earl in Nanny Murder Riddle' it says, and I quote, 'The murderer of children's nanny Mrs Sandra Rivett is believed to have mistaken her for her employer, the Countess of Lucan'. I'll say you did!'

'Shut up.'

He tossed the paper aside and picked up another from the pile. He scanned it before letting out a terrific roar of laughter. 'How is it that I've missed so much while I've been in France?' he said. 'These just get better and better. Apparently you've been spotted in Cape Town — oh, and here's another one from the *Express*, and I quote, 'Other detectives yesterday watched the homes of 21 close friends of Lord Lucan, who is being sought after the Upstairs Downstairs Murder Mystery'. Though I do think they could have done better than to dub it an 'Upstairs Downstairs Murder Mystery'.'

And on he droned, raking over the papers' front-pages and chuckling to himself as he read the highlights. 'But this is just priceless!' he said, his great chins quivering with laughter. 'May I quote from the *Express* again? 'Did a friend unwittingly help Lord Lucan evade arrest?' I do so love their use of the word 'unwittingly' as if somehow your friends hadn't realised that you were Britain's most wanted criminal.'

Goldsmith was nearing the bottom of the pile, discarded papers strewn all about the end of the bed, and his fingers grimy with newspaper ink.

'Incredible!' he said, throwing his head back he was laughing so loud. 'They've arrested that bovine MP John Stonehouse after he faked his death in Miami!'

For a while, I'd been on my side, staring at the white wall a few inches in front of my nose. 'Should I know him?' I whispered.

'You don't know? It seems that just a month after he was presumed to have drowned off Miami, our one-time Postmaster General has been discovered in Melbourne holed up with his secretary. Shall I tell you the best bit?'

'Please don't.'

'It was all down to you!'

I was so tired of his games and his incessant chatter. I continued to stare at the wall. 'Please leave the room.'

'Hear me out! They only arrested Stonehouse because he'd tried to withdraw some money from a bank and the cashier had got suspicious at the sight of this tall stuffed-shirt of an Englishman, and . . . ' Goldsmith took a last long pull on the stub of his cigar, 'And the cashier thought Stonehouse was you! Isn't that too perfect?'

'Get out.'

'Who'd have thought that you'd be indirectly helping to catch a fraudster?' He surveyed the stub of his cigar and had a half-hearted glance round my room to see if there was anything to stub it on. Then he dropped the glowing stub onto the floor, grinding it under his heel as he stood up. 'I don't think that you'll be moving anywhere soon, Lucky. So *ipso facto*, I will be seeing much more of you anon.'

I continued to stare at the wall long after he'd turned out the light. I'd found the story of John Stonehouse deeply unsettling — it had reminded me just how many lives had been blighted by my crime.

When I had first conceived of killing Veronica, I could never — never, never — have believed quite how many people's lives would be so comprehensively fouled and ruined. I well knew that, along with actually killing Sandra, I had wrecked the lives of both her family and mine.

But what I was coming to realise was that there were many other people who had been incidentally affected by the fall-out of my crime. The worst and most tragic of these incidents was that of my dear friend Dominic Elwes and his family, and I will return to his story later.

But who could have dreamt that my one act of reckless folly would directly lead to the arrest of John Stonehouse? Truly, it sometimes seems as if a single flap of a butterfly's wings can cause a tornado in Texas — and continue to cause tornadoes nearly 20 years on.

9

That first interview with Goldsmith was to set the tone for the rest of our meetings. Even though he lived in London, he'd come down a couple of times a week to see me, almost as if I had become his personal pet.

He seemed to delight in despoiling the bunker — my bunker, effectively — with his wretched cigars. Not that I'm averse to the odd cigar, but down in the bunker it was impossible to clear the fug of stale smoke. So that's what the place always smelled of: Goldsmith's cigars. I hope one day they kill him.

An hour after that first interview with Goldsmith, Aspers came down to visit me.

'I'm sorry,' he'd said. 'I didn't have any option. You were bleeding to death. I had to get Jimmy.'

Aspers was sitting on the edge of the bed, just as Goldsmith had done an hour earlier. He'd brought along a vast cornucopia of the most exotic fruit that you could come across in the 1970s — grapes, tangerines, pomegranates, guava, passion-fruit, starfruit — all of it, I later gathered, the staple fodder that he used to serve up to his gorillas.

'Jimmy will be fine,' Aspers continued. 'It's good to have him on our side.'

'I know.' I'd replied automatically and said what had to be said. But, in my heart, even at that early stage, I sensed that having Goldsmith on board was going to be a disaster.

'Nothing to worry about,' said Aspers. 'Have some more of that sweet tea. Good for blood donors, as I remember. I'm afraid it's slightly the blind leading the blind at the moment. Now — promise me that you won't do something like that again.'

'I — '

'You owe it to yourself. And you also, I think, owe it to Sandra. She's dead. What's the point in you dying too?'

'A small atonement?'

'Nonsense.' Aspers' logic may have been flawed, but at the time I was mollified.

'Ok, I promise,' I said. 'You have my word.' And, what's more, I have kept that promise — though often-times I have thought to break it.

'Good,' said Aspers. 'You'd have made a good blow-out though for the tigers. Couldn't have all that fresh meat going to waste.'

I did smile at that one. And later, as it turned out, this was a theory that was seriously mooted in the press. Just a year afterwards, it was widely surmised that

Aspers had actually fed me to his damn tigers.

Must have been Goldsmith who put that one about. Almost certainly, come to think of it.

Aspers took a huge ape-like bite out of an apple and munched on it meditatively.

'In a way, it's a good thing that we've got Jimmy onboard,' he said. 'He's got many more contacts than both of us put together. He knows the sort of solid low-lifers who wouldn't turn a hair at smuggling a man out of the country.'

I sighed. It was impossible for me even to conceive of a life outside that bunker. My entire world had been reduced to those book-lined walls and the tang of stale sweat.

'He says he'll get to work on it tomorrow. You'll be out of the country, free as a bird. Whatever happens, old cock, we'll look after you.' He looked at my arm. 'How you feeling?'

'Weak as milk.'

'Better sleep. And no more suicide attempts — you've promised.'

★　★　★

I had another two months in the bunker, gradually getting better from my little piece of self-mutilation. My slashed wrist cleared up within a few weeks, though the scar is white now in the Indian sun. It will be with me till the day I die.

My time was spent reading and, of all things, a little light exercise. Aspers had brought me down a skipping rope and an army fitness manual — stretching, press-ups, sit-ups. I'd not touched this sort of thing since my National Service days, as a Second Lieutenant in the Coldstream Guards.[8] But it's surprising what can amuse you if you're locked up in an underground cavern. As I got my strength back, I'd spend 30 minutes a day with that wretched skipping rope. By the end of it, I was as good as any boxer you've seen, cross-overs, doubles, ten minutes at a stretch.

Not much, but along with the library it took my mind off things; took my mind off Sandra, the children and the blizzard of bile that was being written about me in the national press. During my four months in the bunker, I don't think the papers ever let up on me, not for a single day.

There was one other thing that I recall of those days. For a while I'd let my hair grow, until I had a half-inch of stubble and another spiky half-inch on top.

You know how they say that a great shock can turn your hair grey overnight? I'd always thought it an old wives' tale — but it was precisely what occurred to me. The spiked hair on my head was completely white — white as parchment. Around my face it was more salt and pepper, though within the year that too was a match for my hair. I remember fingering it for the first time, looking at myself in the mirror, and not quite believing that that thing who was staring back at me was myself. In under a month I had turned into a silver fox — and have remained that way ever since. Add to that the disfigurement that came courtesy of Goldsmith and there was never going to be the slightest need for plastic surgery.

I suppose it all helped to alter my appearance. But even though I was a fugitive, it took me an age to get used to that white hair. Still, could have been worse — I could have gone bald. It was one thing, at least, that distinguished me from Goldsmith. As a boy, Goldsmith had had a fine head of hair, but one year, when he was barely in his thirties, he lost nearly the whole lot. Doubtless, it was a bodily reaction to all the many gross iniquities that he had visited upon the world. And I was to experience a couple more of those iniquities during my time in the bunker.

In those four months, before I made my final flit, I only left the bunker twice: both trips absolutely insane beyond belief, and both of them at the behest of Goldsmith. But what did he care if I was caught? In his eyes, I doubt I ever ranked much more than an experiment in revenge — and he'd still sup it up whether it was hot, cold, or even 20 years old.

The first time I left the bunker was after I'd been down there about a couple of months. I was almost into a routine by then, biding my time until Goldsmith and Aspers had plotted a way to get me out of the country.

I'd just had some coffee and an apple for breakfast and was starting on my morning press-ups when Goldsmith tore into the bunker, not even knocking as he burst into the library. 'My,' he said, taking in the scene of me in the classic press-up position. He was wearing a blue suit and tie, as if he were about to go into the City. 'Better come quick, Lucky.'

'What is it?' I was alarmed. Were the police onto me?

'Later,' he said, finger to lips.

'Where are we going?'

'Just put your shoes on.'

So of course I followed him — I was hardly going to stay there in the bunker. How did I know what had happened? It was all too possible that I was undone.

I followed Goldsmith along the passage, up the stairs and bent low as I emerged into the reception pit, slamming the trap shut behind me. The garage doors were closed, so there was not a glimpse of daylight to be seen, but after two months underground the sudden change of environment was shocking.

Goldsmith was already up and out of the reception pit — and, of all things, going down into the second reception pit just a few yards over. I'd hardly noticed this one before as the hole was usually covered with railway sleepers. Five of these sleepers had been hauled off and were lying beside the wall.

Goldsmith beckoned to me. I don't know what I was expecting to see. I don't think I was expecting anything at all; I was beyond expectation. But it was a surprise nonetheless: a second trap-door set into the side of the reception pit, very similar to the one that led to the bunker, and it was already open. Those trick doors were always like some extraordinary *trompe d'oeuil*. You expected the wall just to be a plain stretch of bricks, and your mind couldn't quite compute that part of it was at the wrong angle and swinging inwards, the line of bricks broken by a square of blackness.

'Come,' said Goldsmith, bending down into the trap. Oh, but didn't he look reptilian, leering up at me as he squatted down there amid the filth. 'Come on, Lucky. A sight that is positively not to be missed.'

So I went down the stairs and realised that, just as with everything else in his life, Aspers had told me exactly as much as I'd needed to know. No reason, of course, that he should have told me, but somehow over the previous month, and because I had taken Aspers into my trust so completely, I had assumed that he would accord me with the same level of confidence. Not a bit of it.

Although our friendship was now far deeper — and far more honest — than it had ever been before, he was still a long way away from laying all his cards on the table. I don't think it was personal. Even with Goldsmith, Aspers always kept a little in reserve. Just in case the cards fell awry.

What I realised as I went down the steps into the reception pit and peered through the second trap was that Aspers had a second secret tunnel — leading to heaven knows where. I stooped through the trap-door, to be confronted by another set of steps. Before I followed Goldsmith down, I clicked the door shut behind me.

At the bottom was a passage, arched and brick-lined with a concrete floor. It was a good height, well over six feet tall, and broad enough for three men. Goldsmith was already sauntering on ahead, hands in pockets, head a little stooped, as if he was doing nothing more than ambling by the Thames. The passage was long, far longer than the one to the bunker, and I could see the lights on either side winking into the distance as it inclined upwards.

I hadn't walked such a distance in weeks as I padded after Goldsmith. I'd asked him once where we were going, but he'd stilled me with a curt cut of his hand.

The tunnel was going fairly straight, but I had no inkling in which direction. Was this it, I wondered? Had I seen the bunker for the last time? Not that I'd enjoyed my time there, but it had been a haven of sorts; better by far than anything else I could have hoped for.

Occasionally I glanced at the dry, dusty bricks, but it was impossible to age them — they could have been anything from 30 to 300-years-old. But well constructed, even I could see that, with not a single brick out of line.

I don't know how far we'd travelled — could have been a half-a-mile or so. Eventually, we reached the inevitable trapdoor, though this one was full height.

Goldsmith stood in the doorway and gestured for me to bring my ear close. 'Don't say a word,' he whispered. 'Don't make a sound.'

What on earth were we doing? Where were we going? Was Aspers in trouble? I just couldn't make it out. All the while as we'd tramped along I had been going through every conceivable permutation as to why Goldsmith had brought me out of the bunker.

But even my wildest conceits were way off target. That, though, was because I had still not begun to appreciate the warped nature of Goldsmith's brain.

Beyond the door was a staircase, a very narrow staircase with walls that were barely more than a shoulder-width apart. Very old wood, dark oak, lit by a couple of lights in the ceiling. The plastered walls had once been white but were now dusty and cobwebbed, and the smell was musty as if it hadn't been aired in decades.

At the top of the stairs was a passage, again very narrow. There was no electric lighting along this stretch, but there did appear to be a window at shoulder-height, which gave off a very weak light. I peered briefly through. It was a grille of some sort. I needed a moment to make sense of what I was looking at — I was looking into an office, though my eye-level was right by the floor.

It was Howletts, it had to be — and I was being led through a warren of passages that ran right through the guts of the building.

We wormed our way further into the house, periodically passing these dusty grilles with their little colanders of light, snatched glimpses of rooms, some opulent and some used for nothing more than storage. All of the grilles seemed to be situated at ground-level in Howletts' actual rooms; I started to realise that, more than likely, on the other side they'd been disguised as air-vents.

Goldsmith was soundlessly padding ahead of me, occasionally stooping under a flight of stairs or a beam. He knew exactly where he was going and it was quite apparent that he had used this little network of secret corridors many times before — either for bed-hopping from one mistress to the next, or just for plain snooping. He was addicted to both.

By now we had been in the house some minutes, and had been up — and down — several flights of stairs. At first I'd thought that Aspers had put in this elaborate network of passages himself, but it was soon clear that they were part of the very fabric of the house.

Another stretch, again with walls so close that they practically brushed my shoulders. Goldsmith stopped and held up a warning hand. Ahead of us, I saw a glimmer of light from another carefully-positioned air-vent and could hear the quiet murmur of voices, one of them quite distinct. I'd have recognised Aspers' voice anywhere.

Goldsmith took up position at one side of the grille and made for me to join him. Squinting through, I could make out a desk, a couple of chairs, and two sets of men's legs — one of them, which had to be Aspers, was in work-boots, while the other was wearing the black lace-ups that are so beloved by officialdom.

I recognised the room — it was Aspers' office and I had been in there many times before, sometimes to gamble, though more often to square my debts.

Aspers himself, or as far as I could see, was lolling in a saggy-looking leather armchair, feet kicked up onto a matching pouffe, while the other man sat more soberly in an armchair facing him, knees bent, feet tucked together on the lush Astrakhan carpet. There was a pot of fresh coffee, still steaming on the walnut table between them along with — funny how I can still picture this — a vast plate of doughnuts and Danishes. There must have been at least 20 pastries there, all doubtless for Aspers' amusement.

'Have another éclair officer, why don't

you?' said Aspers. 'My pastry chef made them up specially.'

'No. Thank you.' The man in the blue suit — I could not see his face — flicked a speck of lint off the line of his trousers. 'Just to be clear about this, Sir. You have not heard in any way from Lord Lucan?'

I started at the sound of my own name. Of all the many reasons why Goldsmith had taken me into Howletts, it had never occurred to me — never for the first moment occurred to me — that he'd brought me in to witness Aspers being grilled by the police. I stared at Goldsmith, his face half in light, half in darkness, looking like nothing so much as a malignant fiend from hell.

Now it all seems so obvious. The sheer inevitability of it was almost staring me in the face. But at the time, the sheer nerve of what we were doing took my breath away: standing not five yards from one of the very detectives who'd been charged with hunting me down.

And he wasn't getting much change out of Aspers, I could see that. Aspers had gone into story-telling mode. This was, of course, fraught with danger, as the more he talked, the more chance there'd be of contradicting himself. But Aspers was such an accomplished bullshitter that this sort of spiel was just gammon to him. Besides, it wasn't especially his neck on the line; it was mine.

'Officer, I would like to be quite, quite clear about this. I have not heard in any way from Richard John Bingham, also known as the Seventh Earl of Lucan. He has not phoned, he has not written, and nor has he appeared here in person. Is that unequivocal enough for you?'

'It is.'

'Lift up the floorboards if you like, be my guest. Might take a bit of time, but if you feel the need to make absolutely certain that Lucan is not on these premises, then bring in the crowbars.'

'I don't know if this levity is appropriate.'

'Appropriate? What do you mean appropriate?' Aspers scratched himself at his fly buttons. 'Would you prefer me to be wearing a black suit and black tie? Would that be appropriate enough for you? Would you like me to have gone into mourning for this woman I never knew? Would that be appropriate? Perhaps you'd have liked me to have gone to the funeral too and made some simpatico speech. I daresay that might be appropriate behaviour. Should I be wearing sack-cloth and ashes on account of my friend being Britain's most wanted fugitive? Would that be appropriate? I just have no idea of what, two months after the event, would be considered appropriate behaviour. So why don't you just spell it out to me, officer, what by your lights would be appropriate.'

The officer flicked another imaginary speck from his trousers and crossed his legs. 'We understand that on the day after Sandra Rivett's death, you organised a luncheon party at your home in Lyall Street for Lord Lucan's closest friends. Why was that?'

'Why was that indeed?' Aspers said with a laugh. 'Because one of our closest friends was wanted for murder — and we wanted to find out what the hell had happened to him! What do you think we were going to do, play whist and sit there eating cucumber sandwiches like a bunch of wizened spinsters?'

'Had anyone heard anything from Lucan?'

'Not a thing. Not a bloody thing. And more's the pity. If I saw him now, I'd have shaken him by the hand.'

'So you're proud to have a friend who, we believe, attempted to bludgeon his wife to death?'

'Proud to have Lord Lucan as my friend? Of course I am — you don't imagine that I chop and change my friends just because they are presumed to have broken the law. And I use the word 'presumed' because, as you are doubtless aware, Lucan is still very much innocent. Wanted by the police, of course, but still a long chalk from being guilty.' Aspers was in full flow, his words tumbling out. 'But I tell you one thing, if she'd been my wife, I'd have bashed her to death years ago — and so would you.'

The officer took out a notepad and scribbled for a few moments. 'Will you call us if Lord Lucan makes contact?'

'Is that my duty? My duty is a thing I never do. On principle.'

Goldsmith nudged me, whispering, 'Only Aspers could quote Oscar Wilde at a time like this.'

Aspers paused a moment to tock, his tongue clicking against the roof of his mouth. 'No, I very much fear that if Lord Lucan makes contact, I will not be contacting you. Sandra Rivett's death was lamentable, but — even if Lucan is somehow connected to it, which I altogether deny — I don't see why I am especially beholden to the British police. You think, no doubt, that I have some higher calling and that the law of the land should take precedence over my friendship with Lucan.'

'I haven't heard that sort of piffle since my school-days at Rugby, when the masters used to encourage us to believe that it would be for the greater good if we started shopping our friends — and it sounds even more ridiculous now than it did then. So, to answer your question, hell will have frozen over before I start passing on to the police any confidences that I've received from or about Lucan — and, just so that we can be clear on this, I'm quite certain that his other friends would tell you likewise, though they may possibly lack my candour. And I'll tell you just one thing more, and that is that if Lucan wants money off me, I'll give it to him.'

After this tirade, there was silence. I doubt that the detective had ever heard the like. Eventually he got up, 'I don't think there's anything more to be said. Don't trouble yourself to get up. I'll see myself out.'

'I wish you joy of the day.' Very cool. Aspers didn't bother to stir himself in the slightest as the officer left.

The officer stalked out of the room, shutting the door behind him, and for a minute or so, there was just the sound of the grandfather clock and the slight click of Aspers' tongue, which was always the clearest indication of him ruminating.

I'd thought that Goldsmith was going to take me straight back to the bunker — but he was not nearly finished.

'Very impressive,' Goldsmith said softly through the grille.

Aspers started, just the slightest of

twitches. It was the only indication that the man had any nerves whatsoever.

'Hello Jimmy,' he said. 'Should have known that you couldn't resist witnessing something like that.'

'A command performance,' said Goldsmith, lips close up to the begrimed vent. 'Guess who I brought up to watch.'

'You didn't bring Johnny along too?' Aspers let out a snort of laughter and was up and out of his chair and squatting down at the grille, squinting through with his face not a foot from ours. His eyes suddenly caught mine. 'So you did, you cheeky bastard! Listening in to my private conversations — the sheer bloody nerve of it!'

Oh, but how he laughed, kneeling on all fours. At first it was just a chuckle, but it grew into a great roar of merriment, his great shoulders quivering. 'Quite the most idiotic thing I've ever seen you do,' said Aspers, red-faced now as he leant back on his haunches. 'What did you make of it? Didn't over-cook it, did I? I do know that I have a tendency to overplay my hand.'

'Spell-binding,' said Goldsmith.

'And you Johnny? Was it worth risking your neck?'

'It was,' I whispered. I could say no more. I was still reeling. Because — for once — I had been in that remarkably privileged position of watching a friend fight my corner, and fight it, mind, without any knowledge at all that I was there to witness it. It's a loyalty beyond price. And I tell you one thing, that although my life has been such a calamitous disaster, almost from start to finish, I have always felt blessed to have had the friendship of John Victor Aspinall.

Aspers laughed as he got to his feet. 'You must be out of your cotton-picking minds.'

10

So what turned Goldsmith into such a malicious swine? You may as well ask me what it was that first drew me to Veronica. I have no idea.

Who knows what childhood aberration turned Goldsmith into a monster — not just with me, mind, but with the vast majority of human beings that he ever chanced upon.

They say it was his short-lived marriage to Isabel Patino that hardened his heart, but that's nonsense. He'd been an unscrupulous hound long before Isabel came into his life. It's just that, with age, he's become much better practised at it.

I never quite grasped why Goldsmith's love affair with Isabel so captured the public's imagination — but it was a story that hogged the front pages for weeks.

He must have been about 20 when he met this fabulously wealthy heiress, and it was love at first sight. She was petite, very attractive, the daughter of a South American tin magnate — and if Isabel's idiot of a father had played his cards any better, then he might not have ended up with Goldsmith for a son-in-law.

But of course the clownish Antenor Patino had to forbid his daughter from seeing Goldsmith, and from then on the result was never in doubt. It was exactly — exactly — the sort of fight that Goldsmith thirsted for. Anyone who even remotely knew the man could have predicted the inevitable elopement to Scotland and their marriage.

What no-one could have predicted, however, was that a few months later Isabel would die from a brain haemorrhage while she was eight months pregnant with Goldsmith's child.

That — I admit — was a tragedy. She was by all accounts a vibrant, charming woman, and ever since her death, Goldsmith has always held her up to be his perfect embodiment of womanhood.

Now I don't wish to seem churlish. But, since I'm past caring, I'll say what I think. Goldsmith has behaved despicably with practically every woman he's ever met, and the fact that he didn't treat Isabel abominably is only because she died when they were still in the first flush of honeymoon love. I have no doubt whatsoever that if his first marriage had lasted even a year, then he'd have been cuckolding her just like he did with every other woman in his life.

Some people believe Goldsmith's endless bed-hopping had a sort of roguish charm. (It's always helped that he's been as rich as Croesus.) But for me, it has always been indicative of his complete contempt for humankind, where even the women that he's loved most in the world are eventually ground to dust under the wheels of his monstrous ego.

That, then, was how he treated the women in his life.

With men, it was more complicated. He had a few intimates, such as Aspers, but his general position was that men were there to be competed against, beaten and then dominated.

There was one other category of men who, for whatever reason, had irked Goldsmith to such a degree that they became his playthings, and he would periodically return to them to see if there were some new way that he might make their lives more miserable.

And I was one such.

★   ★   ★

By now my time in Aspers' bunker was almost at an end. There was nothing that I personally could do to effect my escape from

Britain, so all I could do was sit there like some fledgling swallow and await my daily scrap of news.

Goldsmith, it turned out, was doing the bulk of the planning and had been trying to organise a freighter. They'd thought initially about flying me out from Biggin Hill, or some other Kent aerodrome, but it was eventually deemed too risky. A freighter, on the other hand, was thought to be less likely to arouse suspicion.

Or so Goldsmith told me.

Since I'd never been in any sort of bargaining position, I was happy to go along with whatever Aspers and Goldsmith suggested. More fool me.

But at the time, I'd fancifully imagined that whatever Goldsmith was arranging, he had my best interests at heart. I had believed that since Sandra's murder, our various tensions had been resolved.

Not one bit of it.

My escape from Britain was — I believe — conceived and drawn up by Goldsmith with one aim and one aim only: to be the most hellish experience of my life.

* * *

It was the beginning of March, about a couple of days before I was due to leave

England for the last time, and I was filled with first-day-of-term excitement. I didn't know how it was going to turn out, but I hoped — I hoped — for a chance at a new life and the possibility of making amends. Anything had to be better than that stifling limbo in the bunker, with its lingering fug of Goldsmith's cigars.

I was reading in one of the armchairs, a cup of afternoon tea by my side. Those were the days when I was reading so much that I could devour a Dickens or a Dostoyevsky in under two days.

I heard the slight thump of the trap-door being closed and put down my book. I hoped it would be Aspers, but my head told me it would be Goldsmith; Aspers tended to come much later in the day.

It was indeed Goldsmith — and I goggled as he walked in. He was wearing a cream toga with an imperial purple border, while over his shoulder was slung a sack.

The sweat was dripping off his bald head and he mopped at his face before sinking into the other armchair.

I stared at him for a while, cool as you please. I was in no hurry to talk.

Goldsmith dabbed at his face again, the toga rucking up at his feet to reveal criss-crossed leather sandals.

'God that bag's a weight,' he said. 'Carried it all the way from the house.'

'Really?'

'Yes, really,' he said, delving into the sack. 'Got something for you Lucky,' and he handed over a crisp white invitation on which my name had been written in swirling black copperplate: 'The 7th Earl of Lucan'.

'I'll get some champagne,' he said, stalking off to the galley.

I was vaguely aware of him tinkering with some glasses, but I only had eyes for the letter. I had seen many of these invitations before, and just like all the others, it was thick and engraved on the most expensive card that money could buy.

Aspinall's parties were legendary. The planning alone took months and months, and as for the cost, well all I can say is that during Aspers' pomp, there wasn't a magnate in Britain who held parties on quite such a scale of lavish opulence.

So as I sat there, invitation loose between my fingertips, I knew exactly the sort of thing that I was being invited to. But what was the point of dangling this little morsel in front of the world's most wanted fugitive? It wasn't as if I'd dare set foot into the party.

Would I?

The invitation, engraved on gilt-edged

card, extended to ten pages, complete with illustrations and a typical piece of Aspers' creativity. For every one of his parties, Aspers would indulge himself in over 2,000 words of scene-setting, just to get his guests in the mood.

I can, at least, remember a little of how it started: 'Three millennia ago, the people of Ilium celebrated the end of a ten-year war. The ships of their oppressors, the Greeks, have already quit the shores of Troy and in their stead is a wooden horse, an offering to the Gods for a safe passage home. It is a remarkable horse, accurate to the last detail, with its head so high that it practically peeps over the city gates. It has wheels too, for ease of movement, and this morning has been dragged up over the slick sand of the shore and into Ilium itself.'

'The King, Priam, has finally vanquished the Greeks and is celebrating with the most uproarious party of his life. His son Paris, a one-time shepherd, has been forgiven, and by his side is the world's most beautiful woman, Helen of Troy. And who is that lurking in the background? Who but Priam's daughter Cassandra, looking half-mad and for ever screeching prophecies of doom and destruction — but no-one will ever believe her . . . '

And so it went on. How ever bizarre it may seem, Aspers' party was celebrating the fall of Troy — and, as I was soon to discover, a group of workmen had spent the past fortnight constructing a huge wooden horse to stand outside the front of Howletts.

To anyone who didn't know Aspers, the fall of Troy might have seemed an eccentric theme for a party, bordering on bad taste. But Aspers had always loved his historical heroes, and thought nothing of spending half-a-million on recreating such obscure events as 'The Banquet of the Diadochi' or 'The Feast of Mithridates' — whatever the hell they were. I can even recall once going to 'The Banquet of Guatemoc' to celebrate the birthday of some Aztec emperor who'd caught Aspinall's fancy.

This, then, was the sort of all-night party to which I had just been invited. In my prime, I'd have done anything for an invitation. But now . . .

Goldsmith handed me a glass of champagne. We chinked and I drank, thirstily. It tasted odd, a little bitter. That was because Goldsmith had spiked it. I'm sure he had. Otherwise there wouldn't have been a chance of luring me out of the bunker.

'The party's tonight,' said Goldsmith, nestling into the other armchair. 'And seeing as I'm paying for the bloody thing, I'll invite whom I please.'

'You're paying for it?'

'The dear old sod's gone practically bankrupt again. It happens occasionally. But appearances must be maintained, parties must continue to be thrown, and *ipso facto* I must support him.'

'Really?'

'Oh — don't worry about Aspers. I daresay he'll win it all back at poker, just like he always does, the cheating hound.'

'And there's my uniform?' I nodded at the sack on the floor.

'Exactly,' he said, stretching inside his toga and producing a small envelope. He casually stroked the top edge before opening it. 'Strange theme for a party, but I believe that Aspers is currently obsessed with Priam's son Paris. Not that I know much, if anything, about Paris, but I suppose that he did have much to commend him. Ran off with the world's most beautiful woman and thereby caused the death of every one of his countrymen. For that, alone, you have to admire him.'

'He sounds a lot like you.'

The champagne — or whatever had been mixed into it — was jangling at my nerve endings. I felt this sudden surge of energy. It was like nothing I'd ever experienced before, as if I'd been given a shot of raw power. I'd even lost the edginess that I usually felt when Goldsmith was in the room.

Already I was up and pacing the library, pouring out more champagne as I stalked the chairs.

'Aspers isn't seriously expecting me to come? How can I come?' I swilled back more champagne. 'I couldn't possibly come.'

Goldsmith screwed up his face and made a dismissive flip with his hand. 'It's all been taken care of. You'll be standing at the door dressed as a Greek soldier. Aspers has got a score of actors in for the night. You'll be there among his gaggle of soldiers, midgets, priestesses and whoever else he's thought fit to hire for the evening. All you have to do is be one of the gatekeepers. Stand at the front door, sword in hand, looking grim and sentry-like. You won't have to say a word.'

'It's crazy,' I said, but I could sense this rip-tide of bravado.

'It is crazy!' said Goldsmith, pouring the contents of the letter onto the desk and chopping it with a knife. I recognised dully that it was cocaine, which was not my usual vice of choice. (No — us peers generally like to get our kicks from the quaint, old-fashioned addictions of our forefathers such as gambling and drinking.)

He cut the cocaine into four lines, rolled a ten pound note, and sniffed up a line with each nostril. 'They're calling it a 'rock and roll breakfast' these days,' he said. 'Here. Put a bit of colour back in your cheeks. You could certainly do with some.'

Not that I'd got anything especially against drugs. But under normal circumstances I wouldn't have touched them with a barge-pole. Even then, even before my first tentative snort, I realised that I had what's now known as 'an addictive personality' — and the very last thing I needed was a coke habit.

But suddenly it seemed like the most sensible thing in the world. A 'rock and roll breakfast'? Just the ticket. Just the thing to raise me out of the unutterable tedium of life in the bunker.

I took the rolled-up note and, mimicking Goldsmith, closed a nostril and snorted one of the white lines. A moment later, I did the same with the second.

It's difficult to recall the actual sensations of that first hit of cocaine, but I remember how the effect was almost instantaneous. The powder seemed to have hooked straight into my brain's pleasure zone. Every thought of my children and my wretched existence was erased from my mind to be replaced by this great wave of euphoria. As good a feeling as winning a fortune at backgammon — possibly better. It was as if every single button in my brain had been pressed at the same time. I was fizzing, unstoppable — no longer a fugitive on the run, but Superman. The possibilities were limitless.

One of the things about cocaine is that you can't stop talking. You talk and you talk — though the next day you never have the faintest recollection of what you were actually prattling on about.

An hour later, I was looking at myself in the mirror. By now, I was used to that two-inch shock of white hair on my head with a beard to match. But as I stared, my mouth was actually moving up and down, as if trying to spit out the great raft of inane ideas that were teeming through my head.

After the cocaine, the thought of dressing up as a Greek soldier to join the party seemed like the most extraordinarily brilliant idea. It would be a chance to see all my old stalwarts for the last time — even if I was unable to utter a word.

Goldsmith was, if anything, even more jubilant than me, helping me tie up the heavy-duty sandals and buckling the back of my leather and iron tunic. But instead of a proper Greek battle skirt, I was kitted out with a faux leather swimming costume that clung to me like a second skin. The better, said Goldsmith, to show off my lissom legs. At the time, I found those skin-tight Speedos uproariously funny — after all, who on earth would be able to recognise me from my bare legs alone?

My uniform was capped off with a floor-length red cloak and a plumed helmet, with great side plates that hid all but my eyes and chin. The helmet, with its sweeping horsehair plume, must have made me nearly eight-feet tall; quite an imposing sight for a gatekeeper.

'Very good.' Goldsmith nodded. 'A fine figure of a man. Very *distingué*,' he said, switching to French, in which he was fluent.

Minutes later I was following Goldsmith in the long tunnel to Howletts. I hadn't noticed it before, but there was a trap-door leading from one of the stairwells into a scullery. Goldsmith had a quick peek through the air vent to check no-one was there before opening the trap. We crawled into the scullery from underneath some crockery shelves.

'And here we are,' said Goldsmith, grinning again at the thought of yet more mischief-making. 'I daresay you better put your helmet on — though frankly with that hair and that beard, not even Veronica would recognise you.'

As I slipped on the helmet, tying it tight beneath my chin, I'd never felt so pumped. Goldsmith led the way out of the scullery and into the heart of the house. From all sides, I could hear the chatter of voices as Aspers' team made ready for the party. A glimpse into the kitchens, where a dozen people were prepping for dinner. Florists tweaking and snipping at great haunches of flowers that flowed down the stairs in a waterfall of colour. Teams of waiters and waitresses laying up the round tables in the vast marquee. Dozens of Greek and Trojan soldiers casually having tea in the drawing rooms, giving no more thought to their costumes than if they'd been dressed in jeans and t-shirts. An immense wooden horse, menacing black, to greet the guests as they came up the drive. And, most bizarre of all, Aspers in the library dressed like Julius Caesar and surrounded by at least a dozen toga-ed midgets. (You might not realise the difference, but midgets are normally proportioned, while dwarves are not. When Aspers discovered that midgets were much rarer, he never hired another dwarf again.)

Aspers had several bottles of brandy and the midgets — with, presumably, their midget tolerance to alcohol — were already well on their way to becoming, as my grandmother used to say, 'fusionless with drink'. Aspers was coaching them on what to say to the guests.

And here's another thing that you might not believe about Aspers: he was teaching those midgets the very grossest insults that you could hurl at a woman.

'Mutton dressed as lamb!' they'd chant, and Aspers would let out a great peal of laughter. 'What an old tart!' they'd say. 'Who's been dragged through a hedge backwards?'

All good knock-about stuff — if, that is, you were thick-skinned enough to take it.

Although Aspers spared no expense at his parties, serving up only the very finest wines and foods, his guests did have to expect a fair level of teasing. Sometimes it bordered on downright abuse.

The drunk midgets were generally placed in various niches around Howletts, especially above the staircase, from where they would rain down insults on any woman who dared walk through the front door; the more glamorous the woman, the more lewd the insult.

Aspers had also spent an inordinate amount of time over his seating plan — to make it as offensive as humanly possible.

How on earth can a seating-plan be offensive? Not a problem at all — if you decide to group the guests by type.

So, as I wandered through to the main marquee, I could not help but smile as I saw that Aspers had divided his guests up into tables of 'Whores', 'Jews', 'Pimps', 'Poofs' and 'Poodle-fakers', as well as a catch-all table for anyone who could not readily be pigeon-holed: 'The Wunch of Bankers'.

Aspers caught up with me as I laughed at his seating plan. 'Astonishing!' he said, clapping me on the back. 'I laid Jimmy ten to one that he wouldn't be able to lure you out of the bunker! How did he do it?'

'He spun me a line,' I replied, pleased with my *double entendre*. 'You know me. Never one to resist a challenge.'

'Let me have take a look at you then,' he said. 'Guards on parade, please.'

I squared my shoulders, head up, eyes on the middle-distance, as Aspers inspected me from close-quarters like some pernickety Sergeant-Major.

Finally, after a minute, he stood in front of me pursing his lips. 'I think it will do. Those rubberised pants were a very good idea.' He squeezed the bridge of his nose. 'I can't really be objective about it. I've no idea. But it's your call. Do you really want to go through with it?'

'Of course.' That was the cocaine talking, mark my words.

'Should be all right, so long as you keep your mouth shut.' Aspers nodded as if he was talking himself into it. 'We'll have you with another Greek soldier by the front door. You'll be like a pair of Guards at Buckingham Palace: At ease, but with lips sealed, whatever the provocation.'

'Fine,' I said.

'Stay there as long as you like.'

'I'll just see them in.'

'Would you like a sword and spear? Give you something to do with your hands?'

By dusk, I was standing guard by the front door of Howletts in that vast porticoed entrance, with one hand grasping one of Aspers' Zulu spears. I'd not exchanged a word with the other Greek sentry, who'd taken up position by a brazier about 10 yards away.

Such a delight to breathe in fresh air and to be able once again to see the sky, the trees and the crescent moon. We all of us should be denied these simple pleasures for a time, just so that we can appreciate them all the better.

A moment of wonderful tranquillity as I stood there in the sundown-light with a zephyr of wind tracing over my bare legs. The monstrous wooden horse was dead ahead of us, brooding black against the rippling orange skyline.

The first guests started to arrive and for me it was as if I had a mute but starring role in *This is Your Life* — for, whether by accident or design, the guests appeared to come from every single chapter of my life.

It was, I suppose, my last farewell. I never saw anything of them, not a single one of them, again. And they were all there, almost every man that I had ever thought of as a friend. How strange it was to stand there, stony-faced, as the likes of Charles Benson and Bill Shand-Kydd strode past arm in arm without even glancing at me.

Oh how I had to restrain myself from talking to Ian Maxwell-Scott; just to have touched him on the arm and wished him well.

But, even with the cocaine in my system, I knew it would have been criminal folly to have said a single word. Regardless of my disguise, just a single drawling word from my mouth would irretrievably have blown my cover.

I'd been on guard duty for nearly an hour when from out of the darkness I recognised a voice. It was one of my most treasured friends

— Dominic Elwes. Dominic was one of the great wits of our generation, who when he was on form could make even Aspers play second-fiddle.

Dominic was not just a charmer, but with his blonde hair and blue eyes was strikingly handsome. If he had a fault, it was that he adored mixing with the super-rich. And it's not easy when most of your friends are multi-millionaires and you haven't got a bean to rub together — because no matter how funny you are and how devastating your repartee, sooner or later you'll get tagged as a freeloader.

But that wasn't how I saw Dominic. For me, he was just another traveller who, like myself, had never had much luck with money and was happy to accept whatever scraps fell from the top table.

Dominic was dressed in a Greek soldier's uniform, complete with a red helmet plume that was even more garish than my own. He was chatting and laughing as he bounded up the stairs two at a time. At the top he waited for the two women who were accompanying him.

He was standing in the doorway, just a couple of yards to the side of me and silhouetted in a blaze of light.

'What ladies!' he said. 'It must be Helen of

Troy and her younger sister!'

The women laughed, but they loved it all the same — and all the while I stood there stony-faced, not moving a muscle as I stared stubbornly at that wooden horse.

Dominic ushered the ladies in and was just about to follow when he caught sight of me out of the corner of his eye. I don't know whether it was my stance or my aura, but suddenly he stopped in his tracks.

'Ladies — ' I heard Dominic say. Did I detect a slight catch in his throat? 'I'll be with you in just one moment.'

I sensed him padding softly towards me. I steeled myself to stare at the wooden horse.

Dominic stood not two feet in front of me, puzzlement playing over his features as he peered through the deep shadow into my face.

I was as immobile as if I'd been on parade before the Field Marshal. I tried to fix my eyes on the horizon; on the crest of his helmet; on his forehead.

My gaze wandered, and for just a single moment, our eyes met.

Up until then, he hadn't been quite certain. He had been intrigued, doubtless seeing some old echo in my posture. But he didn't know for sure until he'd looked me in the eye. I was staggered at how quickly he'd recognised me. The eyes are indeed a window to the soul. You can lie and you can dissemble, but your eyes are going to give you away every time.

'Johnny?' he whispered. 'Is that you?'

What torment it was to have to stand there, unable to say a word to one of my dearest friends. A part of me, naturally, wanted to embrace the man and to toast his health with champagne; I loved him as much as I loved Aspers. But another part of me had long ago realised that Dominic was the very last person with whom to share my secret. He was a blabber, simple as that.

He stared at my face a moment longer before his eyes darted down to my legs. The red cockade of his hat almost brushed against my chin. I wondered what he was doing.

I felt a ripple of shock as I realised that he was searching for some of my old scars. One of them, from an old water-skiing accident, had turned into a white blotch on my knee. A total giveaway.

Dominic was so surprised he staggered a pace backwards. 'It is you!' he whispered. 'My dear, dear Johnny.'

I'd clenched my teeth, but the spear was trembling in my hand. I snorted a great lungful of air.

'Oh my good God,' Dominic said, his face

just a few inches from mine. 'My dear Johnny. I am so glad you're still alive.'

He continued to stare at me, before impulsively taking a step forward and embracing me. Never in my life have I so welcomed a hug — and been so unable to reciprocate.

I screwed my eyes up tight, trying to stop the tears. But they came anyway, nothing could stop them coursing down my cheek. Tentatively, I rested my chin on his shoulder. How good it felt to be held like that. For a few moments I just stood there, leaning into him and letting the tears fall. He soothed me like a mother soothes her child, hands stroking my shoulders. It was just how it's been throughout my life. I can take any amount of insults, any amount of derision, but just offer me a crumb of kindness and I turn to mush.

Dominic gave me one last squeeze. I believe that I may even have let out a whimper at the unbearable pain of it all.

'I know you can't talk,' he said, cupping my face lightly to stroke my cheek. 'But wherever you go and whatever you do, I'll always think fondly of you. If you ever need help, I'm only a phone-call away.'

Without another word, Dominic leaned over and kissed my cheek. I think it was the first time that I'd ever been kissed by a man like that; it is quite different from the kiss of a woman — much rarer, and all the more meaningful because of it.

Dominic gave me one last hug and then was gone, flickering through the front door in a haze of red horsehair and glittering armour.

I was reduced to a shambling shell of a man. I was still trying to present the stolid, imperturbable soldier, but my mask was falling all to pieces. Even as I clasped onto my weapons, digging in my fingers until my nails ached, my shoulders were heaving and the tears streaming soundlessly down my cheeks.

It wasn't just the uncharacteristic affection that I'd received from Dominic, so very different from anything that I'd seen from Aspers or Goldsmith. It was also the damning realisation that I'd never see any of my friends again. I hadn't given the matter much thought before. I suppose I'd believed that in the usual nonchalant Lucan fashion I'd make friends wherever I went. I'm a man's man; I like male company and I attract it.

But friends like Dominic, like Charles and Bill? The men were one-offs and I would never see their like again. I would that I had appreciated their friendship more at the time; and that I had been better able to repay it.

All I can say is that there have been times when I have missed those men as much as I missed my own children.

Eventually my shoulders stopped heaving and the tears dried in the wind, streaked white salt on my cheek-bones. I was benumbed, not knowing why I remained on guard-duty, yet standing there still for the hope of a last glimpse of an old friend. And what would I do when I saw him anyway? It was pitiful, pathetic. I looked about me one last time, and then skulked, tail between my legs, back through the pantry to my cigar-fugged hell-hole.

It was the last time that I would ever lay eyes on Dominic or any of my other old stalwarts.

And seeing as Dominic is about to leave my story, I may as well tell you how it all turned out for him. And, just as so often happens with people who've fallen foul of Jimmy Goldsmith, it turned out badly.

Now I'm aware that so far in this narrative, I may have given you a few indications as to Goldsmith's bullying manner and general viciousness. But — quite apart from what he did to me — if ever you wanted to see Goldsmith in action, you only had to see what he did to Dominic.

And it all so tragically stemmed — of

course — from the botched murder of Sandra Rivett.

What occurred was that about seven months after Sandra's death, and long after I'd quit the country, the *Sunday Times* ran a colossal feature on the murder and all its subsequent fall-out. Apart from being a re-hash of all the most salacious stories about myself, it concentrated on what has come to be termed as 'The Clermont Circle'. This circle included Goldsmith, Aspers and a few other of my so-called cronies — and it was these men who were widely perceived to have spirited me out of the country.

Like all the stories about my disappearance, it was part fact and part supposition. Most of it was very wide of the mark. But, unfortunately for Dominic, both he and Aspers had collaborated with a young Old Etonian, James Fox, in writing the story. Both of them, I'm sure, believed that they were helping me out by muddying the water.

Dominic then compounded the error by doing an oil painting of the Clermont Circle, including in it the ghastly visage of Goldsmith — who, as you may remember, was about the one person who hadn't attended Aspers' lunch the day after Sandra's murder.

The thing that sent Goldsmith into a white rage, however, was a photograph that the

Sunday Times had dredged up of me alongside Annabel Goldsmith. It had been taken while we'd all been on holiday in Acapulco, and although the setting was innocent enough, the picture had been so cropped that it looked as there was a sniff of a romance between the pair of us.

Goldsmith went mad. For a man who was as legendary for his bed-hopping as his billions, he was an inordinately jealous man. And it was my dear Dominic who had to take the rap. Goldsmith blamed him for collaborating with the paper; he blamed him for painting that picture of the Clermont Circle; and he blamed him chiefly for selling that private photo of Annabel and me (which Dominic never did, by the way — he didn't know one end of the camera from t'other.)

The upshot was that Dominic found himself ostracized from all the swells and the nabobs whom he had once considered his closest friends. Goldsmith just froze him out and the rest of them followed suit.

Dominic had no money and had lost all of his closest friends — but it was Goldsmith alone who assassinated Dominic's character with such remorseless ferocity.

Within six months of that Fall of Troy party, Dominic committed suicide by taking a cocktail of barbiturates. Along with Sandra, my children, and even my dear wife Veronica, Dominic was to be yet another hapless victim of my crime.

Have I mentioned that — like me — Dominic was a father-of-three? Just three more innocents who were to become incidental casualties of the murder. It makes me weep to think of it.

11

I suppose I had better record the last incident from Aspers' party.

I'd tried to get some sleep, but after the cocaine and my meeting with Dominic, it was impossible. I read for a while, did some skipping, drank champagne and by the time I went to bed was completely over my earlier outburst of maudlin self-pity. When I next got up, there was Goldsmith reading the papers next door in the library. The bunker had become a proper little *pied-à-terre* for him.

His toga was a sight — frayed and spattered with wine and mud. He looked up from the *Daily Express*, puffing on another of his repellent cigars. I have never been able to abide them since. 'I have made an important discovery . . . that alcohol, taken in sufficient quantities, produces all the effects of intoxication.'

'Christ — now even you're quoting Oscar Wilde.'

'Tell me Lucky, did you really use to tape all your inane conversations with Veronica?'

'What?' I poured myself some champagne

and sat opposite him. 'What are you talking about?'

'Just listen to what it says here in the *Express*, and I quote, 'Lord Lucan hoarded 60 tapes totalling 70 hours of conversation he had with others in the society world in which he moved. He bugged the telephone of his home in Belgravia and even intimate talks with his wife'. Is that really the act of a gentleman?'

'I don't really think you're the person to be telling me how to behave like a gentleman,' I replied. Yet how distasteful it was to be reminded — again — of my own unsavoury behaviour. I had, as it happened, been taping many of the conversations that I'd had with Veronica, and, in mitigation, all I can say is that I did it for the children. I had thought that the tapes might help me win the custody battle.

But I was certainly not going to embark on a conversation with Goldsmith about the rights and wrongs of phone-tappings. So I changed the subject.

'Who have you been sporting with tonight?' I asked, nodding at the grass stains on his toga.

'Lovely girl,' he said. 'Aspers introduced me over drinks. I must say that he does his best to look after me. Had her before dinner.'

'Who was she?'

'You don't seriously expect me to remember those sort of details?' He placed the cigar on an ashtray and started to play with his lump of lucky amber, slipping it through his fingers. 'So how did you get on Lucky?'

'Dominic recognised me.'

'Did he now, the blighter? Well that's not good.'

'No, it's not.'

Goldsmith raised his eyebrows and peered at me before returning to his paper.

I'm sure it was the cocaine and the champagne talking. They're a lethal combination. Out of nowhere, I suddenly asked, 'Would you like to break my nose?'

'No thank you.' Goldsmith didn't even look up as he turned the page.

'I'd appreciate it.'

'What — now? Just because you were recognised by Dominic? Don't be ridiculous Lucky. It was a fluke.'

'I think it's best.'

Goldsmith shrugged and got to his feet. 'If you insist. Though I'd rather not use my fist. Maybe there'll be something in the kitchen.'

He returned with, of all things, a steel hammer with dimples on the front. I believe they're used for tenderising meat. 'You're quite sure?' he asked. 'You know you're completely unrecognisable with that beard and crew-cut.'

'I'm sure.'

'Just sit back in your chair then, nice and easy.' He hefted the hammer in his hand. 'I daresay that I'm going to enjoy this. Never had the pleasure of a free hit at a man before.'

Well, all I can say is that I was still high on coke and I'd just polished off three bottles of champagne. I seriously thought that a different nose might better disguise me.

Goldsmith stood over me, inspecting my face in minute detail. 'Daresay it's the only way,' he said. 'That splendid patrician nose of yours could only belong to an aristocrat. Don't tell me — it's been in the family for generations.'

'Do we need a towel?'

'Let's just get on with the job, Lucky.'

I nodded glassily. I was so spaced out that I'd probably have agreed to eating off my own arm.

Goldsmith stood in front of me, feet set like a boxer. Oh, that demented smile on his face — I'll never forget it. For a moment he nodded at me, eyebrows raised, as if to say, 'You've had this coming a long time.'

An explosive swipe to my face, the steel hammer landing square across the bridge of my nose. I heard the snap of the cartilage.

Blood spurting everywhere, spraying over my face before gushing down my front. The metal tang of blood in my mouth. Goldsmith on the very verge of giving me another hit just for the sheer hell of it. And only then, only after my numbed brain had registered all these different sensations, did the pain kick in. Even with the booze and cocaine, it was one of the most excruciating moments of my life. It felt as if my nose had been sliced off at the root.

I moaned, feebly pawing at my face. Goldsmith now clucking around with towels and the like, but there was little he could do.

He led me to the bathroom and endeavoured to clean up. Eventually, after 30 minutes or so, the torrenting blood crusted up to a trickle. I almost fainted.

'Looks very painful,' said Goldsmith, eyeing me judiciously. 'Should have done the trick though. I think it's crumpled nicely.'

I was sitting mute on the end of the bed. 'Must pop off now,' he said. 'I'll come round in the afternoon to see how you're getting on.'

And you know how I replied? I can't believe what I said — for what I uttered were the words that we had to say to the headman at Eton after being given six of the best: 'Thank you'.

The pain when I got up was a full ten on the Richter Scale. Combined with the hangover, my whole head had become one ragged, raw nerve-ending.

My nose looked as if I'd been kicked by a steer. It throbbed black and purple, an angry smear across my face. I'd tried to look at myself in profile in the mirror. It was difficult. My nose seemed to have been flattened.

I dabbed at the dried blood with a wet flannel, the snapped edges of cartilage grating as they rubbed against each other.

I had the most monumental queasiness — and mixed in with it was this extraordinary anxiety.

I know now that it's called 'the doomies' and it is one of the many side-effects of cocaine. The coke can give you a high, which can last for almost 12 hours. But the downside is that for the next two days you're a jumping bundle of nerves. I can't really explain it any more than I could explain what it's like to have heroin for the first time. But the nagging anxiety is akin, I've always thought, to that feeling you get when you've forgotten to do something of the utmost importance.

There's no getting round it though. If you

want the thrill of cocaine, there is always a price to be paid. Much as there is a price to be paid for all of life's pleasures.

★ ★ ★

A day or so later, Aspers came round to take my picture for the new passport that was being made up for me. He was wearing his usual country gear, torn raspberry pink cords and a well-worn check shirt, frayed at the collar. His sideburns were as thick as I'd ever seen them, huge mutton chops covering almost the entirety of his cheeks.

'God, my dear chap, you do look a sight.' He inspected my nose from all sides. 'Every day there is a new colour to the rainbow on your face.'

'And all because Dominic recognised me.'

'He's a fly one, isn't he?' The tongue clicked against the roof of Aspers' mouth. 'It's fortunate that you've only got a couple of days till you're out of here. Dominic has many sublime qualities, but keeping his mouth shut is not one of them.'

'And is it Botswana?'

'I don't think it is,' he said, fiddling with the settings of the camera in his lap. 'I think you're off to India.'

India. In four months in that bunker, it was

164

the first time that India had ever been mentioned as a possible hideaway. 'Where the hell did India come from?'

Aspers pointed the camera at me, firing off five shots. Five pictures of a wild-man, black eyes staring out through a thick hedge of grey-beard, my nose still a livid purple, and haggard stress-lines rucking deep into my face. A man old before his time. And how do I know this? Because since I left England, it is the only picture that I have ever seen of myself.

'You know Jimmy. As capricious as the wind.'

'But India? India! Didn't he think fit to even sound me out beforehand?'

'Actually, no,' said Aspers. 'I don't think he did. When he's got a good idea, he usually just goes ahead and does it. It's always a hassle asking for permission.'

'He didn't have to ask for my permission! It just might have been courteous — '

'Calm down, dear boy. You're not really in much of a bargaining position.'

'But still! India — of all places! I don't even like curry.'

Aspers chortled. 'That is going to be the least of your worries. Cheer up! What I wouldn't give to be having this sort of adventure. I don't know what Jimmy's plans are for when you've arrived in India, but I'm sure everything's in hand. Very good on the detail is our Jimmy.'

Indeed so.

I never really found out how much of the deadly detail of my demise was down to Goldsmith, and how much was just down to hubris and bad karma. Whatever. It did turn out badly and I deserved nothing less. But, with hindsight, it does seem as if all along Goldsmith had had a 20-year plan, playing with me and poking at me, before finally tiring of the whole game and dispatching me with all the indifference of a schoolboy stamping on a spider.

★ ★ ★

Within two days, I was quitting that vast, book-lined bunker for the last time. And, although I'd had a wretched time of it in there, I was sorry to be leaving. The bunker had been a hell of sorts, but I'd had my routines and my creature comforts, and such a fantastic supply of books as would last you a lifetime.

But, being in that airless pit had been driving me half-crazy. Aspers' party had reminded me of what I'd been missing — of fresh air and new-mown grass, and even the simple pleasures of seeing a white cloud scud across a blue sky. I was thirsting for more of it. I wanted to immerse myself in nature and I dreamed of swimming naked in the sea as the salt water roiled and cleansed my cankered soul.

In all my fancifulness, I imagined myself at the helm of my getaway ship, with the water stinging at my face and the wind howling in at the beam as huge Atlantic rollers swept us from stem to stern. That, to me, was my idea of perfect heaven.

It's funny how, during my whole incarceration at Howletts, I'd never thought to ask Goldsmith how he planned to get me out of Britain. I'd presumed that there might be a flight, or several flights, or perhaps a long trip on a sturdy trawler. None of that I would have minded in the slightest; in fact, after four months' barren pampering in the bunker, I was yearning for something a little more Spartan.

Only Goldsmith, however, could have contrived to dream up the exquisite hell that I was put through over the next 100 days. And I use the word 'contrived' quite deliberately, because I am certain that Goldsmith wanted it to be as awful an experience as he could make it. One hundred days I was stuck on that boat, with not a soul for company, and the wonder of it is that I didn't go stark staring mad.

I didn't go mad. Not quite mad, anyway. But sometimes I think that even madness might have been preferable to what did occur — because in just three months, Goldsmith managed to turn me into the most craven drug-addicted junkie that ever walked the earth.

Was it his fault? Surely all of us most take responsibility for our lives and our addictions? Surely it's only the most spineless fops who continue to blame others for their misfortunes?

But I do blame Goldsmith. I blame him entirely for turning me into the pathetic, crawling heroin addict that I once was — and now I will explain why.

12

'Well goodbye old cock.' Aspers reached out and enveloped me in a great bear hug. 'It's been one of the more amazing experiences of my life. Awful for you, of course. Terrible. But — but . . . glad to be of service.'

It was past midnight and I was wrapped up in jumper and oilskin to keep out the coastal mist.

The pair of us had left Howletts after lunch, sedately skirting London before arriving at Felixstowe docks at around midnight. Aspers had packed me a duffel-bag of clothes and washbag.

'It's like being packed off to Eton for the first time,' I said.

'A walk in the park compared to Eton.'

'Thank you,' I said, in as heartfelt manner as I could. The words didn't remotely do justice to the occasion, or my feelings for the man — but how else do you thank a man for saving your life?

'I think I owe you an explanation too,' I said. 'It — it wasn't just about the children — '

Aspers held his hands up. 'No need.

Honestly there's no need.'

But I ploughed on. 'I had to. I had to do something. I was as good as bankrupt. I find it amazing now that I could ever have thought of myself as a gambler. But — ' I stared down as I tipped my toe into a puddle. 'But you have shown me nothing but kindness. Even when I'd gone belly up, you gave me back my cheques, kept me on at the Clermont. It was more than I deserved, I know. But in the end, I just couldn't live with being a bankrupt.'

'It was — ' Aspers whistled low, his head tick-tocking from side to side. He was unexpectedly tongue-tied. 'It was the very least I could do.'

'No friend could have done more.'

Aspers clicked his tongue against the roof of his mouth, making the same sound with which he used to call in his animals. 'You weren't nearly as bad a poker player as you thought.'

I snorted derisively. 'The proof of the pudding — '

'Every man's loss is another man's gain,' he said softly. Suddenly he clicked his fingers, as if remembering himself. 'Oh, you better have this.' He patted his coat-pockets and pulled out a half-inch thick envelope. 'Some of my winnings from yesterday. Just a few dollars. They're all I have on me.'

'Really?' I cuffed a tear from my eye. 'You have been so incredibly kind.'

'Nonsense.' Aspers ignored my proffered hand to sweep me up in a great bear-hug. 'Do give me a call when you're settled down. I'll come pay you a visit. Just make sure it's luxurious.'

I laughed. 'I'll do that.'

'I suppose, then, that this might be an appropriate point to quote you one last line from Oscar — 'Laughter is not at all a bad beginning for a friendship — and it is far the best ending for one'.'

'*Dorian Gray*?'

'But of course.' He waved as he walked back to the Land Rover, and as I waved in return I felt such a surge of affection for that bear of a man who, without a thought for himself, had done so much for me.

But I never did make that call. And when I did finally think to make it, there had been too much water under the bridge. Or so it seemed. I'm sure that if I had made that call, he would — once again — have done everything in his powers to help me.

All I can say is that you're not really capable of making the most informed decisions if your brain's been addled by drugs.

★ ★ ★

'That's that then,' said Goldsmith. He tossed his cigar-stub into a puddle.

'I suppose so,' I said.

We'd met up in Felixstowe a few minutes earlier. Goldsmith was going to see me onto the freighter before catching a lift back to London.

'Think you'll ever see any of this again?' Goldsmith asked.

'Haven't given it a thought.'

'If you do, it'll probably be from the inside of a police van. But I don't think you'll be missing much. Just think what you're leaving behind — the IRA running rampant, the three-day week, inflation at 18 per cent and the stock market in free-fall. And now the Tories are even being led by a woman. The country's gone to the dogs.'

But in my mind I was saying farewell to Blighty, my dear old homeland. At the time, I presumed I'd never see it again — and I was right. So my last glimpse of Britain was rain drizzling onto the tarmac and yellow street-lights winking in the darkness. The outline of a few blocks of houses in the distance, past the grey perimeter fencing. Water slapping at the quay, the familiar stink of the dock and the shadowy freighters towering up out of the mist.

Not as romantic, perhaps, as the White

Cliffs of Dover, but for me it was a moment that was symbolic of everything that was so solid and down-to-earth about my home country. The dismal rain; the great trading freighters; and in the distance, all the tidy homes at midnight, with Ovaltine being sipped, newspaper crosswords being abandoned, and couples snug abed with the curtains drawn tight.

A light blinked three times from the ship nearest us.

'Let's go,' Goldsmith said, moving off directly. 'We're clear for ten minutes to get you on board.'

I slung the duffel-bag over my shoulder and kept step beside him, boots splashing through the puddles. The ship we were heading for was an immense-size, twin funnels jutting out stark from behind the bridge. I could just make out her name, *Dido* — and there was only one *Dido* that I knew and that was *Dido* Queen of Carthage. It didn't end well for her either. Killed herself in the most wretched fashion after being abandoned by her lover Aeneas.

Goldsmith led the way up the gang-plank. At the top, there was not a person in sight — no-one on the deck, nor on the bridge. Goldsmith looked as if he knew where he was going, walking towards the stern, before

173

darting down a staircase into the hold. I lingered for a moment at the top, the rain smacking into my face. It was goodbye, goodbye to every thing and every person that I had ever cherished. I don't know why, but on a whim I stood ram-rod straight and gave a formal salute. It seemed an appropriate way to be taking my leave.

'Come on!' Goldsmith hissed from the bottom of the stairs, waving his torch at me.

One flight, two flights, three flights, right into the very bowels of the ship. The lower we got, the more I could smell the rotten, fusty stench that is endemic in ship's bowels the world over. Even at the time, it seemed unnatural, to be replacing that glorious scent of the sea with this filth, this foetid canker. Stygian gloom and the creak of a ship as she settles for the night. It was so awful that for a moment I nearly turned on my heels to get back to the rain and to the docks. I don't know what it was that was giving me the creeps. Some sixth sense, perhaps, telling me that I'd be better to take my chances in an open row-boat to Europe than to fall in mutely with Goldsmith's schemings.

By now we were right in the guts of the ship, as low as we could go. All about us were containers — lines and lines of containers, enormous great boxes stretching as far as the eye could see. Goldsmith took a left, a right, and another left; everything looked the same to me. It was a vast ocean-going labyrinth, every sound from inside and out echoing off the walls.

Goldsmith stopped by a container and started to minutely inspect one of its corners. It was seemingly identical to all the others — and I can tell you its dimensions very precisely. It was seven yards long, three yards wide and three yards in height — and for the next three months it was to be my prison cell.

'And here we are,' said Goldsmith, who was squatting on the floor. 'See these chalk markings? That's about the only way you'll be able to make this container out from any of the others. It wouldn't do to get lost, you know.'

There was a panel, two-foot square, in the side of the container; I hadn't noticed it. Goldsmith eased it slowly sideways. The door had been well greased and it didn't make a sound. He stuck his head into the container and flashed the torch round for a few seconds.

'Seems to be all in order.' He smiled at me — in, or so I thought, a good-natured way. More fool me. Now I am quite certain that the only reason he was smiling was because he had just seen the hell-hole into which he was consigning me.

'Let me tell you the drill.'

I squatted down beside him, our knees almost touching.

'There's only one person on board who knows you're here. His name is Hammel and he is going to be the sole conduit for food, water and the rest of it. Hammel knows only that you're a fugitive — but he does not know your true identity. I daresay it might be best to keep it that way.'

'Fine.'

'He'll bring your provisions every morning, as well as disposing of your ablutions — '

'My ablutions?'

'In a bucket, Lucky, the best that was available in the circumstances. It goes without saying that it would be dangerous to leave your container. If they even suspect there's a stowaway, you're done for. Is that all clear?'

'I can't even leave the container?' Even before I'd set foot in that wretched box, I felt uneasy at the prospect of such a lengthy incarceration.

'Wouldn't advise it. There are crew milling around all the time, just going through their routine checks. Plus there's the fact that you might never find your way back. One container looks very much like another. Hammel will try to get down each morning between eight and nine. He will do his best to make life comfortable for you. But — '

'But?'

'He has limited resources.' Goldsmith stood up. 'Oh — I almost forgot. Your passport. You're an Australian, would you believe, going by the name of, ahmm,' he riffled through the passport. 'Jeffrey. Jeffrey Steadman.'

'Jeff Steadman?' I mulled my new name over, looking at the picture Aspers had recently taken of me. It was hard to think that, not four months earlier, this grey-haired wreck had thought of himself as one of London's great playboys.

'You might want to do something about the accent, Lucky. Plenty of time to practice.' He laughed to himself and thrust out his hand. 'By the by, have you had any thoughts about what you'll be doing with yourself in India?'

Well funnily enough, I had. And like an idiot I told him. And this one thing, more than anything else, really screwed me.

It was just a passing whim, but it had tickled me nevertheless. For over the previous week, I'd been giving quite considerable thought to what I wanted to do in India. I wanted — I needed — some sort of project. My life in London had been nothing but the most endless pampered routine, a seamless cycle of gambling at the club and regrouping at home, whilst fitting my family in wherever I could. Such a wonderfully gilded experience, but the sort of aimless hand-to-mouth life that cankers a man's soul and leaves him dreaming, thirsting, for any way to cut loose. Now that I had been given a second chance, I was determined not to fall in to the same rut of mindless routine.

And the project I had conceived might seem schoolboyish — but then its origins stemmed from my school days. At Eton, I had a history master, a Major Morris, who'd been besotted with one of the school's old boys, the Duke of Wellington, and a small level of his enthusiasm had been passed onto his pupils. One summer the old Major had even had us out recreating the Battle of Waterloo on Agar's Plough — where, of course, it's said that Wellington really won the Battle.

As a direct result, I'd spent one of the happiest fortnights of my life milling through Belgium and Portugal, wandering around a few of those epic battlefields at Badajoz and Torres Vedras; funny how they always seem to be far more glorious than any of the battlefields that we have now, but I daresay they all look better with age. At the time, they were probably nothing but unmitigated hell.

One of the lesser known facts about

Wellington is that although he carved out his name with all his battles in the Peninsular, he learned his trade in India. He was known as the Sepoy General, and it was in India that he learned about tactics, logistics and the gruelling business of siege warfare.

He'd had several big battles in India against the Mahrattas, who had — correctly — believed that they might have been able to strike a better deal with the French. But it wasn't the Real Politik that interested me so much as the battle-sites themselves, with, to name a few, Assaye, Seringapatam and that mountain-top jewel, Gawilghur.

I had been mulling it over during my last days in the bunker and the more I thought of it, the more it appealed. My plan may not have been much, but it was at least a project of sorts — and even half viable, which is more than can be said for most of my efforts.

What I planned, hoped, to do was visit Wellington's battlesites in India. I was going to immerse myself in Wellingtonia, would stay in the Mysore mansion-house where he had squired so many of his mistresses; would visit the Seringapatam jail where Major General David Baird had been incarcerated for nigh on four years; and would climb the great breach in the walls at Gawilghur.

'Come on,' repeated Goldsmith. 'What are

your plans for India? A grand tour, perhaps?'

'I don't know,' I said. 'I'd been thinking of visiting some of Wellington's battle-sites.'

Goldsmith's brows contracted in thought. 'There's a picture of one of them, isn't there? The Tippoo Sultan of Mysore?'

'Cut down in the Water Gate at Seringapatam.'

'I remember now,' he laughed. He was still shaking his head as he thrust his hand out. 'I'd hazard that no-one will ever call you this again, so I might as well be the last. So this truly is goodbye to Richard John Bingham, Seventh Earl of Lucan.'

I shook his hand. 'Goodbye.'

'Better have my torch,' he said. 'I think Hammel has provided you with candle and matches, but this will get you started.'

'Thanks.'

I saw him waving over his shoulder, as he walked off, that great bulk silhouetted against the light. 'Wellington eh? See you on the other side.' A nonchalant wave of his hand. He didn't look back.

As the clump of Goldsmith's footsteps receded into the distance, I slumped to the floor with my back to the container. So this was what my life had come to — skulking at the bottom of a freighter on a slow boat out to the Indian sub-continent. What would all those illustrious ancestors of mine have made of me? What indeed? They'd probably have thought it was all of a piece with everything else that has been committed in the name of Lucan.

I sighed and looked about at all those long alleys before ducking head-first into my own container and dragging the duffel-bag in behind me. I slid the hatch back tight and only then did I peer about me at my new surroundings.

Now I've been in some awful places in my time. Yes, Goldsmith ensured that I lived in a few truly repellent holes in India. But this container was the worst of the lot — the worst by far. It was my hell on earth.

By comparison, Aspers' bunker was a palace — but then Aspers' bunker had, at least, been designed for human habitation. This container — this seven-yard-long container, with not a breath of fresh air nor a glimmer of natural light — may have had a token nod towards habitability, but had been designed to be as unpleasant as humanly possible.

Which, of course, is just how Goldsmith had planned it.

On the floor was a pallet bed, which had been made up with immaculately laundered sheets and a few blankets. The top corner had been turned back, just as you sometimes see in the swanky hotels, and, to complete the joke, a little gold-wrapped chocolate had been placed on the pillow. I sat on the bed as I surveyed the rest of my 'room' and could feel the wooden struts of the pallet digging into my buttocks through the thin mattress.

By the side of the bed was a wooden fruit-box on its side, with a candlestick, some spare candles and a box of matches. Over in a corner, a metal bucket and wooden lid, along with a box of the cheapest, shiniest toilet paper that money could buy. In another corner, of all things, a deckchair. And on the walls, some posters that could only have been handpicked by Goldsmith himself. It was like some grotesque parody of the inside of a travel agent's shop. 'Welcome to Goa!' said one, above a picture of a golden crescent of beach. 'The wonder that is India!' said another, alongside a picture of the Taj Mahal. And there were several more like them, Sellotaped slapdash around the inside of the container, but the one I particularly remember had the tag-line, 'India — history that lives and breathes', atop a picture of the Amber Fort at Jaipur, along with a great vista of blue sky. Oh, how terribly funny — to be taunting me with all these exotic pictures while in actual fact I was stuck in a hellhole.

If I hadn't realised that Goldsmith was taking the piss before, I certainly did when I came to examine the one last item in my room, a Fortnum and Mason's hamper that was lying on the floor at the foot of the deckchair. How I'd used to love the sight of those wicker hampers, which had always used to promise so much in the way of exotic dainties — but this . . . this was the work of an utter bastard.

Goldsmith had even left a note on the top. 'Welcome to your new home,' it said, as if I'd just moved into some pile in the country. And on first inspection, it looked like a very fine hamper indeed. A magnum of Crystal champagne; a bottle of Absinthe and another of Crème de Menthe; a tin of Jacob's cream crackers; a large tin of Beluga caviar, so heavy it could have been a door-stop; various other tins of Heinz ravioli, Heinz baked beans, and Heinz Spaghetti; a couple of tubes of tomato puree; a bottle of HP sauce; plus — and even at the time I remember goggling at them — at least ten cans of tinned mince. There were some other things in there too, but what they all had in common was that they were singularly useless for a man who had no tin-opener, no cutlery, no crockery, and — above all — no cooker. A magnum of Crystal champagne, for instance: very pleasant indeed when it's ice-cold and quaffed with friends. But to leave me a Magnum — a bloody Magnum! — of Crystal to drink all by myself, and completely tepid at that. The Absinthe and the Crème de Menthe — need I say more? Cream-crackers, but with not a knife to be had and nothing to spread on them. That monstrous tin of Beluga must have cost a fortune, but if caviar isn't chilled, you might as well be eating fish-paste. And as for all those tins of Heinz and those tins of mince — what did he expect me to do with them? Rustle up a shepherd's pie?

As I sat there on the deckchair, surveying the contents of the hamper, which I'd placed all about me on the floor, I had the first glimmerings that this unholy allegiance with Goldsmith was a monumental mistake. It's true that the décor of the cabin and the Fortnum's hamper might — just — have been a little joke, if I'd been going to spend just a single night there. But this smacked of genuine malice aforethought.

It took me a few more minutes to appreciate fully just how unpleasant my first night on the *Dido* was going to be. Idiotically, I had not brought along any water. And I had nothing to read, absolutely nothing at all. It was this that caught me worst of all, given that in Aspers' bunker, I'd had such a splendid library at my very fingertips.

If I'd given my journey but a moment's thought, I'd have taken with me the complete works of Dickens, or even the complete works of Mills & Boon, to while away my time on board. But as it was, I had brought along not one single thing to keep me occupied. I was all set to be bored out of my mind — and this, I'm sure, was why Hammel's proposed solution was to fall on such fertile ground.

From all the banging and buffeting, I could tell that the *Dido* was nearly underway. Every sound seemed to be magnified in the hold, the mooring lines thumping against the side of the ship as we cast off, followed by a strange serpent slither as they were reeled in. A series of enormous crashes as we were buffeted by the tugs — it was deafening. In time I wouldn't even notice the droning roar of the engine and the perpetual thrum of the waves against the hull, but that first night it was as if I'd been locked inside some vast bass drum.

It was well past midnight, but I was so geed up that I wasn't nearly ready for bed. So I lit a candle and made what sort of repast I could for myself: a handful of cream-crackers smeared with tomato puree, washed down with tepid Crystal champagne that was swigged straight from the bottle.

I dozed for a little while in the deckchair, woke up, saw the candle guttering in its stick, and when I woke again the candle was out and I was in utter darkness. For a moment I thought I was back in my bedroom in the bunker, but the smell wasn't right. I stumbled out of the deckchair and crashed out onto the pallet bed. The thumping hangover had kicked in even before I'd fallen asleep. My penance had begun.

★　★　★

I was woken by the sound of knocking. The hatch slid back to reveal a rectangle of grey light in the corner, and a darting beam of torchlight poked through.

A man's head poked into the hole. All I could see of him was his silhouette. He had longish, curly hair, strapping square shoulders.

'Good morning, Chico,' he said. A Hispanic lilt to his voice, though whether from the Continent or South America, I couldn't tell. 'You sleep well? You sleep good?'

All I could manage was a croak before I finally found my voice. 'Hello Hammel — good morning.'

'Hi Chico.' His torch played over my face for a few seconds. I must have looked like a badger in its burrow. 'You in big trouble if you want to live here. A long trip ahead of us, you hear me Chico?'

'So I'm told.' I clambered out of the bed and squatted next to him in the dark.

''kay Chico, I will try make it as, er, as 'kay as I can for you.'

'Thanks.'

'Every morning, I bring you food and water. I take away your bucket.'

'That sounds very good, Hammel.' I never found out why he called me 'Chico'. It must have been the name that Goldsmith gave him.

'I not spend long. Here is — how you say? — your nosh.'

'Thank you.' Whatever he'd provided, it wasn't going to be any worse than Goldsmith's hamper.

'Give me your bucket now. I clean it.'

I slopped out, just like they used to do in jail. Even in the few short hours since I'd used it, the bucket was already humming.

'I go now.'

'Where are you from, by the way?'

'No — you tell me. Why you here Chico?'

'I see.'

'He pay me well. Goodbye.'

He was just sliding the hatch back, when

my brain kicked in. 'Hammel!' I said. 'Wait! One more thing. You couldn't find something for me to read. I've got nothing to read here — nothing at all. And a tin-opener and a knife.'

''kay,' he said, though I could hear the doubt in his voice. 'What language?'

'English, of course.'

''kay.'

The hatch slid shut.

I didn't bother to get a light, but thrust my face straight into the bucket of water, if only to clear my muzzy head. Then, squatting beside it, I scooped up mouthful after mouthful of water with my hands. It tingled as it trickled down my neck.

That occupied me for about five minutes. I felt my way over to the bed, found the matchbox and lit a candle — no easy task, I can tell you, when you're effectively blind. That must have taken about another five minutes.

I surveyed Hammel's provisions. A loaf of bread, an apple, an orange, a hunk of Edam, a large wedge of cold roast lamb, and half-a-pack of Bourbon biscuits. I gnawed on the bread and the lamb. That maybe took 15 minutes.

I took stock of my room again. The posters were already beginning to grate. I made my bed and found that the chocolate treat was now engrimed into the pillow. I neatly packed all my various bits of food into the Fortnum's hamper. Another 15 minutes. I sat in the deckchair, twiddled my thumbs and stared at my watch and stared at the candle. Can you imagine it, nothing but a candle and complete darkness. It does strange things to your mind — even just a few minutes of it.

And if, perhaps, you're not in the most robust state of mental health, if there are any chinks at all in the armour, then you will be found out. At first your thoughts leap-frog willy-nilly from one to the next. But as you calm down, they begin to cluster.

Dreams, first, of my childhood, and of being evacuated from London to America during the war, where, compared to most of the benighted souls in the world, we lived out our lives in the utmost luxury. Along with my brother Hugh and my sisters Sarah and Frances, I had six years in Florida and New York State, before returning home to England and to Eton. Even as a teenager, I had already acquired a taste for late-night cards, and our poker schools frequently lasted till sun-up. Add to that my penchant for racing, and you have in embryonic form the wastrel that I was later to become.

The army, perhaps, might have been the

making of me. I did a couple of years National Service with the Coldstream Guards in Germany, but even that I managed to turn into nothing more than a training-ground for the Clermont. I was known as the best poker player in the Regiment — but I'm afraid that reveals far more about the low standard of play of my fellow army officers than it does about me.

Initially, I'd thought my memories were going to be in chronological order. But somehow that solitary candle, standing there in the darkness like a disembodied beacon, kept reining me back.

These days, I believe, it's known as the elephant in the room — and so far in this manuscript I have largely skirted round this huge elephant in my life.

But now I may as well have done with it. There's no avoiding it any longer, as throughout my three-month trip on the *Dido*, this was to be the central vortex for my thoughts and visions. No matter how my dreams began, no matter what I wanted to think about, within minutes my thoughts would always be sucked back into that one great whirlpool of horror.

The murder.

The thing was: I should never for a moment have got somebody else to do it. I should have kept things simple; should have been a man. I should have killed Veronica with my own hand.

But, although I had planned to do away with Veronica for well over a year, there was something about it, at the last, that stopped me from actually doing the deed myself. I had married the woman and even though I hated her having the children taken away from me, there was still something that prevented me from killing her in cold blood.

When you first conceive of it, you might imagine that in the heat you'll be able to steel yourself to commit murder. But killing your spouse — even though it's the most common form of murder there is — was not for me. Even a month beforehand, I knew I wouldn't be able to do it.

So, in all my clinical insanity, I decided that the way round the problem was merely to hire someone else to do the job. Tony was his name, a former soldier who I'd met somewhere along the way. I don't know if Tony is still alive, but seeing as he has kept quiet about that whole fiasco I shall pay him the same compliment. No names, no pack-drill.

One drunken night together I made my proposal. He asked if I was serious — and although I laughed, I said I was more serious than I'd ever been. We discussed how much he wanted — £6,000 as I recall, half paid up front, and the remainder after the deed had been done. After that we got down to the nitty-gritty.

It was such a seemingly simple plan. We'd wait for a Thursday night, when Sandra the nanny had her night off. Tony would let himself into our house in Belgravia, and would lie low in the basement; he'd extract the lightbulb from its socket so that Veronica would be walking down into darkness; and then with one crisp blow to the back of the head, Veronica would be dead and my problems would be over.

After this, the plan was for me to enter the house and, while Tony kept watch, I'd bundle Veronica's body into a mail-bag. Just in case he hadn't finished the job off, I'd even prepared the spare bludgeon.

As for alibis, these were already taken care of. I'd arranged to meet three friends for dinner at the Clermont at 10.30pm. I planned to have a light supper, not too boozy, before heading home for the night. My alibi now established, I'd drive through the night to Newhaven, drop Veronica's crumpled body to the crabs at the bottom of the ocean, and then motor back to Town in time for breakfast; feigned surprise at Veronica's disappearance — but then she did have some previous for bolting. The police informed that she'd gone missing; a cursory manhunt; a mild hubbub in the papers; Tony paid the second tranche of his money. And that, I hoped, would have been the last of the Countess of Lucan.

It had seemed simple enough at the time. But as I write now, it does appear to be unnecessarily complicated. Why did I need to get Tony involved in the first place? Why couldn't I have just done the thing myself, made a proper job of it? It would almost have been more fitting for me to have killed her. I'd married the damn woman, had stood by her side and pledged to be with her 'till death us do part' — and since it was me who wanted to snuff out her existence, it was surely right and proper that it was me who finished her off.

My chief fear had been that Tony would blow the whistle on me. What if, years hence, he were hauled up for some other misdemeanour and decided to try and ease his sentence by turning Queen's evidence? Well, it was a possibility. I considered it, but thought it unlikely.

As for the murder and the disposal of Veronica's body — well, there might be a few glitches, but nothing that couldn't be sorted out on the day.

The one thing that I had never conceived was that Sandra would change her night off; that she'd be in the very house with Veronica that night, and would go downstairs to make tea for her mistress; that in the darkness, Tony would mistake Sandra for Veronica and attack the wrong woman; and, finally, dismally, that he'd then make such a bloody hash of the job. Poor, poor Sandra — she must have fought like a wildcat. Over and over again he had to hit her until she finally succumbed.

The first I knew of it, Tony was bolting out of the house. I'd been waiting nearby in Stoop's Ford Corsair. Tony climbed into the car beside me, hands and legs trembling, and even in the dull streetlight I could see that he was spattered from head to foot in blood.

'It's done,' he said, legs jittering against the seat.

I already have my gloves on. I pick up the mail-bag from the back-seat and slip into the house, oblivious to all those fusty Lucan relics than line the entrance hall. I walk down the stairs to the basement, adrenalin pumping at the thought of what I will find. A scene of utter carnage. Far from being a clean kill, there are flecks of blood all over the stairs and the walls. Smashed cups and saucers. A vast pool of black blood on the floor. It was a slaughter-house, nothing like what I'd planned. And the smell, the rich cloying stench of fresh blood. But given enough time, I'd be able to clear it up.

My torch plays over the blood and the flowery dress. I see the tiny body lying on the floor. And that horrific moment as I catch a glimpse of her hair. Not fine blonde hair, but a lustrous brown mane.

We'd got the wrong woman.

Heart-stopping. I'm utterly dumbfounded. It had to be Veronica. How could it not be Veronica?

I don't know what to do next. The next few minutes have about them a dream-like quality. I suppose that I'm still intent on sticking with the original plan. I'd just get on with it and dispose of the body; Veronica would be dealt with in her own time.

It's a hell of a job trying to put a body, even one as slight as that of Sandra's, into a mail-bag. I'm panting with the exertion of it all. It took about ten minutes. Cleaning up the blood and mess was going to take much, much longer.

At this stage, I'm just about on top of things. Things had gone wrong, but I'm still on track.

Then, just as I'm bending over the bag, I

hear a call from upstairs.

'Sandra!' The electric realisation that Veronica was actually in the house. And coming down the stairs.

The next few minutes are a whirling blur. Too late by far to make a run for it. Then and there, I decide to kill her. Like Macbeth, I am in blood, stepp'd in so far that should I wade no more, returning were as tedious as go o'er. I don't have time to think of how I'd dispose of not one, but two bodies, or how farfetched it would seem to the police that both Sandra and Veronica had disappeared on the same night. No, all I know is that if I were to stand even a prayer of getting away with it, Veronica has to die.

I attack her on the stairs, attack her like a maniac, thumping her head and trying to throttle her with my gloved hands. How she fights me, tooth and nail, until she lands the blow that does for all men, catching me right clean in the testicles.

At that stage, I think, my brain goes into temporary shutdown. We sit there on the stairs chatting quietly to each other. It's surreal. Not two minutes earlier, I'd been trying to throttle the life out of her, and yet there we are talking as if we were a couple of lone survivors from a cyclone. At least that's how it seemed to me. I actually thought we could sort things out.

I excuse myself and go to the bathroom to get a wet towel for her wounds.

And Veronica, bless her, takes her chance and flees from the house to run screaming all the way to the Plumber's Arms.

I remember washing my hands at the basin, the soap turning pink in my fingers, as I hear the first screams from out on the street. I look at myself in the mirror, dull weariness etched into my eyes. I'd played the hand out, had seen the turn of the last card. And the game was up.

There is no time even to say a proper farewell to the children. I dry my hands on the towel and calmly leave the bathroom. I'm in a total daze. All I know is that I have a minute or two, at best, to get out of the house.

But, in all the blood and the ghastly mayhem, a single moment of such sweet poignance. I am able, in my own mind at least, to say goodbye to my daughter Frances. All the shouting must have woken her and she comes out to see what is happening. I see her standing at the top of the stairs, and oh, if only I had grasped her in my arms and told her that I loved her and that I would always love her. But we rarely any of us get a chance to rehearse our goodbyes, and so I did none of that; no, like the stand-offish blue blood that I used to be, I just tell her to go to bed and without a backward glance I quit the house for the last time.

The car is parked a few yards up the street and it's empty. Tony must have fled as soon as he saw Veronica come screeching out onto the street. I never found out what happened to him, though karma being what it is, I am sure that he, too, has had his own penance to pay.

I drive a few miles south before calling my mother from a phone-box and tell her to look after the children. But after that's taken care of, I am plotting, scheming, probing, trying to see if there is any possible loophole. For a little while, at least, I still hope that I, Lord Lucan, might be able to brazen it out.

But of course I'm sunk — finished. My life as a peer and as a familyman is over.

And as for the rest of it, I think, you know.

★   ★   ★

A small but defining episode in my life and it's no surprise, perhaps, that during my hellish sojourn in the *Dido*, I would keep returning to it.

That very first day, as I sat in the deckchair staring at my candle, I fancied that I could see Sandra's body sprawled out on the black

198

pallet. I looked more closely. From the kink of her arms to the very position of her limbs, it was as if she were lying there, there, right in front of me. I could even see the blood dripping down the walls.

At times I would jolt myself out of my fascinated stupor, and would cast back to some of the happier occasions in my life. Dandling George on my knee. The thrill of a win at the races. And that sweet ecstasy of being far out at sea with a mighty power-boat thrumming beneath my feet.

But no matter how I sought to detach myself, always it came back to that one luminous point in my life, which had become to me like the candle in the room. Even when I shut my eyes, I still couldn't escape the sight of Sandra's body for ever slumped in the corner.

By the next morning, when Hammel returned to me, I was a nervous wreck. I could feel the beam of his torch playing over me before I opened my eyes.

'Hey Chico, good morning!' he said, pointing the torch full into my face. 'Chico, you look like shit, what you been doing in here man?'

I scrambled out of the bed. 'Hammel — Hammel — I'm going out of my mind in here. Have you got anything for me? Have you anything to read?'

'Cool it, Chico.' Although I couldn't see it, I could feel that he was smiling. 'I found some stuff for you.'

And, along with food, water and a tin-opener, he handed over a week-old copy of *The Sun* newspaper, a copy of *The Lady* magazine, and a well-thumbed navigation manual.

'Is this it?'

'Eh, Chico, the best I find. We don't do Inglese on this ship.'

I grimaced with distaste. *The Sun* and *The Lady*, indeed. I read them through from cover to cover, mind — many times over in fact — and can still recall every single article of that hideous magazine, which included a full four pages on knitting patterns, as well as a risible spread on how to make the most from your herb garden. Stomach-churning stuff but I read it so often that I'd practically memorised it.

'But, but — ' I was trying to get across the urgency of my predicament. 'I'm bored out my mind! Haven't you anything? Isn't there anything at all?'

'I don't know, Chico,' he flashed his torch in my eyes again. 'That face of yours, it really something. Break your nose?'

'Even a pack of playing cards?'

'Hey Chico, we got no cards. We watch TV, we do the radio. But hey — you wanna try this? Eet's good.'

He reached into his pocket and, as if by chance, pulled out a little polythene bag, complete with Rizla papers, rolling tobacco and a lump of hash resin the size of a walnut. Yes — Hammel just happened to have about him all the ingredients that I'd need to turn myself into a Class A drug addict.

Of course it's just about possible that Hammel might have had all that drug paraphernalia for his own personal use — and that out of the kindness of his heart, he'd decided to lend it me.

But, having been bitten so many times during my latter years, I have come to realise that when things have gone wrong, it's not happenstance, but generally down to the evil hand of Jimmy Goldsmith.

So let me make it plain: although I have no evidence, I am quite certain that, right from the first, Goldsmith intended to turn me into a drug addict.

And on what fertile ground did his seeds fall.

For if ever there were a plunger in this world it was me. I have that addictive personality that can't be content with a single sip, yet has to sup the whole pot. So whether it was power-boat racing, poker, backgammon, or even dining off smoked salmon and lamb cutlets, I was incapable of moderation.

And I haven't even started on the especially addictive qualities of cannabis, not to mention all the other drugs into which I immersed myself on that slippery slope.

In my youth, I had dabbled in drugs — I'd lived through the Sixties, after all — but had usually sought out my addictions elsewhere. On the *Dido*, however, and thanks to Hammel's seemingly limitless supply of drugs, there was not a shadow of a doubt that by the end of the trip I would become the most helpless, hopeless drug addict that walked this earth.

Coincidence? Was it just chance that led to Hammel having such a wealth of drugs at his fingertips? Not a bit of it. It had Goldsmith's sticky finger-prints all over it.

After Hammel had gone, I didn't stand on ceremony. Not for me the heartfelt agonising of whether I was doing the right thing. Be damned to the right thing! That is, by the way, one of the few advantages of being in it up to your neck: you may do as please and convention and all her prissy hand-maidens can go to hell in a hand-basket.

I squatted on the pallet by the candle, and although I'd never rolled a spliff before I'd seen friends do it enough times to know the drill. I splayed out the Rizla paper on top of the fruit-box, laid out a few threads of tobacco, and topped it all with a corn pellet-size crumbling of hash. I was inept at the lick and the roll as I tried to seal up my first spliff — but within a week I would be doing it like an old hand. Not the most perfect roll-up that I'd ever seen, a little lumpy at the ends and straggly in the middle. But it would suffice.

I touched the end into the candle, and, as that oh-so familiar scent of hashish began to permeate my nostrils, I took my first drag.

It's not easy trying to recall the sensations of that first spliff, but I'll try. A little while afterwards, my memory becomes a total blank and for at least 13 years of my life I have no recollection whatsoever. But, while I was in the very act of stepping out into the abyss, I do still retain a few memories from all those years ago, so I may as well share them.

As I puffed away, I could feel my whole body relax into the bed in the most delightful way. The candle took on an almost numinous power, as if I were in the glowing presence of some mystical force; a heightened awareness of the coarseness of the blanket at my fingertips. Even the blackness around me seemed to be richer, dissolving into various grades of grey through to purple and magenta black.

But I couldn't be doing with staying in that shitty, cramped container, with its fug of stale air. What the hell had I been thinking of?

In an instant, I'd whipped back the hatch and was worming my way out onto the cargo deck. What an extraordinary environment in which to have my first trip, with those vast containers rising all about me like the narrow canyoned streets of New York City. Everything, from the murky striplights overhead to the endless avenues of containers had about them a raw power and intensity that was entirely new to me. The wall of noise from the thrashing engines seemed to infuse my whole body, as my every cell vibrated in tune with the ship. We were like two living beasts, both of us perfectly attuned to the other.

I went up to the very front of the ship. It sent a shiver of delight up my spine to hear the hull cleave through those monstrous Atlantic rollers. I touched the metal and could feel it quivering, alive, beneath my fingertips. It was like putting out to sea in a high gale, and as I leant my cheek against the cold hull, I felt as one with the *Dido*, the pair of us fused together like a horse and its rider. Such exquisite joy to be there in the hold, carving through the ocean; for one blissful minute I believed that I was the ship's figurehead, staring out over the waves as we sliced through the sea.

I was staggered that, two days earlier, I hadn't recognised the essential beauty of those long lines of containers, each line so very similar and yet subtly different; and the way, also, that the dust spangled in the air, glowing yellow around the lights before it turned to an iridescent brown; and even the quiet sound of me padding along the floor had a metronomic charm. Why had I never before observed the exquisite pleasure of seeing my feet moving back and forth, and the quiet, authoritative slap as they hit the floor?

Or some such. It's all bunkum. If you're high on drugs then even a steaming pile of excrement will have its own peculiar fascination. What I'm trying to get across though was the sheer wonder of my first toke; the scales had fallen from eyes.

I don't know how on earth I made it back to my container. I'd left the hatch open and I vaguely recall that I could see the candlelight glimmering out onto the floor. I was starving. It's commonly known as 'the munchies' and is one of the many side-effects of marijuana; I duly munched my way through the food that Hammel had left me and a few tins from the hamper.

And that, for the next week or so, was my routine. Sandra would still be there in my visions, either slumped on my bed or occasionally lying sprawled in the corner, but I found that the first spliff of the day had this magical ability to lift my mood. Just a few drags, and everything became lighter, more ethereal — more, almost comprehensible. It was as if the hash gave me a better handle on my life and my situation.

Eventually I was having five, six spliffs a day. Each morning my faithful servant Hammel would bring me fresh supplies, the grin stretched across his face as he saw that I was completely off my head. I was so stoned that most of the time I left the hatch open to get in a little air. God knows what the place must have smelled like.

But, as anyone but a senseless British peer could have predicted, there had to be a downturn. You don't get all those highs and all those moments of wonderful perception without having some knock-on effect. It's Newtonian mechanics for the modern-day: for every action, there is an equal and opposite reaction. And for every spliff, and every ecstatic insight thereby gained, there is an opposite and equal amount of agony to be experienced.

At first I didn't really realise what was happening. I'd been using the hash to block Sandra out and suddenly — suddenly . . .

It was terrifying.

It was my second spliff of the day, sitting in the deckchair and gazing at the candle as Sandra lies on the bed. And she moved. I genuinely saw her move. She's more than moving, she's struggling to her feet. Almost in mime, she's defending herself from a rain of unseen blows that are being delivered to her head. Not four yards in front of me, she's fighting for her life, biting, gouging, doing anything she can to tear herself away from the relentless attack. A blink and she's now looking pristine, hair made up; she's now walking downstairs without a care in the world, turns the corner and reels from an invisible blow to the head. More and more blows come crashing down onto her skull, the blood showering round the walls.

I ran screaming from my hash-filled container, and when I returned, spent and parched with thirst, I saw that Sandra was now lying comatose on the deckchair.

With or without the hash, that murder scene was to be played out in an infinite number of variations, sometimes backwards, sometimes forwards, sometimes in slo-mo, and sometimes it even felt as if it were me who was being bludgeoned to death, the torrent of blows cracking into my skull and neck. As I sat eating in the deckchair, Sandra would squat beside me, the blood from her head dripping onto my knee. She never spoke, but the worst of it came when she started to look at me. How to describe the expression in her eyes? There was a certain tenderness there, but they had about them a look of rueful regret; the look of an ex-lover, perhaps, who has the memories but knows that it has all come to naught.

Sandra had become a permanent presence in my life, and when she wasn't in my dreams, she'd like as not be there with me in person.

I don't know how I stuck it for so long. I'd smoke more spliffs, and more spliffs, in an attempt to expiate the situation — but of course that only made things worse and the nightmares more vivid. I kept a candle burning morning, noon and night.

And one morning, I woke up with her. I had been dreaming about I know not what, but when I woke up, Sandra was in the bed, there right next to me. The pillow and sheets were covered in blood, and her slick hair was wet on my shoulder. I screamed a great whinny of terror. I was sure it was still part of the dream and pounded my head into the wall, head-butting the steel to wake myself up. But Sandra's body was still there, her arm draped across my stomach. I punched my hand as hard as I could into the floor, knowing that it could be nothing more than my imagination. My knuckles throbbed with the pain — but it made no difference. I could actually feel Sandra's cold body beside me, her limbs like ice and her hair claggy against my neck.

Panting with the horror of it all, I wormed my way out of the pallet bed to sit on the deckchair. I watched her body, waiting for movement, but there was none. She was nothing but a chimera that had been invented by my brain. She had to be. How could she be here with me on the *Dido* — and, as if to prove this very fact to myself, I got up and gave her body a poke with my finger.

The quite extraordinary surprise as my finger pressed into hard, unyielding flesh. I had expected that, like a bubble of foam, she'd disappear into the ether at the first touch of my hand. But she did not. It was as if her very corpse, in cold flesh and blood, was beside me.

13

I scrabbled out of the deckchair as soon as I heard Hammel at the hatch.

The trap slid open and, as ever, the beam of his torch played round the container.

'Jesus, Chico!' he said. 'What you been doing in there?'

'Hammel — please, please, you've got to help me. You've got to. I can't take it.'

'What the problem, Chico?'

I stared at my fingers, flexing and unflexing as if of there own volition. 'It's a nightmare. It's hell. I don't care what happens. I want to come up.'

'No,' he said with brusque certainty. 'That is not possible.'

'But . . . but these things I see. I can't take it.'

'Maybe you leave off the marijuana for a little while? Take it easy.'

'It's not like that. I just need — ' I suddenly noticed my fingernails for the first time. Every one of them had been bitten to the quick. 'Do you have any valium? Anything like that? It's like I need something to calm my brain down.'

'Valium?' he shrugged, his ringlet hair bouncing lightly on his shoulders. 'I got no valium, Chico. I see what I can find, 'kay? You 'kay Chico?'

* ★ ★ ★

And find something he did. Oh, but with what finesse they lured me into that grotesque world of the junkie. It was done with such panache, I never once felt the bite of the hook nor realised how I was being inexorably reeled in.

'Here you are, Lucky,' said Goldsmith, his bald pate shining in the candlelight. What the hell was Goldsmith doing on board the *Dido*? I have no recollection whatsoever. I tell you merely what I can recall. And one of my most distinct memories is of Goldsmith visiting me on board, sporting his usual three-piece suit, complete with silk tie and gold tie-pin.

'Try this,' he said. 'It may help.'

I didn't know what to expect. But in place of the tobacco and sweet-smelling marijuana, he gave me a pouch containing some sheets of silver foil and some white powder.

'What is it?' I squinted through the clear plastic.

Goldsmith smiled that wicked smile of his;

the smile of the devil. 'I'm told it's first-class. Just put it on the foil and heat it up. When the smoke comes, you sniff. You sniff it up, Lucky.'

'And that's it?'

'Give it a try Lucky. You may like it.'

★   ★   ★

And over the edge I went.

Barely before the trap was shut, I was huddled round the candle. I could feel the weight of Sandra's body behind me. With trembling hands, I crimped a sheet of foil down the middle before pouring out a thimbleful of the powder. It didn't even occur to me to think what I was doing — to rein back. It was probably powerful stuff, but then it had to be if it was going to give me any sort of release from the private hell in the container.

I held the corner of the foil between thumb and forefinger and began to waft it lightly over the flame. Nothing happened at first, but gradually as it heated up, the powder went black and started to wriggle. Wriggling like a snake — and that, if you didn't know, is how those great exponents of the opium trade, the Chinese, came by the expression 'Chasing the dragon'.

That first time, I sniffed it up direct from the foil, but later on I made myself a little paper tube, the better to suck up every last trace of the smoke. And its effect?

It did just exactly what it's done for so many millions of people over so many centuries — it dulled the painful wretchedness of my existence. Sandra may have been in the container, or she may not. It didn't matter any more. I was so used to her existence that she was a part of the bleak furniture.

For the beauty of heroin — which is what I soon realised that I had become addicted to — is that your every feeling, from ecstasy all the way through to sorrow and rage, is squashed flat. It was like my brain and my whole body had slipped into neutral. Sandra had gone back into the shadows. Thoughts of the murder and my flight from England were just that — little bubbles which drifted through my head, but to which I paid no heed. And even when I thought about the loves of my life, my three children, I was so detached that they might have been sitting there outside my very container and I'd not have climbed out to see them.

So that, then, is the joy of heroin. It has none of those epic, giggling highs that you can get from marijuana or cocaine — and none of the lows. It irons things flat, erases all the mile-markers, so that in the end there is nothing ahead of you and nothing behind. All it can promise is the sheer beauty of experiencing nothing at all — but it is so exquisitely painless. Almost another version of transcendental meditation, though without the need for years of self-discipline and practise. My little one-way ticket to oblivion.

★   ★   ★

It never lasts. Nothing ever does. Even with something as powerful as heroin, things are still in flux. So, although chasing the dragon worked for a month or maybe more, there came a time when simply sniffing the smoke was no longer enough. I started to notice Sandra's presence in the container again. Sometimes I'd wake from my trance to be confronted by the shocking sight of Sandra lying at my very feet.

So Goldsmith, with all the diligence of a Florence Nightingale, sat tight beside me to explain some of the more direct routes of obtaining my rush.

It was a total blueprint for how to create a heroin addict. First the marijuana and when that failed to cut it, the switch to heroin. First the smoking, then the skin-popping and finally the full-on mainlining — and then, over the years, back to skin-popping again after all my good veins had been used up.

It seemed so easy, so natural, when Goldsmith showed me skin-popping the first time. All he did was scoop up a teaspoon of heroin, add a little water, and heat it over the candle, the better to ensure that the powder was properly dissolved. He had a couple of syringes already with him.

'Just pop it into your arm, Lucky,' he said. 'In the fat under the skin.'

Not for a single moment did I think to hold back. I was craving the hit so much that it didn't occur to me that I'd become a heroin addict. You're desperate. Would do anything for it.

A year earlier, of course, as I'd sat languidly sipping gin martini at the Clermont, I might have thought that the life of a heroin addict was not totally maximising the potential of the Seventh Earl of Lucan. Compared to my illustrious forefathers, it might have seemed like just a little bit of a comedown.

But still — we all of us do the best we can in the circumstances, given the limited abilities at our disposal.

And my circumstances were dire in the extreme. I'd been responsible for Sandra's murder — and now, deep in the bowels of the

Dido, I could do nothing whatever to escape her. So I did what I had to do. When you're at such a stage in your life that you're injecting heroin into your body, there can be no question of right or wrong in your mind. It's what you do when you've run out of options: when your world and your outlook has shrunk to such a small focal point that you can think of nothing else but the dream of release. The candle in the darkness was a perfect analogy for what I had become: incapable of thinking of anything except for my little beam of heroin, and as for the rest of my life, my past and my future, it was nothing but an infinity of darkness.

Goldsmith squatted beside me as I injected myself. This time he was wearing one of his creamy suits, a bit grubby at the knees from hauling himself into the container. Somehow he'd managed to retain his Panama, which was at its usual jaunty Goldsmith angle.

I don't remember much more — but then I'm not really much of a reliable witness. Everything about the next 13 years of my life was seen through a glass darkly, and when I look back I get the occasional flash, like the beam of a far-off lighthouse. Very occasionally, something occurs that will trigger a long-gone memory. Or is it a dream? Sometimes it's hard to tell one from t'other.

But for the rest of it, my life as an addict was nothing but an impenetrable black fog.

I watched with complete dispassion as the needle slipped into my arm for the first time. The squeeze of the syringe, as the plunger slides home, and a dim awareness that I'm injecting this sticky brown treacle straight into my body. And, quickly, that great glorious release, starting warm in my belly before suffusing my whole body. The rush is a feeling of warm contentment, like a return to the womb, everything safe and my troubles diminished to the status of a peripheral blur. Sandra's presence never actually left my side, but it did at least become bearable; the guilt and the rage dropped away from me like a cloak to the floor, leaving me with all the calm of the dead. And that is heroin for you: it's a halfway house to death. You might as well sink yourself into a deep freeze. You're not doing anything, you're not feeling anything much — apart, that is, from the noticeable absence of pain. It's like Socrates as they released him from his tight bonds so he could drink the hemlock and die. Rubbing his leaden hands together, he observed that it had almost been worth having his arms cuffed together, just for the wondrous relief in having them unbound. And it's the same with heroin. For those who can't face up to the awfulness of their lives, there is much to be said for the moment of release — and the more wretched your existence, the more sublime it is to be freed from it.

Goldsmith patted me on the back as he saw my eyes glaze and the tension ebb from my body. This fantastic lightness was suffusing my body, so very different from the deadweight of living. I sank back into the deckchair and let out this blissful sigh of relief, like one who aches with weariness and who has finally come to the end of a long journey.

It might have been a week or a month before I was mainlining the heroin straight into my veins; for this period of my life, I have only the vaguest recollection of timings. Initially I would target that big blue vein that runs the length of your arm, but as it turned into a pin-cushion over the years, I ventured further afield round my body, searching out for fresh veins in my feet, my wrists, neck and even behind my knees. It's disgusting — but does that matter to a junkie? He does what he can to get his next hit, and would even inject it into his eyeballs if that was the only way of going about his business.

I have only the haziest recollection of how that voyage on the *Dido* came to an end. I think I was stretchered off, before being dumped into the back of a pick-up truck. Gazing up at the stars with the cold air whisking past my face. I'm carried to a little hut. It has a door, a window, a pallet bed. It's been whitewashed both inside and out. Bakingly hot, the sunshine so bright that my eyes screw up in pain. There is a garden of sorts with a few vegetables, sandy underfoot. Some palm trees, a rockery, and around the periphery a low wall marks the full extent of my kingdom.

Thirteen years I lived in that little hut in Goa, from the years 1975 to 1988. That's a hell of a long time to live in a place and yet to have next to no recollection of what it was like.

14

And what, meanwhile, of Goldsmith? What was happening during these 13 years to my nemesis?

These facts, by the way, I only learned much later — during my time as a heroin addict, I was in no fit state to take on board anything about even my family or my closest friends, let alone someone like Goldsmith.

But I was eventually able to piece together what was occurring to Goldsmith during my hiatus from the human race — and much to my regret, he was going from strength to strength. The women still loved him, the luck was still with him and the money just poured in.

The one thing that really did stick in the craw was that he'd actually managed to garner a knighthood. Sir Jimmy Goldsmith indeed! Even for a truly ex-peer like myself, it still galled me to see that Goldsmith had become not just a part of the establishment, but was now dining at the top table. He was terribly young to be knighted, only 43. I was never quite sure how he'd managed it. He was a financier of sorts and I think had prevented a blue chip firm from going to the wall — I have no idea. I once had a brief stint as a merchant banker, but it was never for me. Somehow Goldsmith had got on side with the Prime Minister, Harold Wilson. I can imagine him turning on that bewitching charm that lured so many women into the bedroom. Wilson, it has to be said, was losing his marbles by then.

It was known as 'The Lavender List', because Wilson's secretary Marcia Falkender typed out the names on a single sheet of pink notepaper, and it was the most controversial honours' list in decades. Many thought that it was the work of Falkender, but in fact all the names came straight from Wilson. Funny how an old Leftie could have his head turned by such an out-and-out Capitalist as Goldsmith. Another of the fellows to receive a Wilson bauble was Sir Joseph Kagan, whose firm, of all things, manufactured Wilson's gannex overcoat. Kagan eventually got his come-uppance and was sent to jail, and more's the pity Goldsmith didn't meet the same fate.

As for Goldsmith's love-life, it was as tempestuous as it had ever been. About four years or so after my flight, he'd married his long-term mistress Annabel Birley, or Anna-bel Vane-Tempest-Stewart as was. I'd met her a few times, and, now that I remember it, had even helped celebrate Goldsmith's 40th birthday with her at Cuixmala, his immense estate in Acapulco. She was far too good to him; but then most women were. He might have been married, but I imagine that he continued to whore his way round London and the Continent just as he'd always done.

One thing that did tickle me, however, was that the great British public had found him out. They'd rumbled him to such an extent that he'd even quit the country.

Goldsmith had always loved calling in the lawyers. They'd served him well during his first marriage to Isabel Patino and later on when he'd been fighting the Patino parents for custody of his daughter. So when *Private Eye* wrote something unpleasant about him, he'd had the libel writ served within the week — and then another and another. In a matter of months, it had turned into all-out war. I don't doubt that *Private Eye* may have got a few of their facts wrong. But the general thrust of what they were saying was spot on the mark. That Goldsmith was a selfish, repellent buccaneer.

Did I mention what the original writ was over? It was, naturally enough, about me. Yet another unexpected piece of fall-out from Sandra's murder, though this one certainly had to be chalked up on the credit side. It all stemmed from the lunch Aspers had organised in London the day after Sandra's death. Goldsmith, as I've already said, had not attended, though *Private Eye* claimed that he had. And even though Goldsmith had been up to his neck in it all, he absolutely went for them over this one factual error. 'Twas ever thus. The more Goldsmith screamed and raged, the more you knew that you'd got him on the run.

What I enjoyed most was that Goldsmith eventually won his victory — but what a Pyrrhic victory it was. For although he may have beaten *Private Eye* on a point of law, in the eyes of the British public, he'd lost everything. By his very actions in the courtroom, Goldsmith had shown himself up for the unscrupulous, vindictive swine that he really was.

One thing about the end of the case was that, apart from the cash and the fulsome apology, Goldsmith had insisted on having dinner with the editor of *Private Eye*, Richard Ingrams. How very typical of the man. Only months earlier he's been trying to get Ingrams thrown into jail and the next he's wanting to shake him by the hand and toast his health.

But Goldsmith had certainly found his métier in life. Several times over he'd been on the brink of bankruptcy but — every single damn time — had at the very last minute managed to stave off the creditors. If only I could have had some of that luck. What made his name though and what truly restored the Goldsmith family fortunes was a singularly appropriate trade for a financial mercenary such as Goldsmith: he became an asset-stripper. Now forgive me if I haven't fully got my head round the detail, but the nuts and bolts of it appear to be that you buy up these big, old firms and then make a tidy profit as you strip it down and sell off its parts. Along the way, he'd also discovered a dazzlingly simple tax dodge that had enabled him to snap up millions of acres of American timberland for an absolute song. Again, I'm damned if I know how he did it.

By 1987, and at the age of barely 54, he'd officially retired, but would still occasionally turn his hand to a bit of corporate piracy as and when the opportunity arose.

He'd left the country too — had to, really, after his *Private Eye* debacle. He may well have been rich as Croesus but his reputation in Britain was finished.

It was Aspers, of all people, who helped go a little way to restoring Goldsmith's reputation, for it was Aspers who got Goldsmith hooked on ecology; although I always thought that Goldsmith's Green credentials were a bit of a joke.

For Aspers, the Green movement was the real thing. It was his life. He'd put his money on the line with Howletts and Port Lympne, and frequently reiterated how much he preferred the company of animals to human beings. But with Goldsmith, I always had the impression that he was dabbling in ecology as some sort of way of ensuring his legacy. Certainly throughout the time I knew him, he never evinced even the slightest interest in Green issues — far from it. But I daresay it kept him out of mischief, and the sop of saving the world's rain-forests was a good enough excuse to buy his luxurious 18,000-acre estate in Mexico. He had 300 people working there, catering for his every whim. Three hundred! As Goldsmith was so very partial to saying, 'Luxury is the most addictive substance in the world.'

With all these various ructions going on in his life, you might have thought that Goldsmith would quickly have lost interest in the small but awful story of the erstwhile Lord Lucan.

Far from it. I may have been halfway round the world from him but he would periodically have a little poke round, just to see how his specimen creature was getting on. Boredom was probably a part of it, but with a man like Goldsmith you should never underestimate such a simple factor as plain old vindictiveness.

I've often wondered why he never turned me in. Imagine the humiliation of it as I was dragged back to Britain to stand trial for Sandra's murder. But that was never part of the plan. As revenges go, just handing me over to the police was going to be far too mundane. Hang it — I might even have got onto speaking terms with my children again.

In India though, he could observe the spectacle of my wretchedness in all its revolting glory. Much pleasure it gave him, I don't doubt, to see how this loathsome British peer had been turned into a junkie who was eking out his existence in little more than a swineherd's cottage.

As for me, I was so far gone on heroin that my earlier life, not to mention the Spartan nature of my new home, was an irrelevance. The junkie has a total lack of awareness of what's going on around him. I might have been staying in a palace for all the difference it would have made to my life.

So this, for what's it worth, is all I can remember. My life was centred around a little mud hut with a reed roof. Every few months I'd help cake the wall with a paste that was made up of cowpats and water. Inside was my charpoy, with a thin mattress and a few musty old blankets. And that, I think, was it. Every day, I spent many hours on that charpoy, gazing out of the window at my little square of sky, which was framed with the fringes of a palm-tree. There was a rickety bamboo chair outside and next to it a tree-stump, which I sometimes used as a table.

For my ablutions in the morning, there was a little privy hut adjacent to the pig sty. Frankly I'm surprised that Goldsmith, with all his eco-credentials, never took to this particular style of lavatory, seeing as how it speedily disposes of one's waste matter while also providing a nutritious and flavoursome diet for the pigs. Though I must admit it was a bit unnerving the first time I used it. Before I squatted down, I had a glimpse of a pig's pink snout already snuffling around the bottom of the outflow.

It was all situated, as I later discovered, on the edge of a farm near Anjuna Beach in Goa, and the farmer and his wife, Jay and Neeraja, were effectively my gatekeepers. Not that I was going anywhere much, but they were the people who looked after me: who nursed me back to health when I fell ill; who gave me a daily ration of curry, rice and a few chapattis; and who kept me well dosed up with heroin, along with occasionally sterilising some of my equipment.

I think Jay and Neeraja were also responsible for keeping Goldsmith briefed as to my various goings-on, but I only twigged this much later. But, even for dullards like myself, there can come a moment in your life when the penny drops and you have this blinding revelation that would have been plain as a pike-staff to anyone else. For me, it was a moment of the most choking mortification at my own culpable stupidity, as I realised that, for all his earnest blandishments, Goldsmith actively wished me ill.

I'd be shooting up about five or six times a day. Not that it ever gave me a high, but it did dull the relentless pain. It's difficult to describe the general feeling of pain that is part and parcel of being a heroin addict, but it's as if your whole body is in a vice. You're in a constant state of tension and the only release comes out of the end of that little syringe. Most of the time I was stoned, and if I wasn't stoned I was ill. The weight just dropped off me. I was nothing but a skeleton of a man, constantly out of breath and with my nose dripping like a tap. I was always coughing, from dawn to dusk, as I hawked up these disgusting globules of phlegm from my lungs. And, just for good measure, although I was never much interested in food I used to suffer from the most crippling constipation.

Welcome to the wonderful world of the heroin addict.

Before we get on with the story proper, and the one golden high-point of my life since Sandra's death, I may as well mention one of the few things that I do recollect from those addicted days: the time I saw myself in the mirror.

In India, my looks, not to mention my clothes and my general health, were a matter of no consequence. But one day, as I was pouring some water outside the hut, I happened to get a glimpse of my face in the jug. I'd not seen my visage for so long that I was staring at a stranger. I placed the jug on the tree-stump and peered more closely at the water inside and this shambling apparition with white hair and beard.

It was the opposite of Narcissus staring at himself at the river as I was hit by this wave of revulsion. That was me? It couldn't be me. Not possible. For the first time in many years I had been hit by a trace of self-awareness and remembered that once I'd had another life. I'd sat in the House of Lords. I used to gamble daily at the Clermont. I'd had a wife, once, and three children.

I tottered through the fields to the main

house where Neeraja and Jay lived, stumbling up the veranda in my haste before knocking on the chicken-wire door.

'Mr Jeffrey Sir?' said Neeraja, eyeing me warily through the door — and well she might. I rarely visited. She had a homely plumpness, with her orange silk sari straining to retain the great folds of flesh around her midriff.

'Neeraja,' I said. By that time, I spoke so infrequently that my voice was barely above a whisper. 'I wondered if I might be able to borrow a mirror.'

'A mirror? Yes Mr Jeffrey.' A moment later she returned with a wooden hand-mirror. I thanked her and, while I was still standing at the front-door, I had the first proper look at myself in more than a decade.

'Godfathers!' It was impossible to see one single point of common reference to the vagrant that I was looking at and the man that I once used to know. It wasn't just the wild hair, or my corrugated skin, the flattened boxer's nose, or even the gaping grey holes in my mouth which had once held such strong white teeth. No, it was the dull, cloudy eyes, which had so little spark in them that I might have been staring at a dead man.

It's not that I wanted my old looks back. But for a moment, I did feel a rare sense of self-realisation: I was pissing my life away. Again, a twitch of a memory as I recalled my old life. Not that I could ever go back. But from nowhere I had this desire to clean myself up.

I must have been staring at myself for five minutes, my fingers occasionally straying to my face.

'Neeraja, do you have any scissors?' I whispered. 'Could you tidy me up?'

It may sound strange that a junkie is capable of suddenly dragging himself out of the mire like this. Well, he's not. But that's not to say that a junkie can't have the odd moment of lucidity. What he is incapable of, however, is any sort of follow-through. They've got no stamina, no staying power. Give them something to do, which will last about 20 minutes, and they'll have a chance. But as for anything that might require more than an hour's commitment, forget it.

I sat on a stool in the garden while Neeraja snipped at my hair. It was the first time in a decade that I'd been touched by another human. A quite exquisite feeling as her fingers teased at my great mane of white hair. She didn't talk, but simply snipped away until I was left with a trim white bob, which she tied into a pony-tail with an elastic band.

I sat rigidly on the stool, not wanting it to

end. Around me on the grass was this ring of white hair, like the moultings of an old sheepdog.

'And the beard too, Mr Jeffrey?' said Neeraja.

'Please.'

How perfect it was to be there in the dappled morning sun, with Neeraja tamping and snipping at my face, filling my lap with hanks of grey beard. You can do without a lot of things in your life, but one of man's most basic requirements is the need to be touched.

When she was done, I looked at myself again in the mirror. The transformation was remarkable. In the right light, the ponytail and the clipped trowel of a beard could almost have looked distinguished; there was even a hint of life winking back at me from those dull, black eyes.

It was a very slight fillip in my drug-addicted life; there were many more bags of heroin to be injected yet. But what it did presage was a desire for company. For over a decade, I'd lived the life of a hermit, and although this desire for solitude was now innate, I started to drift into the local village.

Again, I have no recollection of how it all began, but somehow I found myself becoming a regular in a little coffeeshop. You'll have to forgive the lack of detail. I feel like a young child who returns again and again to his parent's local restaurant; they know with certainty that they've always been going there, they know that the place is so reassuringly familiar that it feels like home, but they wouldn't have the faintest idea about how they'd started going there in the first place.

Normally, I imagine, I'd totter the half-mile into the village, drink a cup of that sweet milk chai, and then amble back. Get my dose of heroin, inject it into any part of the body that wasn't covered in scar tissue and switch off the light for the next six months. I don't know how often I went to that café, but go there I did, like an old arthritic dog returning again and again to its favourite dustbin. Where the money came from I don't know. Presumably Neeraja gave it me.

And now that my scene-setting is done, I think we are ready for curtain to come up for the next act: for hard as it may be to believe, despite my addictions of my life on the run, I did fall in love. And for the briefest of moments, I think there was a small chance it was mutual.

At least I hope it was. We all of us like to believe that at some stage in our lives we have met our love-match. Whether we have made anything of it — well that is a different question entirely. But even a taste of it is better by far than nothing at all.

I was wearing white, all white, thin cotton trousers and a thin white smock with an open neck. On my feet, some old black rubber flip-flops. I liked my skin to be covered, the better to hide the ant-tracks of injection marks that swarmed up my arms and legs. My hair was in its usual pony-tail to keep it out of my face, while my white beard had been recently clipped. A walking stick was by my side. Jay had made it for me.

Down the track I go and out onto the single-track road, which is the usual affair that you get in India: dotted with potholes and with the verges overgrown in verdant abandon. Stray dogs scratch themselves in the sunshine. Some water-buffalo are milling about on the road, chewing at anything that happens to waft in front of their noses. I watch as one of them even tries to enter the Post Office. It's a sandy-coloured brick bungalow with the words 'Post Office' stencilled on the wall in red. The cow is shooed out, but not too briskly. Cows, after all, are sacred here.

There's a small market, selling chillies, water-melons, thumb-sized bananas and those rank-smelling durians, which in looks have always reminded me of a puffer-fish. I

234

can smell the wood-smoke as it curls up from the chimneys. A scrawny ginger Tom pads along the corrugated iron roof-tops. Toothless crones smoking Bidis on their door-steps. Children shrieking during a game of tip and run in one of the yards. The sunshine warm on the nape of my neck, but not blistering. How is it that I've never noticed any of this before? I must have visited the café over a hundred times, yet none of this has registered.

As for the café, well it was more of a shack really, with a little counter at the back behind which was the black kitchen. Now *that* I do remember! Everything, from the pots, the pans to the cooker, the shelves and the walls, was black; it probably hid the mice as they scurried around the food. There were a few rectangular tables, all of them in chipped sky-blue, and overlooking the street was a long bar at which you could perch and watch the world go by. There was no window there as such, but instead a large shutter that swung upwards to serve duty as a makeshift awning. The shack was predominantly used by locals, but the odd traveller would sometimes stray in.

I don't know how it had come about, but my regular spot in the tea-shack was always at the bar by the window, feet tucked beneath me on the stool below; my stick tucked to the side and a glass of chai slowly cooling in front of me. And what was I thinking about? I have not the faintest idea; why not ask me to expound Einstein's General Theory of Relativity? Junkies aren't in the business of remembering; their only desire is to forget. But I think that as usual, I must have been staring, trance-like, out of the window and onto the street — impassive to all the comings and goings in the shop, and certainly oblivious to the woman who'd just walked in.

No, the first I knew of her was when she tripped over my walking-stick. And if I still had that bamboo cane with me I'd kiss the damn thing, just for sheer gratitude at having brought Karen into my life.

It was like a gun had gone off. A terrific bang and I looked down to see this woman sprawling on the floor at my feet with cup and cakelet smeared against the wall.

'Jesus Christ, why don't you look where you're putting that stick?' She was on all fours and slowly hauling herself up.

And do you know what I did? Truly the most astonishing thing — the only possible thing, in fact, that could have disarmed her so completely.

I burst into tears.

I don't know if I'd cried in over a decade,

but this woman's minor outburst was like a dam-burst. It was like ten years of hell pouring down my cheeks.

Her words had just been the catalyst, but once I'd started crying, it was as if for the first time I'd become aware of the misery of my life and the pain of my loss. It'd been a God-awful mess-up. Tears for myself and tears for the children who I would never see again. At first they just dripped down my cheeks, but soon it was the full waterworks, wracking sobs, my whole body quivering as I buried my face into my hands. An entirely new experience for me. As you might expect given my starched Eton upbringing, crying in public was perceived as a weakness which was only indulged in by women and the mawkishly sentimental.

Once I'd started, there was no stopping me — on and on it went, interspersed with these huge racking coughs.

I gradually became aware that this woman was sitting on a stool next to me; that she had an arm round me and was stroking my neck.

I sniffed, sniffed again, braced my shoulders and took a sip of cold tea. The glass rattled against my teeth.

For a while I stared quietly at my lap, enjoying the light touch of this woman's fingers on my neck. Finally I looked at her

— and this is what I saw: a petite woman with a boyish crop of brown hair; a woman who was not going to stand for any nonsense; and a woman, perhaps in her mid-40s, who had been so tempered by life that she had all the durability of cold steel. Her face has that comforting sense of *déjà vu* that you get when you see a soulmate from another life.

As our eyes met, she gave me a little rueful smile before nodding her head. And I did something that, just an hour earlier, would have been unthinkable. I took her hand, cupped it in my own, brought it to my lips and kissed it. I caught a trace of soap, clean and efficient. It was an old-style act of homage, almost fealty, as if I were acknowledging her grace.

'Thank you,' I said.

She was sitting knee to knee next to me on another high stool. Very slowly, she broke off from my neck to cup my hands in her own.

'You're back again are you?' she said. A tough, hard voice, even though she spoke in little more than a whisper. I would have known it anywhere, recognised it immediately from my childhood.

'You're from New York?' Despite the drugs, I could still sometimes slot my brain into gear.

'You like Yankees?'

'I love them. I was brought up in America during the war. They've never shown me anything but kindness.'

She laughed at that. 'Maybe I'll be the exception — '

'I'm sure not.'

'You're being very gall-ant today.'

It was the first time in a decade that I could actually recall myself smiling. And there we sat, holding hands and smiling at each other. We'd spoken barely more than a few sentences, yet each of us somehow knew that we were in the presence of something precious.

'Hello Jeff,' she said. 'Good to have you back again.'

'And you are?'

'I'm Karen.'

'You'll have to forgive me, my brain is addled.'

'That's all right. It usually is.'

'Is it? I suppose it is.' I scratched at the sores on my arm. They were part of my life as an addict. You give yourself five injections a day, you don't bother much about sterilising the equipment and one way or the other you're going to get infected.

Karen rubbed at her knee, which was still sore after her fall. I eyed her glassily. Petite, I saw, but brisk, efficient. I think she'd be known as a no-nonsense type of woman. Or, as they said of her type in my day, she didn't suffer fools gladly.

'How did you come here?' I asked, mind flittering like a butterfly. In those days, I'd moved way beyond social niceties, said the first thing that came into my head. If I had a question, out it came. 'Why are you in this cafe?'

She put on a Bogart voice: 'Of all the gin-joints in all the world, how did I end up here? Jeez you're in a bad way Jeff. I've been coming here for years.'

'Is it fate?'

She laughed, interlocking her fingers in mine. She was shaking her head in disbelieving amusement. 'Fate? You're a goddamn jackass Jeff. But OK, I'll humour you for a while. Maybe I just happened to be sunning myself on Anjuna beach and I heard about this old guy living in a junkie squat who needed my help — '

'And I do need that.'

She sort of rolled her eyes, as if at some private joke. 'A girl can only take so much sunshine. Besides Jeff, I needed a challenge.'

And in that split second, I made a decision. I was going to need her help. In a rare moment of clarity, I saw a way out. And I couldn't have done it without her.

'It's going to be a big challenge,' I said. No smiling now. I was looking her in the eye, pleading for help. 'I'm a heroin addict.'

'I know.'

I raised a quizzical eyebrow.

'Been hooked a long time, haven't you?'

'Over ten years.'

'It's good to have you back in the land of the living Jeff. You look a bit whacked.'

'I do?'

'Do you remember ever trying to give up before?'

'Until you came in to this café, I'd never felt the need.'

'You old charmer — OK, well it's probably about time to refresh you with the rules. The rules are that we're going to take it one step at a time — and this time, you're going to do what I say. Don't want you sneaking off to use your own private stash.'

'Yes.'

'And, as always, there's no sex. I'm here to fix you up Jeff, get you back on the road. I'm a carer. But I ain't ever gonna be your lover and that's the end of it.'

'Right. Rather lost interest in that side of things over the years, I'm afraid.' I coughed, wiping the spittle from my mouth with a filthy handkerchief. 'Could you tell me one thing though — '

'Let me guess? Why am I doing all this for a perfect stranger?'

I nodded.

'Maybe I knew you in another life,' she said.

'Well whatever it is, I'm grateful.'

The reason, if you must know, why she took me on was obvious enough. She was one of those wonderful people who finds themselves attracted to birds with broken wings and who once they've found one want to do nothing so much as make them whole again. Karen had, I later learned, been doing it not just in her professional life as a nurse but also in her private life, when she would collect about her all the waifs, strays, delinquents and emotionally challenged retards that came her way. She'd patch them up, cure their ails, and then when they were sufficiently able to get to get back on their feet, they'd walk straight out of her life. That's how it always happened with Karen — and that, for one reason or another, is the regrettable truth about what happened with me. But, I do think that even my darling Karen would admit that she'd played her part. Of course it was my fault that it came to an end. But women like Karen, who yearn to nurture, do sometimes find it difficult to cope with their broken-winged bird which has suddenly relearned how to fly.

How it had cost her over the years, as relationship after relationship had hit the rocks — and that's not even starting on the physical and emotional abuse that she must have suffered at the hands of all those wrecked men. The first of them, of course, was her roller-coaster of a father, who from the sound of things suffered from the most severe bi-polar disorder, the one moment the life and soul of the party, and the next mired so deep in the Black Dog that slashing his wrists seemed like the only way out. And one day he did just that, slashing his wrists and dying in the very bathroom of Karen's university bedsit. Ever since, she'd spent her life trying to save him and his ilk.

Karen had been travelling some time. She'd hit the road after another grisly break-up with a man whose wing may still have been broken, but who was more than capable of beating the living daylights out of her. And in a moment of Epiphany, she decided to have done with all these benighted characters that she'd drawn into her life; have done with the whole lot of them and travel the world and meet a man, a mature adult man who was able to love and be loved.

That was the plan anyway.

Might have worked too, if she hadn't come

into that little coffee-shop which was to be our haven.

It was the tears that did it. Nothing else would have worked. But the sight of this old man in tears had been an arrow darting straight into her heart. And how could it not have done? You can have as much therapy as you like, a lifetime of working through your hang-ups and the various rackets going on in your head, but you can never go against your nature.

And thank the Lord that it was in Karen's nature to be so attracted to such a spent old relic as myself. Was I the dad she'd always hoped to save? Quite possibly. Even I, with all my addictions and the rest of it, would not be deluded enough to think that she was doing it just for me.

15

I never saw Aspinall again, but I wish I had — if only to thank him for the most remarkable tribute that he paid to me in his new club.

Aspinall made several fortunes in his life and squandered all but the last. And as I've already mentioned, he was on his uppers when he hid me away in 1974. He still had colossal outgoings to pay for the upkeep of his zoos at Howletts and Port Lympne, but after the sale of the Clermont he had little discernible income. So, for several years, it fell to Goldsmith to keep Aspers afloat. Probably the only decent thing he ever did in his entire life.

Eventually Aspers' good fortune kicked in again. He had another big, big win at the poker tables and set about opening another casino. He may never have had the same business acumen as Goldsmith — hence his near bankruptcy in the crash of 1973 — but as regards lavishness and general opulence, his tastes were impeccable.

His comeback club was in Curzon Street and no expense was spared as he turned it into a casino fit for a prince. Well, it had to be fit for a Prince — as the Royals were exactly the sort of clientele that he was trying to attract in the first place. I read later that in the Gentlemen's cloakroom, Aspers had installed a vast fish-tank with its own 'ecologically independent coral reef'. Magnificent stained glass windows of two legendary gamblers, Cleopatra and Genghis Khan. Precious antiques rubbing shoulder to shoulder with old masterpieces on the walls. And — to my mind, at least — the *Pièce de Résistance* of the entire casino, bronze busts in the dining room of the 'four greatest gamblers in history'.

I always knew that Aspers tended towards the bizarre. These four great gamblers would certainly not have made it into most people's top ten. But here, for what it's worth, were Aspers' four gambling heroes.

The first was Marshal Blücher, the Prussian general who turned the tide at Waterloo and helped rout Napoleon. It was Blucher who told his King: 'All my life sire, you have gambled with my bones — now I shall gamble with your treasury.'

Next was Charles James Fox who lost everything he possessed at the tables except his friends.[9]

The third greatest gambler in history was

Pasha Gordon who wagered his life at Khartoum for the Kingdom of God.

And the last of these four epic gamblers? It was none other than my poor benighted self, a man who gambled everything for the sake of his children.

And so I did — and lost it all too. But I did give a weak smile when I learned that Aspers had decided to immortalise my act of monumental folly. A moment of dry humour in what has always been a most bloody business for everyone involved. Would that I were able to thank him for it.

★ ★ ★

Of those first few weeks with Karen, I only have a few snatched glimpses of memory. She had quickly moved into the village, renting a top floor flat close by to the tea-shop. It had a bedroom plus en suite lavatory with the requisite hole in the ground and two ceramic pads on which to plant your feet. In the lounge-cum-kitchenette was a sofa, an arm-chair and two side-tables, though usually we preferred to sit out on the balcony, with its sweeping views over the coconut groves. Far in the distance, you could just make out a thin strip of green-blue sea. Oh, and now that I remember it, there was also a little lumber-room by the front door. I'd some-times store things there; I forget what.

And what's it like trying to break a 14-year addiction to heroin? A living hell. Karen cut back my heroin use by stages, so it wasn't total cold turkey. At first it was like I had a fever, with cramps, twitches and non-stop sweats. For a few days, I experienced something almost akin to euphoria at having had the gumption to quit, but this was soon replaced by a leaden anxiety.

The worst of it was the unbearable insomnia. I'd always found it hard to sleep, but now I'd be lucky to get two hours a night. Without the heroin, Sandra was also back with a vengeance; she'd usually be lying there dead on the floor as I lay on my charpoy.

I am aware though that there's not much interest to be had from reading about some swine of a fellow trying to beat his addiction to heroin. Not much interest either for me in raking over those stone-cold embers. Such an utterly tedious period of my life. And frankly I can't be bothered to go back there.

No — my story, or such as it is, is to be found in my dealings with Karen and my further dealings with Goldsmith.

Much of my rehab I spent in Karen's lounge, with its sliding door that led out onto that bamboo balcony. She had a couple of rattan easy-chairs, with their curved backs shaped like a crescent moon. Side by side we'd sit in those chairs for hours on end, often not saying much but content to stare out to the dusk horizon. But the conversations were always very onesided. I knew everything about Karen's early life, about the men who'd beaten her up and the mum who'd died of cancer — and she knew nothing about mine. I rarely volunteered any information and, if she ever asked, I would duck and weave and dissemble. But sometimes, if the breeze was a cool feather on the skin and the sun was low in the sky, I could be tempted to open up.

One evening, I'd just showered in her flat. In many respects you deal with cold turkey in the same way that you might treat a bout of flu; you need to be cosseted.

She'd brought a couple of lime sodas onto the balcony. For once it felt good to have the sun on my skin. We could see it tipping low over the sea and it warmed my blighted soul.

The feelings I had for Karen were quite different from anything I'd ever felt before. I wonder if I'd ever felt like that during the first flush of my romance with Veronica. Probably not. Throughout my relationship with Veronica, I was besotted with position, class, money and all the other piffling trappings that so obsess the English blue bloods. I never knew myself and I never took the time to get to know Veronica either, so we each of us brought out the worst in the other.

I remember the quiet comfort of knowing that, even in the silence, Karen was sitting there next to me. I was learning to savour the tranquillity of the moment. But then I was no longer quite so up my own lordly arse. God, I must have been a nightmare for Veronica. Of course when we'd married, I'd given her the title that she yearned for. But I was never in any way capable of giving her the support and the husbandly attention that she needed.

From nowhere, I said something that I had not uttered in nearly two decades. They were words that I had never dared hope that I might say again, but they came bubbling out of me completely unbidden, like water spuming up from a well-spring.

'I love you Karen.'

She laughed and looked at me, before taking my hand. 'You probably do. At least you think you do.'

Notice, by the way, how my feelings were never reciprocated. In the end, she never did tell me that she loved me — and, come to that, we never consummated our relationship either. But if not love, then I think she felt a certain tenderness towards me. For myself, I was grateful for anything and everything that was on offer.

'You ever want kids, hey Jeff?' she asked, changing the subject in her usual blunt manner.

'Want them?' I said. 'I've got them. Three of them, a boy and two girls. They were the best thing ever to happen to me.'

'Gee. How come you never told me this before? When did you last see them?'

'I never told you because you never asked.' I paused for thought, taking pleasure in Karen's elfin face. The sun suited her. By now she had a deep tan that crinkled dark around her eyes when she smiled. 'I last saw them 14 years ago.'

'That's a hell of a long time for a family rift.' She took a sip from her soda, crunching the ice between perfect dainty teeth. 'Why don't you go back?'

'They'd never have me.'

'They might do. You never know.'

'Trust me, they wouldn't.'

'Like to tell me what you did to piss them off so much?'

I shrugged and stared out over the tree-tops. Wondered how it might sound if I told her that I'd tried to murder the children's mother — and had ended up killing the nanny by mistake. 'It was . . . It

251

was — ' I said, regrouping. 'I can't go back.'

'Fine.'

I sipped some of the lime soda. Beyond the little snapshots that I had freeze-framed in my mind, what did I remember?

'My favourite memories are of when I had them all to myself. I'd give them a bath in the evening. No splashing on the floor as I was quite a strict father. I'd wash their hair and bundle them up into warm white towels. We'd snuggle into bed as I read them stories.' A memory came darting back into my head, so sharp that it made my eyes water. I'd leaned over once to kiss George on the top of his head — and suddenly I could recall the actual smell of his hair.

'What did you do for holidays? Buckets and spades on the beach?'

'I hadn't thought of that in years.' I smiled at the memory. 'Such a tedious existence I used to live. Stiflingly dull. I used to gamble, you know, most nights of the week, stuck in the middle of this sea of green baize frittering my life away. Paid the bills for a little while — or at least it did at first, though in the end it damn near bankrupted me. But every year we'd try and go off to Portugal. We'd rent a villa and for weeks on end we'd play on the beach, eat langoustine and drink Sancerre. The children's skins would be as brown as shoe-leather by the end of it. I had a power-boat too. We'd go out along the coast, poking our way through the inlets until we found a beach for a picnic. The children loved it. Those holidays must have been some of the few occasions when they couldn't sense the *froideur* between Veronica and myself.'

Karen said nothing, continued to stare out at the picture perfect sunset, with the sun bubbling as it sank into the sea.

'I was quite the expert at building sandcasties, I'd happily spend all morning on them. Huge castles with turrets and moats and even dungeons. I liked the sandcastles from the buckets to be just perfect when you tipped them out. If the castellations started to crumble, I'd have to scoop it all up and start again. We'd decorate the walls with shells, mussels, oysters, limpets, anything we could find — '

'And a little Union Jack at the top?'

'Of course. There had to be a Union Jack on the tower! Seaweed draped along the inside of the moat to deter invaders — and just enough room in the middle for the four of us to stand. We'd wait and we'd wait and then the first wave would come in, just a little tickle, enough to fill up the moat. The girls would be squealing with excitement. I'd pick up George to keep him dry. That delicious feeling of inevitability as the sea rolls in, licking at the outer walls before the towers start to crumble and in the wink of an eye everything that you started has been washed away, and you're all running back helter-skelter through the surf.'

Karen's black eyes had never left me. 'It sounds rather sad when you tell it like that.'

I was enthused — bubbling. The first time in over a decade that I'd ever felt roused. 'Oh no! It was the best bit — the bit we'd all been waiting for. You can't just build your sandcastle and leave it to stand another day. You have to see it all washed away, see how all your work, your towers and your walls, your moats and your bridges have been razed to the ground. And that, Karen, is how it is in life. We say our piece, we make our mark, and then the tide comes rolling in. Everything is swept clean, the beach again reverts to an endless stretch of pristine sand as if . . . as if we'd never existed.'

'And that, I suppose, is how it all turned out with your own castle?'

'Erased off the face of the earth. Surprisingly though, it never provided me with a tenth of the pleasure that I ever had at seeing those sandcastles slip into the sea.'

Karen leaned over and clasped my hand. 'Thank you for sharing that.'

I gave a little snort of laughter, as an old memory slipped back into view, like the hull of a sunken ship peeking up out of the water at a neap tide. 'There was one thing, actually, that we liked to do as a family — all of us, Veronica, me, and the children Camilla, Frances and George. We had an old upright piano and I could play it not too badly. I'd even started having lessons again. I remember it! I was having lessons again, one a week, and I was re-learning all those jolly old hymns and songs that I'd loved at school.' I chuckled as I swung my finger to the beat. 'That old hymn which the Welsh male-voice choirs sing. That wonderful chorus, *Bread of Heaven*!'

I sang a couple of bars, trying to give it the rich vibrato of a true Welsh miner.

'I'd even started learning a great, a sensational hunting song, *Do ye ken John Peel, with his coat so grey*? A lovely one! I think the one that we liked best was *Onward Christian Soldiers*. I'd start off slow and pick up speed, and the children and Veronica would be trying to compete, and I'd be banging it out for all I was worth on the piano, and — '

I broke off suddenly. This time the memory that was surfacing from beneath the waves was of such ugliness that it made me physically flinch. I'd remembered the last time that I'd seen that old upright piano. We'd kept it in the basement — the perfect place for a sing-along.

I closed my eyes and rubbed at my temples. I could see the piano standing there dark in the corner as I tried to stuff Sandra's battered body into the mailbag.

The silence stretched on. The sun had now long gone and Orion was already twinkling high in the sky. Mosquitoes started to drone round the balcony. One landed on my arm. I watched as it started to feed.

Karen hadn't moved for some time. She lay there, legs stretched out in front of her, glazed eyes staring out to the horizon.

And eventually she spoke.

'I've only just realised,' she said. 'You are Lord Lucan.' Not a question but a statement of fact.

You might think that I was shocked that my identity had finally been discovered. But I was not. Like a young homosexual man who is longing to come out to his family, I had been leaving plenty of pointers along the way. And someone as acute as Karen was not going to miss them.

'I . . . I am — ' I had dreamt of this moment so often, the time when I would finally make a clean breast of things. But now that it had come, I did not know what to say.

'I was Lord Lucan.'

I watched as Karen drummed her finger-tips on the arm-rest. She still hadn't looked at me. 'You . . . you killed the nanny. Is that right?'

'Yes. It is. At least . . . I was responsible for her death. It was a mistake. I'd hoped . . . I'd wanted . . . to kill my wife.'

'Well — well,' she said, steepling her fingers in front of her mouth as she marshalled her thoughts. 'Do you want to talk?'

I took a deep breath. Was I ready to confess? Was this the moment when I was going to open my heart?

Of course not. Eton-educated peers — even the addicts — are not in the habit of wearing their hearts on their sleeves.

'It was awful,' I said. 'But it's in the past, locked in its box. And I choose not to go back there.'

'You don't want to talk?'

'No. I don't.'

'Fine.'

'But — but what I can tell you, Karen, is that every day, the shame of it still haunts me.'

And there that scene on that idyllic balcony comes to a close. Forgive me, but all I have left of Karen are these few snapshots of memory — and there are only three more episodes left to tell. As for the rest of it, they have been lost in that great black hole of forgotten memory, experienced but erased like those castles in the sand. What happens to all those forgotten memories by the way? Do they disappear into the ether of the moment, or do they have a wisp of soul that lingers on? I so wish I had some choice in the matter of my memories. I wish I could remember more about Karen and less about my wife Veronica; I wish I could remember more about my parents — and quite considerably less about James Goldsmith. And if I were to have one final wish, I wish that I could remember more about my children — and, along with it, forget completely the inexcusable events of that November night in 1974.

16

The village was winding down as I walked back to my hut. There were a few men smoking by the side of the road, but the children and the animals were all abed. Whiffs of curry and baking chapattis from the little shanty houses, their front doors wide open to reveal scenes of tranquil Goan domesticity. Often there'd be little more than a wooden table and three chairs, a man swilling down palm Feni while his woman was hunched over a pot at the fire. One of the bungalows even had a TV, with its screeching, dancing women. Indian films are an acquired taste — and I have still yet to acquire it.

Further on, I walked past the post office. The counter section was closed off, but it's phone lines were still open, the light blazing out from the door onto the wooden porch. I lingered, drawn to the phone-booth inside.

Two women were sitting on chairs, biding their time, while a man jabbered away in Hindi in the kiosk. The glass door was closed but I could still hear every word. Behind a chipped wooden desk was what I suppose you'd call the operator, dressed in the ubiquitous khaki that serves India's millions of officials so well. He was reading a paper, owl eyes peering through milk-bottle thick glasses; he didn't bother to look up.

I took my place in the queue and as I sat down there listening to the interminable burble from the phone-booth, I had a chance to mull over what I was hoping to achieve. It was partly the talk with Karen, but what had sealed it was seeing those families settling down for supper. As I'd walked past the post office, I'd had this uncontrollable urge to speak to my children. What would they sound like? By then, 14 years on, Frances would be a full 24-years-old; maybe she was married. George would have been 21; perhaps he'd followed me into the army. And little Camilla, who was four when I last saw her, would now be an 18-year-old adult with boyfriends and the rest of it — and to think that I had missed every moment. The pain was unbearable. Birthdays, school sports days, triumphs and disasters, I had missed them all. But the sight of that ramshackle post office had made me realise that my children were only a phone-call away. I'd try our old home number first, just in case they were still there. I could call up Aspers and see if he had any numbers. Hell — I could even try international directory enquiries. I just had this terrible yearning to speak to my children.

As I waited in the queue, and the women made their calls to their far-away families, I wondered what I would say. Who would pick up the phone first, would it be George, or would it be Camilla, eager to hear from her swain? And what would I say? How would the conversation go? I'd ask, 'Is that Camilla?' and when she replied in the affirmative, filled with girlish curiosity at the owner of this aging voice on the other end of the line, I'd say, 'Hello Camilla, this is your father.' A gasp of amazement — but surely she'd have been expecting it. Don't tell me that she and Frances and George hadn't, countless times over, imagined what it would be like if their father called up out of the blue? What they'd say and what they'd do?

So, although it was going to be an initial shock, it was nonetheless going to be a call that they'd rehearsed before. They'd listen in silence, perhaps, as I poured out my apologies, told them how much I loved them. I might even drop them an address in Goa, tell them to come out for a sunshine holiday in India, so that we could meet up, I could explain everything, and I could give them a father's kiss and a father's blessing.

I had it all planned out in my tiny mind. I didn't for a moment think of the possible consequences — that instead of Camilla, I might get hold of Veronica, or that the children might call the police.

The last woman finished her conversation, shuffled out of the phone-booth and handed over her rupees. The operator looked over at me with the glazed eyes of officialdom, and asked me where I wanted to call. I gave him our old phone number in Belgravia. It was the only number that I knew by heart. And to think that I was only minutes away from talking to my children! Why hadn't I done this years before? I'd missed out on 14 years of their lives — but it was still not too late.

I sat on a tatty canvas chair in front of the official and had a look round the office. Funny how I can remember the details of this one room, yet can't recall much of what was important. There was a large calendar on the wall, but it was two years out of date. A wicker basket was on the floor, overflowing with paper and orange peel. One of the beige walls was peppered with black scuff marks, as if a small boy had been using it as a fives court. Through the dusty, cracked window, some palm trees were creaking in the wind.

The official hardly glanced up as he gestured to the phone-booth. It stank of stale sweat, and as I cradled the receiver to my ear I caught a jarring whiff of cigarette smoke. All

I could hear was the ethereal wisp and crackle of over 5,000 miles of telephone line. I stared through the glass at the man at the desk picking his ear. My heart drilling in my chest. And from far off, so far off that I can barely hear it, there is the sound of a phone ringing. Hands clammy with sweat. I'm just moments away from speaking to my children for the first time in 14 years. It rings. And it rings. Towering disappointment as I'm on the verge of hanging up. And finally it's picked up. A man's voice at the end, not a young man. Much older and curt. 'Hello?'

And with that single word, all my dreams came crashing down to earth — I replaced the handset. I hit my head against the wall in acknowledgement at my own stupidity. If my children answered the phone; and if they ever believed it was me; and if they could find it in their hearts to listen; and if they could forgive . . . At best, it was highly improbable. But, as that man had answered the phone, I had suddenly become aware of my own selfishness. It was 14 years on from Sandra's death, and although at the time it must have been traumatic in the extreme for them, they would have coped with it as only children can. It would have been difficult, but they would have found a way of dealing with their father's infamy, and they would have survived. It might not have been the ideal childhood; but few are. One way or another though, my three children would have come to terms with the scandal and to life without their father. I'd wrecked things once for them already — and now who was I to come blundering back into their lives and wrecking what little harmony and peace-of-mind that they had managed to find for themselves?

I'd thought initially that the call would be for my children's benefit. But it was nothing of the kind. Yet again it was just my awesome selfishness shining through.

What a slump I had when I returned to my charpoy. In the darkness, I fumbled for the matches and lit my kerosene lamp. For the first time, it had hit home that I could never see or hear from my children again. If I owed them one single thing, it was never to call, never to write, never to get caught, so that till the day they went to their graves, they truly believed that I'd killed myself.

So that, then, is largely why I got back on the heroin. With dull resignation I went through the motions of adding some water to my white powder, heating it up in a spoon, and that ineffable ecstasy of release as I injected it into my leg. It was difficult, at the best of times, to find a vein.

I didn't get a vein.
I found an artery.

⋆ ⋆ ⋆

Karen, when she found me sparked out on my charpoy and surrounded by all my paraphernalia, went absolutely mad.

She might well have thought me dead, as the floor was slick with blood, but when she realised that I still had a pulse she started hitting me round the head.

'What the hell are you doing, you stupid bastard?' she said. Again and again she slapped me on the cheeks, crying with rage as I slowly jolted out of unconsciousness. 'What are you doing? Why the hell do I bother? What is the point in me helping you if you just keep shooting up every time things go bad? You're a dumb, useless shit.'

My head jolted from side to side and I could feel her tears dripping onto my face. She patched me up with some of the bedding that she'd ripped off the charpoy. Did she take me to hospital? I'm not even sure of that, but all I remember next was sitting together outside the hut; it must have been the afternoon, so it might have been the same day. Fresh bandages were tight round my leg.

Karen had calmed down, but she was still angry.

'You're a wreck, you're a goddamn wreck, you know that? You've probably infected yourself, and serve you right if you do. Why did you have to do it? Why couldn't you just stay with me, talk it through, but oh no, you have to come back here in your uptight Brit way, and you just do what you've always done and shoot yourself up. It's pathetic! You're pathetic!'

I sat huddled in an old deckchair with a blanket around my shoulders. A mug of sweet chai was cupped in my hands. I felt the schoolboy who's disgraced the school and, worse, let down his headmaster.

'I'm pathetic,' I repeated.

'You are pathetic! That's exactly what you are, you shambling wreck! Is this what you're going to do every time something comes up that you're not capable of dealing with? Is that it? So you're a stinking murderer and you're overcome with guilt. Well give yourself up or get over it, but don't ever — EVER — shoot up on me again like that.'

'I'm sorry.'

'Sorry? You couldn't give a damn. You're just saying the first piece of shit that comes into your head. What is it? What do you want me to do?'

Oh, but she was angry, now up and out of her chair and pacing round my scrub garden. Flexing her fingers with pent-up rage. Was it really all me — or had I somehow tapped into

266

all the anger that she must have felt when her father committed suicide in her bathroom? Back and forth she went, her brown linen skirt flaring up round her ankles.

'It was the children,' I said, feebly, barely more than a whisper.

'What? What did you say? Speak to me!'

'I'd — I'd realised that I'd never see my children again. I have to — have to let them go their own way without me.'

'Okay,' she said, abruptly coming to a stop in front of me.

And just as suddenly, it all stopped. She sat down beside me and took me by the hand. 'It's not easy,' she said. 'We'll work on it together. Take it one day at a time, you stinking piece of Limey shit.'

I smiled now that she'd forgiven me so quickly. 'Got it in one,' I said.

I was surprised that she'd calmed down so suddenly, but later it was all perfectly apparent. I was letting my children get on with their lives without me — and Karen, in her turn, had to get on with her life without her father. At least she had the certain knowledge that her father was dead, and that is a luxury that has always been denied to my own three children.

17

Goa is a fantastical hybrid mix of Portugal and Goa. The state is defined by one word, 'Susegad', which means, 'Relax and enjoy life while you can.' It's like 'Manana' in Spain. It means 'Chill out; be cool; don't get too uppity when I'm an hour late'.

The first European to arrive there was Vasco Da Gama in 1498, and the Portuguese very quickly established a foothold in India. But Portugal was never quite big enough to have her own empire and in the 16th Century had the ignominy of being annexed by Spain. So, mindful that their enemy's enemy was their friend, the Portuguese sensibly allied themselves with Britain, and have been allied to us ever since. They're our oldest allies, and in the case of India were allowed to maintain a toehold in Goa while the French were driven into the sea.

They stayed in Goa for over four-and-a-half centuries, but were forced to decamp in 1961, some 14 years after Britain lowered the Union Jack for the last time. But Goa still retains its 'Susegad' motto, still has its Christianity, and still has a much more open attitude to sex and drugs.

The difference in culture is so marked that many people don't consider Goa even to be part of India — not least the Indians. You can even see this in the sport. Anywhere else in India, the national sport is cricket, but the Goans' have always retained the Portuguese passion for football.

And there were the hippies. Goa — and Anjuna beach in particular — is famous for its hippies, those long-haired, sex-addicted dope-smokers. I'd never had much to do with them, preferring to live out my hermit-like existence in my hut.

Or at least I believe that to be true.

★　★　★

Karen had taken me to Anjuna beach. It was via a track through a few farms, but we'd hired a cycle rickshaw. She showed me some of the wildlife along the way, pointing to the bonnet macaques in the canopy of the coconut palms. A riot of colour and squawking from all of the birds, which I might have heard before but had never once noticed. There were Indian rollers in mauve and blue, shiny black drongoes that perched on the posts and harriers and buzzards soaring over the open fields. So much to see, once I had the eyes to see it.

And the beach too. It was if I was seeing the Ocean for the first time in my life, striking a chord in my very soul. Karen lay on a rattan mat while I sank into the sand, working my fingers down, revelling in the lick of surf at my feet.

Karen watched my obvious delight. She was lying next to me, wearing a t-shirt and sarong, and propped up on one elbow.

'We should come here more often,' she said.

I let the sand trickle through my upturned fingers. 'We should.'

'You're on the way, Jeff.'

'On the way where?'

'On the way back to becoming a human again.'

I think I probably was. Thanks to Karen, I'd acquired some sort of normality in my life, was having regular meals, a little exercise. Hell — we'd even gone to the beach for an afternoon outing! How normal is that? I have to say that of all the many beaches I've been to, Anjuna is one of the loveliest. It's up in the north of Goa, and appropriately enough is famous as India's premier hippy-beach. They were clustered all over the sand, some of them smoking on their bongs, some paddling in the water and some lost in the infinity of

270

the moment as they stared out to sea. And I'll never forget that smell of coconut oil: those were the days when the sun-seekers didn't bother with sunblock, but instead basted themselves with pure coconut oil, as if intent on frying the hides off their backs. Every so often, one of the hawkers would wander down the beach offering everything from coconut milk and pakoras to henna-tattoos and a full-body massage. You could even have your ears cleaned, the little men gouging around with their skewers to produce almost a teaspoon of ear-wax.

But it made no odds what they were selling, what services they were offering; Karen gave them short shrift, and very soon they were all traipsing by without a second glance.

My eyes were shut. I could hear shouting and laughter, but what thrilled my soul was that ever same sound of the sea. I think when I am done, I would like my ashes to be cast into the sea, so that I can roll forever on the oceans.

I was out of it. I didn't even realise that the Frisbee had hit Karen on the leg until she screamed out, 'Jesus Christ, why don't you look what you're doing?'

I squinted open my eyes to see a hippie loping down the beach towards us. He had that mahogany skin that comes only with years of sitting in the sun. Long beach shorts down to his knees and long brown hair in a pony-tail. He had a silver ankh round his neck and a large black Celtic knot tattooed onto his shoulder. I'd probably call him a beach-bum, though quite well muscled for all that.

He jogged down the beach to us, sand spurting up around him. 'Sorry about that mate,' he said with an unmissable Australian twang. 'It's the pillock's first time with a Frisbee.'

'Well, why don't you move further away,' said Karen, not remotely mollified.

'Good idea,' said the Australian. As he stooped to retrieve the Frisbee from the surf, he briefly glanced at me — looked and looked again. 'Is that you Jeff?' He squatted down, searching over my face before wringing my hand. 'It is you! How are you mate?'

'Umm,' I said. I wasn't used to dealing with strangers. In fact they frightened me. 'Hi.'

'Jeff!' he said. 'I can't believe it mate! Where the hell have you been?'

'I — I — ' I'd never seen him before in my life.

Karen stepped in to save me. 'Jeff's been in rehab a while. His memory isn't what it was.

Karen, by the way.'

'Vince,' said the Australian, shaking her hand, but still staring at me. 'Jesus, it is you! And you don't remember anything about me? Never seen me before?'

I shrugged. 'Sorry. It's gone.'

'You don't remember anything? You don't remember Tim and Juliet? Jezza and Sue? Angela? What about the Gerbil? You must remember Gerbils!'

'Sorry, no.'

'Wow,' he said, shaking his head as he stood up. 'Sorry to hear that mate. We used to live together. But good to see you're on the mend. Say — if you like, come back and have a look.'

I didn't know what to say. I remember this sense of panic welling up in me as I squinted up at this black silhouette of a man.

'Well, maybe we might just do that,' said Karen. 'Jeff's a bit delicate at the moment, but we'll get right back to you. Where do you live?'

Vince tapped the Frisbee against his hip. 'Same as we always were, same as we always will be. Round the back of Bala's café. Honestly Jeff — the old gang would love to see you again.'

'Bala's café?' said Karen. 'OK. See you later.'

Vince clapped me on the shoulder. 'Good to see you again, Jeff! We thought you were dead!'

Karen watched as Vince strode back up the beach with his Frisbee. She raised an eyebrow.

'I've no idea,' I said. 'I have absolutely no idea.'

★ ★ ★

Nature abhors a vacuum, however — and that even goes for the delicate matter of your brain. You might think that when you start to forget things, parts of your memory just turn fallow; that they're laid off, like uncultivated pastureland. But this was certainly not my experience.

My experience is that, one way or another, your brain starts to fill in the gaps. If it can't remember, it fills your mind with something — anything. Unless you're one of the happy few to have achieved Nirvana, your mind won't be allow to switch off into blankness. And even the most abject sufferer of Alzheimer's, who has forgotten everything about their family, will still dwell upon that single troublesome childhood memory and over and over again will return to it.

In my case, I wasn't quite at the stage

where my brain was orbiting, goldfish-like, around one single silken memory.

Instead . . .

Well instead of trying to explain it, I will tell you how it first started.

It was a Wednesday and we were at the flea market, which I've heard described as 'an anthropologist's dream'. You've got the hippies, the rich Westerners, the round-eyed Indian tourists come to see what Goa has to offer, the businessmen in their suits, and the fakirs in their skimpy orange robes — and these people, mind, are just the punters. As for the vendors, they are even more eclectic; tribal women from Gujarat rub shoulders with traders from as far afield as Tibet and Kashmir.

The flea-market was originally a place for Westerners to hawk their bric-a-brac, but it quickly turned into a black-market for whisky, cigarettes and those new-fangled electronic gizmos which I have seen, but have not even begun to get my head around how they work or, indeed, what's inside them.

We'd gone to the market for a change of scene. If you're in rehab, it's easy to get bored — and before you know it, your hand is straying towards your syringe, your spoon and your little bag of necessities.

Karen and I weren't in the mood for

buying, but just happy to see all the extraordinary things that were up for sale. At one stall you'd see spices and henna and at the next might be a man selling spare parts for Enfield motorcycles, or perhaps a tattoo artist.

Oh yes — and one thing that I'll never forget about the flea-market: the quite extraordinary smell. Smells in India are generally much more vivid, resonant, than in England. But at the Anjuna flea-market, it's as if at every stall you're being hammered with a new olfactory sensation. A man selling sickly-sweet smelling candies will be right adjacent to a tanner with the most rank-smelling hides.

★ ★ ★

We'd pottered over to a vast banyan tree for a chai. Although I've got used to the chai here, which mostly consists of milk and a vast amount of sugar, I do sometimes miss having a proper cup of Earl Grey, lemon at the side. Perhaps that's the reason why I have so few teeth left in my mouth. Most of them appear to have rotted away to black nubs over the years, though this is the first time I've ever realised that the chai might be the reason for it.

And the giddy hippy market swirled by, exactly the same as it's always been. I didn't like it, I didn't object. It was a given.

Karen slapped both hands on the table, the glass cups clattering on the wood. 'About time we had a change of scene,' she said. 'You ever been one for culture?'

'Never really my thing, dear,' I said.

'Come on, you stuffed shirt. Let's go to the museum. Haven't you had enough of watching these people? That's all you do, watch people.'

'I like watching people. But if you want to go to the museum, I would be delighted to accompany you.'

So the Goa State Museum it was, and we caught a bus to nearby Panaji. Seriously, I can't even remember the last time I went into a museum — for me, museums meant dusty relics behind glass. A slightly upmarket version, if you will, of the Anjuna flea-market. I know this may make me sound like a total Philistine — then so be it. But it seems to me that a lot of museum exhibits are revered simply because they're old. Well, it doesn't cut it for me. Not in any way. A 500-year-old pot that was once pissed in by a princeling; some gaudy gilt clothes once worn by a fat Raja; a chess set made of faded ivory that was once a part of the imperial harem; and . . .

Some people, I'm sure, adore gazing at these ancient historical nick-nacks. But they'd always left me cold. It might be different if you had the things in your hand — were allowed to touch the knife that killed the Emperor. But as it is, all we are allowed to do is mournfully gaze at these tufts of history that lie dead on their pedestals as if set in amber.

There — never really been able to put my finger on quite why I hated museums so much.

And as museums go, the Goa State Museum must be one of the more stultifying. Indians seem to have this reverence for all things old. I stumped in behind Karen, resting on my stick as we went up the entrance steps, already preparing myself for an hour of tedium. There were perhaps a dozen galleries, plenty roomy enough, and chock-full of bits of Hindu and Jain art. The sculptures, the bronzes, the paintings. Some of the carvings dated back to the 4th Century, but I did not have the eyes to appreciate them.

This, then, was my benumbed state of mind as I followed Karen from one gallery to the next, my stick tapping at the tiled floor. Maybe it's the museums themselves — regardless of what they contain, they naturally reduce you to a state of torpor.

Totter into another gallery and another, eyes glazing, longing to get outside for fresh air, and we enter another vast museum room, high ceilings with long windows and the blinds pulled down, and in the middle of the room is a wooden table, blackened with age, about the length of a half-size snooker table. It has the most intricate carved legs, lions at the corner and eagles in the middle.

Around it were five equally elaborate chairs. It might almost have been a dining table — but it was quite clearly not used for anything as mundane as food. It had this, this aura about it. How do I explain the feel of this table? For the first time in my life, I had an actual sensation of dipping my toe back through time. I had a sense of what it was once used for. And a sense, too, of screaming. At times it seemed so loud, that I could believe it was genuinely occurring rather than being a construct of my imagination.

I don't know how it occurred — perhaps some of the fuses in my brain had become warped by drugs; perhaps it might even have been in my ancient Irish blood. I still don't know the answer.

For a few minutes I stood in front of this table, wallowing in the sensations that it created. It had the most ornate carving, its patina blackened with smoke and wax and age, and — how do I write this without sounding clean off my head? — it exuded infamy.

Karen had noticed me by the table and had mooched over to see what I was doing. She had a look at the dreary museum guide.

'Sixteenth Century, huh?' she said. 'They used it for over 200 years during the Inquisition. The Inquisition? Seeing you had such a high-fallutin' education, I'll bet you know all about it.'

'The Catholic Church at its very worst. The Inquisitors terrorised most of the Christian world.'

'So how come I've never heard of them?'

'The Inquisition probably didn't get much play in America. But to the British, the Inquisitors were some of our greatest bogeymen . . . '

I have been aware that the table is exerting a strong hold over me. I step over a red rope and with trembling fingers touch the polished table-top.

It was a Looking Glass moment. Although I am still in the museum, Karen at my side, I can see the Inquisitors dead in front of me, sitting at three sides of the table, all bearded, dressed in black, and with this quite terrifying aura of righteousness. A few yards in front of them stands a poor wretch, manacled at both hand and feet, who is held upright by two guards. Blood from his lacerated back seeps through a ragged shirt. I can even hear the Chief Inquisitor talking in calm, detached Portuguese, a man who is bound to do his duty, however unpleasant that may be. Is there a whiff of incense?

As the Inquisitor sends the prisoner on his way, he gives a curt nod, his white beard blending into the ruff at his throat.

And as I continue to stare, the prisoner lets out a terrified shriek and starts gabbling — but even as he begs for mercy, the guards drag him away. I can even hear the sound of his heels drumming on the tiled floor. But the chief inquisitor never once looks up. He is scratching away with a quill pen on a piece of parchment, dipping occasionally into the ink-pot at his side; only when the prisoner has been dragged from the room does he put his pen down. He takes a sip from a silver goblet of wine and makes a quip to the four other Inquisitors, before leaning back with obvious contentment into his chair.

I'm not aware of the expression on my face — but I think I must seem absolutely horrified.

'What's the matter?' says Karen, jostling

me by the arm. 'You look like hell.'

'Can we go?'

And, even as we leave, I look back one last time at the table, hoping that it was just a trick of my heroin-addicted imagination. But no — the Inquisitors are still there, goblets in hand, well satisfied at a good afternoon's work.

★   ★   ★

And that was the start of it. I could never tell when it was about to occur, but ever since I've had these ghastly glimpses into another world. I even had one on the bus back to Anjuna. It was the usual rickety Indian bus, no glass in the windows and with more animals on board than humans. We'd stopped to let yet more people on and I was gazing out of the window at one of the old Portuguese cemeteries.

I've always felt cemeteries are such sad places — because they've witnessed such a wealth of grief. For every single grave, there will have been a score of mourners grieving for their friend, parent, spouse, son or daughter. Such a flood of emotion — and does it all just disappear into the ether?

But as I gazed out over this cemetery, I had another snatched glimpse of the past, could actually see the clusters of mourners gathered round all those century-old graves. Hundreds of them, their heads bowed, widows weeping over white wood coffins, and even as the bus pulled away, the air was rent with the sad sound of their public keening.

18

Goldsmith was waiting for us. He was sitting in a deckchair in the garden outside my hut, with Neeraja bobbing obeisance to him as she placed a Lassi on the side-table.

Goldsmith. I hadn't seen him in years. Hadn't thought about him for a long while either.

He bounced to his feet, his face wreathed in this most ghastly smile — a huge smile, all teeth and lips; the look, perhaps, of a wolf as it's about to sink his teeth into the jugular of a stricken beast.

'Karen!' he said, bounding over to shake her hand. 'And Lucky! How are you? How are you both?' He grabbed my hand and was clapping me over the shoulder, as if after a decade apart he'd finally been reunited with his true boon companion.

It was all rather too much. I was shell-shocked not just at the sight of him — 14 years, I think it had been since we'd last met — but at the sheer overwhelming force of his personality. It's been said many times over that Goldsmith had a 'powerful' or 'electrifying' personality, but during my time in India

I'd forgotten what it was like to be up close to the man. The energy pulsated off him in rippling waves. You could see it in the way he was constantly on the move and, even when he was seated, his knees were for ever jigging up and down and he was constantly gnawing at the dags of his chewed fingernails.

'So!' he said, gesturing to two other deckchairs that had been set out on the grass, 'Let's sit down. Neeraja, you couldn't bring two more Lassis? You are so very kind.'

Karen took a seat and I lowered myself into a deckchair. I was still reeling at the sight of Goldsmith; almost dumbstruck, in fact, at how this skeleton from my old life had re-appeared on the scene.

He looked prosperous and well — and, though it galls me to say it, had hardly aged a day. True, he was practically bald, but he had lost most of his hair years earlier. He wore an immaculately pressed blue linen suit, spit-polished brown brogues, and a dandyish Panama. I remember being particularly struck by the hat. It had a band in the Old Etonian colours, black with a thin stripe of light blue; entirely for my own benefit, I'm sure. Still had all his old superstitions as well, with his lucky gold cufflinks and his amber talisman already rippling through his fingers.

What a contrast he made to me, Goldsmith

the epitome of the prosperous banker, while I was a withered, shambling husk, with leathery wrinkled skin, a shock of white hair and frayed cotton shirt and trousers that wouldn't even have passed muster in a charity shop.

I stared at him for a while, aware of how I had once used to cut a dash in exactly the sort of clothes that he was wearing now. But I couldn't hold his gaze — just as a pack-dog bows its head to the Alpha-Male.

Karen, meanwhile, was quite at her ease, had taken a seat and was chatting to Goldsmith like old times.

'How are you Sir Jimmy?' she asked. She wasn't slumped back in the deckchair, but leaning forward at the edge of her seat.

'Oh do please drop the moniker,' he said, wafting the back of his hand as if the matter of his knighthood was some piffling bauble. 'I am very well, thank you Karen — fit, hale and hearty. And how are you?'

'Happy as a clam. It's a little different from NYC —'

'No traffic, no skyscrapers, no busy-bees for ever on the go.'

'But I'm kinda getting to like it. This business of just doing nothing — it grows on you.'

'And, ahh,' he paused as he wondered how to address me in the third person, 'your patient looks better. I've known him nearly all my life, Karen, and do you know that I would not recognise him from Adam. It is simply unbelievable. Not his mother, not even his own children would recognise him. The nose worked out quite well in the end — smashed it for him myself. And I daresay that not even a Harley Street surgeon could have done a better job of masking his looks. Used to be quite a handsome devil in his time . . . '

Karen smiled, preening her short brown hair and smoothing it behind her ear. She fingered her gold pendant before crossing her legs and leaning in towards Goldsmith. 'He's doing great, aren't you Jeff?'

'Yes,' I said. It was the first word I'd spoken, like some grumpy tongue-tied schoolboy who finds himself in the company of adults. My tongue roamed round my gums, working in through the gaps where once had been teeth.

'And you Karen, you're looking well. You're more than looking well, you're looking, as the French might say, *Sensass!* Love the shoes, by the way.'

Oh how my ears pricked up at that one. Love the shoes? I remembered this old Goldsmith gambit from years back. It's a particularly easy ruse to find out if your interest in a woman is reciprocated: merely tell her that you like her shoes and the reaction reveals all. Feet tucked tight underneath the chair mean, obviously, no interest; feet extended and admired means a degree of interest; and then . . .

'You like them? I only got them at the flea-market,' said Karen, stretching down to touch the looping brown sandal thongs that crisscrossed up her ankles. 'But thank you.'

'They look very comely on you, Karen.'

Neeraja bustled over with a tray from the farmhouse. She set the Lassis and a bowl of salted nuts on the table before bobbing to Goldsmith. She'd never once done that to me — but that was all part of the Goldsmith aura. He commanded subservience.

'By God, but isn't this a pleasant spot? If I'd known about it a few years ago, I might have ended up here rather than Mexico. Anyway — ' Goldsmith raised his glass in salute. 'Your good health.'

'Back at ya, Jimmy,' she replied. She'd called him by his first name. I was struck by her over-familiarity.

My gnarled fingers were trembling as I brought the glass to my lips, the Lassi ice-cold, a tart mix of salt and sour milk.

Up until now, I'd been passively acclimatising myself to Goldsmith's unusual presence, but . . .

I jolted out of my stupor. 'What are you

288

doing here?' I asked. 'Why are you here?'

Goldsmith laughed, the glass shaking in his hands. 'Hark at him, Karen! What do you think I'm doing here, Lucky? I'm here to see how you are, you old devil!'

'To see me?'

'What did you think I was here for? Come back for a tryst with Karen perhaps? Or maybe I just couldn't resist seeing another Goan sunset? No — I'm just here to see how you are, keep you out of mischief. I'm here for the sheer pleasure of your good company.' And with that, Goldsmith leaned forward and grabbed me by the knee, digging his fingers tight into my bony flesh until I winced with the pain.

He laughed and slapped me on the knee. 'Has he been behaving himself Karen?'

She laughed back — oh what a love-fest was going on between them. 'Course he has Jimmy,' she said, 'especially now that he's not quite so stuck up his Lordly ass.'

'Lordly?' Goldsmith cocked an eyebrow, his eyes not even looking at the amber egg as it slid through his fingers. 'Nice to see that all your airs and graces are gradually being pared away. And the heroin? The injections? Are they also a thing of the past?'

I was clearing my throat, but Karen answered for me. 'We have the occasional fall off the apple-cart, but — we're improving, aren't we, Jeff?'

'Yes.'

'I think that calls for a celebration! Care for a Cuban cigar, Karen? I believe you Americans are finding these quite hard to come by these days? It'll help keep the mosquitoes off.'

'Thank you, Jimmy.' She took a cigar, cupping his hand with her fingers as he lit it for her.

'And you, Lucky? No — probably best not.' The cigar was left in its case and tucked back into his breast pocket. And I remember how this one action, a little treat denied me, irked me even more than the flirty banter that had been going on between the pair of them.

'Oh — by the way! By the way! I just remembered. Aspers sends his love and, if it's not too impudent, I thought I'd take a snap, the better for him to see how you are.' And with that he pulled out a small silvery camera from his coat pocket and clicked off a couple of frames. 'Lovely! Aspers will be amused. You must be almost a grandee amongst the hippies now.'

'I don't need this.'

'Bit too much for you?'

'Please go.'

Goldsmith's cigar twirled in his fingers, the

smoke drifting straight up in the still air. 'Like to hear any news from back at the front? Your boy George has followed in your footsteps to Eton, you know — '

I held up my hand. 'Please — I don't want this. I don't want to know.'

Goldsmith pursed his lips, momentarily taken aback, his cigar hovering in mid-air. 'I — I thought you might like to hear what's happened to your family.'

'No. No, I do not. I can't ever go back and . . . It's easier not to know.'

'Fair enough. Daresay it's like with your old girlfriends. Sometimes after the split, you realise that you've made a blunder, thrown away a jewel worth more than half your tribe — and it's a lot more restful just to excise her from your mind completely rather than to dwell on what might have been.'

'Yes.'

'Fair enough. And would the matter of my own company here also now be categorised as 'undesirable'?'

'I think so, yes.'

Goldsmith smiled and pocketed his piece of amber. 'And there, Karen, we have the end, if not of the play, then certainly the act. The curtain swoops, the audience applauds and one of this drama's leading lights must take his exit, stage-left.'

He proffered his hand and I shook it — though I didn't bother to stand up.

'Goodbye Lucky. I wish you well.' Then he stooped to kiss Karen on the cheek, arm snaking round her waist. 'And as for you, Karen, I do hope that I will be able to see you later.'

I could hear him humming to himself as he sauntered down the path, his trademark cigar leaving a hazy trail of smoke behind him. The silhouette of the peaked Panama looked like nothing so much as a devil's horns.

Karen was sitting right back in her deckchair, staring up at the darkening palm-trees, the long fingers of her right hand drumming against her lips.

I slumped back into my chair, overwhelmed at what had just happened — at seeing Goldsmith again and how he'd brought back my other life. When you're gone for a long time from a country, you forget that everyone else's lives have rumbled along plenty well without you. And George, dear little George, had gone to Eton! I squeezed at the bridge of my nose, pinching hard enough to hurt. On the one hand I was fascinated, wanting to know every single detail of my three children and everything that I'd missed during the last 14 years. I wanted to see pictures, letters, drawings; I would have traded my life for a lock of hair. But it was much easier to know nothing — nothing at all about them. It was a simple matter of self-preservation. I was like a reformed addict who craves another hit. If I had but a single whiff of my old life back in England, then I'd be creating just another mountain of misery. Best to leave it all locked in its box. Best not to be reminded of what I was missing.

After a while, Karen stopped drumming her lips, as if finally she had her emotions in check and could allow herself to speak. 'You look all in,' she said.

'I am,' I said, sucking at my gnarled fingertips. 'I am that.'

'I'll see you then.'

I remember those words so well. They were the last she ever spoke to me.

⋆ ⋆ ⋆

I couldn't sleep that night. I'd always been an insomniac, but since Sandra's death the only respite has been in the heroin. And even when I did get to sleep, it would never be for more than a few minutes. Throughout the night you're waking up every 30 minutes, and then as you come to your senses, there's always this feeling of let-down. But with me, the let-down was tenfold, a hundredfold

— because in my dreams I was once again at the Clermont in Mayfair. There is a vast fire in the grand entrance hall and a girl in a satin gown takes my coat. I glide up the staircase; it's one of the most magnificent staircases you've ever seen, a full five yards away and ten yards high. Walls of green and gold, and a brace of Canalettos in the drawing room. My friends are there too — Aspers and Dominic, Stoop and that old podger Raphael. How civilised it is to be back home. Then in a snap, I wake up, blink about me and see Sandra lying on the floor.

I was never going to get any sleep. The news of George following me to Eton had been impossible to digest. Of course, now that I thought of it, it would have been perfectly natural for the boy to go there . . . but, for the first time in many years, I almost felt proud. The feeling was crushed in an instant as I realised the misery that the boy must have been through. There wouldn't have been a boy in the school that did not know that George was the very son of Britain's most notorious fugitive. It would have swept the school, and would have become one of those grim unmentionables, known and discussed by every boy in the house, but never a word of it uttered to George himself.

I'd seen a bit of it in my time at Eton, when there was a boy there, Gordon-Cumming, who was the grandson of Lieutenant Colonel Sir William Gordon-Cumming, who'd been brought low by the great Baccarat Scandal of, I guess, 1895. It was all 50 years in the past — but the Gordon-Cumming boy's career at Eton was for ever dogged by his grandfather's disgrace.[10]

How much worse it must have been for my own son.

I'd hoped for so much for George and his sisters — had wanted to give them the very best in life. But it seems that all I have lumbered them with is this God-awful millstone. And as for George ever taking the title and becoming the Eighth Earl of Lucan . . . well I fear that I have left him in a most ticklish position. Can you imagine calling up to make the restaurant booking? 'And what's the name?' the receptionist will ask, to which the dear boy replies, 'Lord Lucan'. They'd laugh out loud. It would be even worse if he were ever pulled over by the police.

Yes, I'm afraid that, despite all the glory of the six Earls Lucan before me, in one fell swoop I have contrived to wipe the slate clean. Worse than that, actually — I've snapped the slate in half, ensuring that for many generations to come, the name 'Lord

Lucan' will be met only with a snigger and a roll of the eyes.

There were already so many jokes about me. Goldsmith regaled me with the worst of them, of course he did.

I'll tell you one. Not, I can assure you, because I find it funny. But I tell it because it reveals with crystal clarity how most people think of me. Sandra's murder is now all but forgotten. Instead, mention the name Lucan, and all that is conjured up is this image, this revoltingly shallow image, of a moustachioed fop, a chinless wonder, an aristocratic buffoon, a chump, a clown, a wastrel, a damnable, risible, half-witted laughing stock.

So here it is. I hope it gives you even a tenth of the pleasure that it gave Goldsmith:

Knock knock.
Who's there?
Lucan.
Lucan who?
Look an' see what daddy's done to the nanny.

It's just unbearable.
How my ancestors must despise me.

I gave up trying to sleep and stumbled out into the drizzling darkness. I don't remember walking down the path, but I was covered in mud by the time that I reached the road. Not quite as black as the Earl of Hell's waistcoat, as I could see a glimmer from the village ahead of me, but I walked largely on instinct, feeling my way through the puddles. Did I have a syringe with me? I might have; I definitely needed something.

The village was almost asleep, everyone in their beds, save for the lone phone operator at the post office. I glimpsed him through his open front door as I walked past; he was reading a book, content enough to do his duty and keep the phone-lines open.

The street was awash with water, shimmering like a river as the rain swirled over the potholes. I was drenched. Why, I wonder, did I never think to have an umbrella during my entire time in India? It's not as if the monsoons are ever going to stop coming.

Past the café, its front locked down for the night, and over the street to Karen's block, a squat concrete blockhouse as I remember, salubrious even, as houses in the village went. It had a flat roof, with that peculiarly Indian flourish, the steel masonry rods poking up at the corners — ready to take the next floor whenever the owner felt the need to expand upwards.

There was no lock on the front door — nobody ever bothered with locks in the village — and I tapped my way up the stairs in the darkness. The sound of the drumming rain could be heard lightly through the brick walls. At the top, I felt my way in the darkness to Karen's door and knocked on it. 'Karen? Are you in? It's me.' But in answer there was only the hollow sound of the rain on the roof-top.

I knocked and knocked again before letting myself into her apartment. I would not recommend going into a friend's home uninvited; your imagination can start to play tricks and temptation is an absolute devil.

'Hello?' I called, but as I already knew, Karen was not at home. I had a little look round; observed the two half-empty whisky glasses on my balcony. So she'd been drinking with him; and now they'd gone . . .

I know — I know. I was being nothing but the most villainously tiresome dog in the manger. Karen and I were not lovers, nor were ever likely to be. But I did love her and I did feel proprietorial about her. Is it so strange to feel like that about a dear friend? Do you have to be lovers, making the beast with two backs, to feel jealous? No — indeed not, I can assure you of that. It is more than possible to feel jealous about a friend. And that's especially so if in your dark heart, you still harbour some small hope that one day, possibly, maybe, your love might be reciprocated.

But to go off with Goldsmith. Goldsmith! I don't know whether he was married at the time, but he totted up notches on a bed-post like a bee supping nectar from the field. A tryst here, a tryst there, and then he's off on to the next one, with as little concern for the consequences as a dog fouling a lamp-post.

Goldsmith! Even though I hadn't thought of the man in over a decade, all my old hate came surging back into my system. I remembered how he'd crowed at my misfortune; had delighted in pulverising my face; and for good measure had packed me off to India in that hellish freighter.

And now, to top it all, he was in the very throes of bedding my rock, my nurse, my soulmate. I was quite quivering with anger at the thought of it — and at the realisation of how utterly powerless I was to do anything about it. I could not spite him; could not seize Karen for my own; could . . . could do absolutely damn all. How I seethed, how I festered. I went out onto the balcony and poured myself a large whisky.

Still stewing with rage as I walked back home. A slight recollection of going past the post office, and an urge to call my boy George, or possibly Aspers, or God knows who. What I chiefly remember was not just the burning rage at Goldsmith, but also the most bubbling resentment against Karen herself. Caused in large part, I'm sure, by impotent anger at my own wasted life — but more often than not, the cause is an irrelevance. What matters more, much more, is how you choose to focus, to vent, that anger. Just take a look at your spouse, your partner: how often have you had a bad day at work, and yet soaked it all up just so that in the evening you can take it all out on that blameless love of your life?

* * *

When did I come round? When did I come out of it?

I have no idea.

All I can tell you is that the next thing I remember is waking up on my charpoy with a dull sense of unease; that tinkle of a memory that somehow the previous evening you disgraced yourself. You cast back, you try to remember what it is you did, how you managed to insult the host or hostess — or was it even the Gartered guest of honour? But you can only clutch at wisps of memory, as dense and intangible as morning mist. Did you really drink that much? Did you take cocaine or LSD or something else to pep you up? Is it possible? And there follows that numbing 'oh no' moment as you realise that you took at least one shot of heroin and possibly more, and if that's happened — well, anything's possible.

Neeraja had left some chapattis and lentil dhal on the table outside, along with a pitcher of water. I was so thirsty I poured it straight into my mouth, the water sloshing round my cheeks and soaking my shirt. I caught a tang of odour and sniffed it. I must have been wearing it for days. It stank of mildew.

I ate the chapatti as I walked, the crumbs dribbling from toothless lips. The storm was quite over and the trees and foliage were burnished bright, the dust tamped back into the earth where it belonged. But why do I feel so uncomfortable in my skin? Is it Goldsmith? Is it that he's come back into my life?

The village bustling with the usual shrieking children and the pigs snuffling in the drains; the man in khaki still manning his phone-lines at the post office. I glance in to the shanty café to see if Karen's in there.

One of the side-effects of heroin is that it's like a horse's blinkers. You've got no peripheral vision. You only see what's dead in front of you — and only then if you choose to see it.

So, even though the crowd was large and quite raucous, I only noticed it for the first time when I practically blundered into the mass of villagers. I tried to make my way through, but they were too thick, too clustered. I stood limply on the pavement, leaning on my stick, aware that the crowd was blocking my way but not pausing to wonder why. They seem to be surrounding a truck; it must be an official truck because it's khaki in colour. Some sort of markings on it too.

A dog is lying on the pavement. I poke my stick into its stomach and start to scratch her by the nipples. She yawls in ecstasy, unused to being cosseted by a human. I bend to scratch her behind the ear; she's got fleas. They always congregate around the ears, as that is where the fur is thinnest. One by one, I start to kill them. It's quite easy once you know how. You pulp them between your thumbnails. But you've got to do it quick, mind, or they'll have hopped onto your own hide.

I'm aware that the mood of the crowd is changing, becoming more vocal. I cock an eye to see that phalanx of policemen lined up at the back of the truck. Something, someone, is being led out of the door; it's the front door of Karen's building. Some sort of struggle, maybe some screaming. I idly look on as the truck nudges its way through the crowd.

There's still a few more fleas left on the dogs' left ear. I clip them with my thumbnails, one, two, three, quick as you like. The truck eases its way through the crowd and the driver is revving into second. I watch as it trundles past. Inside, I can see a crowd of soldiers and there's a woman too, face red with tears, hands cuffed behind her back. It's Karen. She shrieks as she catches sight of me. I don't wave or smile; I don't feel anything at all, my heart is stone. The dog barks and the caravan still moves on.

19

Oh, but he was a cunning fox.

I realised even before I'd got back to my hut that Goldsmith had done for Karen — and that he'd try and do for me too.

I learned much later that she'd been sent to jail and she may be there still, and all of it, I'm sure, was down to Goldsmith. Who else would have thought to plant the drugs in her flat — not just heroin, but cannabis, cocaine and even amphetamines — and then shop her to the police?

So Karen had been snatched from my life, just as suddenly as she'd arrived. I would have loved to have been in a fit state to fight for her, but I was not even in a fit state to visit her in prison.

Yes, Goldsmith had finished her off and I never knew why.

What I did know was that I had to leave, leave that very night. I'd been in Goldsmith's thrall for too long; and ere long I knew that his grimy fingers would be out to try and wring my own neck.

Jay and Neeraja, I'd realised, were both Goldsmith's hirelings, paid not just to look after me, but to act as my turnkeys. I don't doubt that every week they were reporting back to Goldsmith himself.

So that night I packed up the few belongings I had into an old sack and stumbled out of the farm to a waiting rickshaw who'd put me on an overnight bus out of Goa. And as for money, I had plenty of it — a whole satchel stashed full of crumpled dollars and rupee notes. It had been tucked away under my charpoy, presumably all that remained of Aspers' parting gift. I never counted it but the money never seemed to run out.

And so over the weeks, I had meandered directionless across Southern India with no thought in my head but to get away from Goa and to be rid of Goldsmith. But gradually a thought did crystallise in my mind. Why not travel to Wellington's old stamping ground at Seringapatam? It was as good as anywhere, and it certainly piqued my interest a little, so to Seringapatam I went.

I wasn't happy as such. There was always this uneasy tension lurking at the back of my head. But as I stared out over the walls and across that broad stretch of river, I was touched by its grandeur. I pictured Wellington's troops making their final assault — the screams and the savagery as those brave men stormed into the breach.

Let me tell you a little about Seringapatam. I've had it up to the gunnels with writing about my soulless life in Goa. That's what heroin does to you — sucks all the joy out of your life. And, I suppose, all the pain too. I do miss the sunsets though. I loved the sunsets, sitting on Karen's balcony and watching the palette of the sky go through its evening miracle. Strange that in 14 years there, I never once went swimming. I must have been the only foreigner in history to have spent so long in Goa and never once dipped his toe into the water.

Isn't it odd which memories stick — and which don't? I can remember nothing from the past week. I can remember precious little from the past ten years. Yet I can still recall with the utmost clarity one blissful term at Eton, when for a full summer I immersed myself in Wellington's India, circa 1800.

Seringapatam, just near Mysore in the south of India, is to many just another notch on the Duke of Wellington's baton. But seeing Seringapatam first hand was of a different category altogether. I spent two days walking the walls and examining them from every angle to find the exact position of the breach[11]. It was hard for me. I was a little stronger than I'd been during the worst of my heroin addiction, but I still couldn't manage

306

half-a-mile with my walking stick without stopping to rest.

By now I'd been gone from Goa for about six months. At first I'd been despondent that Karen was no longer in my life, but after a time I saw it as just a part of my penance. For I'd come to view the hell of my life as nothing more than just punishment. It was the price that I had to pay for the crime I had committed. I would not even allow myself the easy get-out of suicide.

So Karen, like my children, was another throbbing empty hole in my heart. I would have liked to have been with her. But I had come to accept that since she was a boon to my life then the fates had decided she could no longer be a part of it.

Goldsmith, at least, was out of the picture. It was a very small mercy, but he was out of my life. I was shot of him. Not that it made my life any more pleasant, but for a while it had felt good to know that I'd never again have to lay eyes on that grinning, jittering old goat.

If only he'd felt the same way.

★   ★   ★

I had been saving the most famous part of Seringapatam for last. It is the Water Gate, a tunnel of 50 yards or so which cuts low through the outer wall.

Wellington's men had stormed the breach and were slaughtering the garrison. With Redcoats streaming all over the fort, Seringapatam's ebullient leader, the Tippoo Sultan, was making a run for it. The Tippoo Sultan and his bodyguards raced for the only possible exit from Seringapatam, the Water Gate — and it was here in this stinking hell-hole that every man jack of them was hacked to pieces.[12]

The Water Gate, then, was the place that I was intent on visiting. If you were even remotely interested in Seringapatam as a battle-site, you couldn't not go there.

Stick in hand, I totter along beside the mud track that runs alongside the main outer wall, following the signs. It's a creepy place when you get there. Possibly it's just my warped imagination, turned mad by over a decade's worth of heroin abuse, but the gun-shots and the butchery seem so close that I only have to draw back a veil and I'd be in the thick of it. Cutlasses slashing back and forth, and salvo after salvo of rifle-fire as the Tippoo's men fall to their knees; the tunnel is so clogged with bodies as to make it all but impenetrable. Sandra's there too, of course she is.

The images are so vivid, flashing across my

eye, that I break into a trot as I splash through the mud out of the tunnel. I stand panting at the entrance, back braced against the grey wall.

Gradually in the sunlight the ghastly scene of the massacre begins to fade. As I stare back down the tunnel, all I can see now is Sandra lying in the mud, silhouetted against a circle of light at the far end.

I begin to notice a little of my surroundings. The words 'Water Gate' are written in large black letters on the wall above the entrance. Some parakeets are squabbling in the trees nearby. A beggar is squatting in the dust by the entrance, wearing a grubby white dhoti and turban. I hadn't seen him as I'd gone in.

'Namaste.' I toss him a rupee.

I haven't particularly been watching what he's doing. But as he looks at me, he gives an actual physical jerk. I can't describe it any other way. His whole body appears to shudder. You'd think he'd recognised the devil.

Maybe he had.

I look over my shoulder as I walk away. Goldsmith is rummaging through the folds of his loin cloth, staring intently.

I quit Seringapatam within the hour, so Goldsmith didn't manage to nail me there. I was pleased about that, for I did at least get the chance to visit Gawilghur. Gawilghur. It is a fort like no other fort you have ever seen before.

★ ★ ★

I travelled by taxi. It was safer than travelling by bus or train, where any number of Goldsmith's hoodlums were waiting to pounce.

Didn't I just take my time getting there, zig-zagging along the little byways. With a man like Goldsmith, you can never take too many precautions. Who knew how many people he'd have after me?

I'd sometimes go days at a time without seeing the white face of a westerner, as if I knew my adventure was coming to an end and was delaying the moment till I tackled this final jewel in Wellington's Indian crown. As we weaved up the 2,000 feet from the Deccan Plain below, the sight of it had me transfixed.[13]

I've spent the previous night in a small village on the plain and taken a taxi up after breakfast. The taxi is returning for me at dusk. They've made me up a little packet for lunch, as the fort itself is all but deserted. But nevertheless, there is still a chaistall, situated

310

just by the car-park. The man is already up and has his stove going; around the back I can see his charpoy. He sleeps there too, lives in this rickety hut — though I can't imagine he gets much business; any business. Tourists just don't go to Gawlighur. But, of all the places on earth, I wouldn't have believed that Goldsmith could have one of his agents actually waiting for me there.

The shop-owner is sitting on a stool, stirring a pot of chai, and I can smell the sweet milk and cardamom. As he stirs, he hums a tune from one of the Bollywood movies. It sounds familiar — but then they all sound the same to me.

I shamble over, poking at the dust with my stick. I'm a little fitter than I was. As fit as you could hope a one-time drug addict to be. I'm not yet a cripple.

'Namaste,' I say, cupping my hands together as I bow over them.

'Namaste,' says the man. He's in a grey shalwar chemise which is flecked and stained with milk, bits of food and doubtless other unmentionables.

He doesn't look up from his fire, continues to stir and hum. How tranquil it is on top of that hill. The smell of the tea lingers in the air as it simmers over the fire.

The tea-seller clanks with his ladle, stirs the

tea and pours it into a chipped glass cup. What a pleasure it is to see a master at his work — even something as simple as making tea. I find it utterly absorbing to watch an artist, a first-rate artist, going about his craft.

The tea-seller shuffles to his feet and brings the cup of tea to the counter. At a shop like that, you take what you're given. The man is wizened, ridges and valleys all over his face, though not necessarily with age; it's just what the sun does to you in India. As far as I can tell, he could be anything from 50 to 90.

And this is the moment that still haunts me. He sets the steaming cup of tea at the side of the stall, and for the first time looks at me, his first customer of the day.

The spasm that shot through him was startling, a great twitch that ran through his body and sent his ladle clattering to the floor.

I eye him blearily as he bends to retrieve it. He's tutting to himself, avoiding my eye.

'You all right?' I ask, handing over a 50 rupee note — a handsome amount of money for a chai-seller, probably a day's takings.

He snatches up the note and fiddles around for some change.

'That's all right,' I say. 'Keep it.'

He scoops up the money and returns to his pot, stirring and muttering to himself, but never once looking at me.

I sit on a rock, stick by my side and sip my tea. Never had it with cardamom before I went to India; I'm surprised that it's never really caught on in England. Admire the fort standing stark against the blue sky. A little belch and I return the cup. My guard's down, of course it is. I've got the world's most amazing fort to see; why should I give any mind to Goldsmith? The tea-seller is now polishing up the cups that will never be used that day. But he still doesn't look at me; his eyes are fixed at about my midriff.

As my dear old papa used to tell me, never trust a chap who won't look you in the eye.

But why should I be bothered by a tea-seller when I'm itching to tackle the fort? Dare I say, even, that I was excited, like a quivering spaniel as it longs to plunge into the covert. For the true wonder of Gawilghur is that it still retains its original breach. Most breaches have either been mended, or the entire wall has been destroyed for house-building and the like. But not Gawilghur. It's got the only breach left from the entire Napoleonic era.[14]

The sun is already high in the sky as I start to climb the wall. It's a little overgrown at the top, but in every other respect the breach is exactly as it was 200 years ago. Using both hands, I climb a few yards up and pause to catch my breath and survey the scene. It's hard to believe that Redcoats were once swarming up this very spot, clutching onto the actual rocks that I am touching now. What bliss to have the fort to myself. My energy is not what it was, my muscles have wasted away to nothing, but I'm enjoying the physical activity. I think I am. I drink some water before making the final assault.

The breach itself is laced with bushes and shrubs. I'm standing on the exact spot where the Redcoats would have been fighting like demons. These battle-sites have an especial grandeur about them, almost a romance, as you think of the men that lost their lives there. Not like that at the time though. No — at the time, it would have been every bit as bloody and ferocious as hand-to-hand fighting always is, and to hell with trying to behave like a gentleman, just stab the man in the goolies and trample him underfoot.

I rest up at the top of the breach, sitting easily on the wall, so still that soon the geckos and the lizards have taken me for part of the scenery. I give one a poke and it scuttles away. How times have changed. Once I'd have killed it without a thought.

Wellington must have stood at the exact spot where I sit now, sipping from his brandy flask as he surveys the inner fort that still lies ahead of him — because what is apparent is that Gawilghur's reputation has not in any way been exaggerated. I have my first glimpse of the inner citadel, which lies about half-a-mile away on the other side of a deep ravine. From all sides, it seems that the fort is surrounded by sheer precipices. Off in the distance lies the endless brown desert of the Deccan Plain.

I pick my way down the ravine, feeling like a little old man, pausing frequently to catch my breath. It is a strange Communion with the past. You cannot help but imagine all the scores of men who died there.

Out of the sunshine and into the shade as I start the walk up the little winding track that hangs on the side of a precipice and leads up to the Gawilghur gate-house. It's a narrow L-shaped passage with high walls on either side and five thick gates one after the next.[15]

Through the shade of the gatehouse, and then I'm blinking like a mole as I walk out into the blazing sunshine. The inner fort is massive — at least a square mile, far bigger than I'd dreamed of; squint my eyes and I can picture the stampede as 4,000 Mahratta troops were put to the sword. How they must have run, dropping over the walls and scurrying from the fort like rats from a sinking ship.

I stop for some lunch by the lake,

meditating on Gawilghur's tragic end as I chew on cold rice and a samosa. From the day it was captured, Gawilghur was abandoned to its fate. Not a thing of it, from the walls to the once great palace buildings, has been touched since.

I slump in the shade of a banyan tree and fall asleep exactly where I lie. When I wake up, the shadows are already getting long.

My eye is caught by a small, squat summer-house that stands on the other side of the algae-green reservoir. It's not much to look at, overgrown with vines and black with age. Immediately I realise what I'm staring at. I hadn't realised it was so close. I make my way towards it through the scrub, drawn like a moth to the flame. Tendrils of weed twitch at my stick, but apart from the click of the geckos, there is not a sound to be heard.

As I walk inside that cool summer-house, the goose-bumps tingle on my arms. I know all about it — have known all about its horrid history since my schooldays.

I'd experienced it before at the Inquisition Table in Goa's museum. But nothing as severe as this. It's far more than just a dream. The stuff is happening right in front of my very eyes. I have become a part of it.

The walls of the summer-house are lit with candles, and as I walk through I see that every room is furnished in the height of luxury, thick carpets underfoot, plumped up cushions on the floor, low tables with the most exquisite mother-of-pearl inlay. A decanter lies shattered in the fireplace, its contents still dribbling red down the wall. In the air, I can smell jasmine mixed with the heady punch of incense.

From the next room, I can hear the sounds of women and children whimpering with terror. The door is ajar and I slip through to see a vision of such perfect horror that the hairs prick at the nape of my neck. My hand flies to my mouth as I let out an involuntary squeal of fright.

The Killadar of Gawilghur, James Goldsmith, is killing the last of his family rather than let them be captured by the Redcoats. Women lie prostrate on the floor, some of them dead and some of them in the very act of dying, spasming like stricken beasts, eyes rolling back into their sockets and with the foam-flecked poison still on their lips.

Goldsmith is muttering to himself, half-crazy with grief, as he forces his son to drink from a silver goblet. The boy squirms his head from side to side, until Goldsmith pins him to the ground, forces his mouth open with thick bejewelled fingers and pours the poison straight down his throat. The boy coughs and splutters, his whole body twitching from side to side as the sad father looks on. A woman in the corner is crying over a dead baby that lies in her lap. She pulls a black dagger from its scabbard and without flinching drives it into her breast; dead before she's even hit the floor.

The shouting and the gunfire from outside is louder now as the Redcoats turn from murder to looting and pillage. Goldsmith stands in the midst of his dead family, all of them sprawled about the carpet and the pillows in the most shocking tableau of death. Sandra is there too, lying in a pool of blood between two of the children. She is with me everywhere now; she is my albatross.

As I stand in a corner of the room, Goldsmith gives a start as he catches sight of me for the first time and beckons me over. I step towards him, stepping over the slight bodies of the children. I know already what is required of me and kneel at his feet for absolution.

I can see the steeliness ebb from his face to be replaced by the most uncomprehending horror. I open my mouth to share his last Communion, for we the pair of us are united in wickedness, and through our actions and our selfishness we have come to destroy the very things that we love the most. With a caress to my cheek, he pours the wine into my mouth. I swallow two mouthfuls of the bitter gall, my body wracked with instantaneous pain. My vision begins to fade, but my last glimpse is of Sandra. She nods as I slip into oblivion.

It's quite dark when I wake up, the candles all burned out. I stumble to my feet, hunting for my stick; all about me are bodies, I can feel them with my feet. Terror is bubbling up in me to the point that I'm on the brink of madness. My visions and my nightmares have, in the past, been cured by sleep. But this is the first time that it's all still with me, just as vivid as when I first saw it. I can even still smell the jasmine mixed now with the bloody taint of the slaughterhouse.

As fast as I can, I flee from that summer-house. Outside, there's a full moon and the stink of gun smoke lingers in the air. Bodies, hundreds of mutilated bodies lie all about me, floating in the reservoir and sprawled in the parched earth. I screw my eyes up tight, slap myself hard in the face, but it changes nothing. Goldsmith is screaming out orders, bellowing at the chai-seller and the Seringapatam beggar. Even Karen is there, kukri in hand, hunting me down to slash my throat.

Oh but it was terrifying. They were hunting

for me everywhere, Goldsmith bellowing like a madman as he marshalled his troops. I crawled through some undergrowth and could hear Goldsmith screaming behind me, 'He's here! He's here! I see him!' I wormed my way into a pile of dead bodies that had been tossed by the side of a well, the blood sticky as it smeared my face. In the flicker of the firelight, I watch as Goldsmith's bayonet scythes up and down. He's even got his cigar stuck in that fat, leering face, jab-jab with the bayonet as the smoke trails into the sky. Eventually the hue and cry moves on. I pull myself from the pile as cold hands cling to me. I can still hear the shrieks as I find my way to the outer wall, duck through a gate and tumble down a goat-track onto the Deccan plain far below.

20

It made no odds. Goldsmith did for me in the end. I know that I have my demons, for ever chattering away dark thoughts at the back of my mind. But even demons can sometimes be right.

It happened like this. I was in a town. Don't ask me which one — I have no idea. All I know that it was as far away from Gawilghur as I could get. I don't know where I was, I don't know where I was living; and I don't know how Goldsmith's men had followed me there.

Ideally in a memoir, you go sequentially from one place to the next and from one event to the next. For me, that is not altogether possible. I don't know how it comes across to the reader. But I only ever intended this to be a record of what happened to the world's most wanted fugitive.

And this is how it ended.

I was living in a hostel by now. It might even have been a commune. Whoever was living with me, I was not having any interaction with them.

I know how useless this all sounds. I can't remember the town, the place, the people — or what I was doing there.

So what can I remember?

I can remember one night, about four years ago, coming out for the evening. I was going off for a wander through the littered park. Maybe I'd stop off for tea somewhere.

It's night-time, no street-lights, nothing for light but the moon, which is so bright that it casts shadows on the ground. Like a fox coming out of its hole, I stand at the edge of the pavement sniffing the wind. And just as I normally do, I cross over the road to the park; it's a park that has so much trash strewn around it that it could pass for a rubbish-tip. Cross the road without a problem, there's not a car moving. It's not a tarmac road, but dusty — I can recall that because I can remember its taste. Dust is quite different from tarmac. It cakes the tongue and dries out the back of your throat.

I'm tottering between two cars when a man comes up to me. He stands on the pavement and asks, 'What is time?'

What is time? One of the great philosophical questions of our age — from an Indian beggar. I didn't recognise the man then, but I believe he was the same beggar that I'd seen outside the Water Gate at Seringapatam.

I opened my hands out. I hadn't worn a watch in years. 'I'm sorry.'

As I recall what happens next, the scene moves to the wholly surreal. It lasted barely a few seconds, but in my memory it spans an age. A car starts up to the side of me. I'm aware of the roar of the exhaust spuming out over my ankles. The beggar in front, the philosopher who wants to know the meaning of time, has leapt back onto the pavement.

I see the car's reversing lights flick on, am bathed in their white glow. I squeal even before I've been hit. The car, an old Humber, is revved once and sweeps back. I'm trapped, sandwiched between two bumpers.

I'm screaming but I feel no pain. The horrific sight of my legs sandwiched between two sets of bumpers. It's caught me at exactly knee height. My knees appear to have imploded, I can hear the crack of the bone long before I feel the pain. Both knees shattered beyond repair. The reversing car stops. Its bumper is the only thing that is keeping me upright. With a flick of the wheel it pulls out into the night. Goldsmith leans out of the driver's window, and gives me a thumbs-up. Over the wind, I can hear the sound of his crazy laughter. I watch as the Humber's red lights disappear down the dusty road and, like an axed tree, slowly topple to the ground. Nothing I can do to prevent myself pitching head first into the dirt. I'll always remember the taste of the dirt. My tongue lolls out of my mouth, touching the ground, and I don't even have the strength to slip it back into my mouth. At first I'm in shock. The pain, the unremitting pain, kicks in much later.

And that is how I became a double amputee. Both legs chopped off a few inches above the knee. I've been wheelchairbound ever since.

* * *

I've been in this hospital in Lucknow for four years. It was a year or so before Goldsmith started to visit and shortly after that I learned that I was HIV Positive. Goldsmith again — no doubt about it. I saw him bribe one of the nurses to make the injection.

I had it coming, I suppose. Can't really complain. I've lost everything I had, lost my children, my reputation and now I've also lost what little health I possessed. Still, I accept that it is all a part of my dues.

I spend most of my days in a whitewashed barrack-room that I share with 26 other men. Many of them are missing limbs. Most of them are — like me — a little crazy. I can hear them gibbering into the night, muttering to themselves in their madness. It gets worse during the full moons. I wonder why that is. I've always heard that the full moon brings out the madness in people, but I don't know why. But it's true. The screaming is always worse during a full moon.

There are a couple of lines of Kipling above the wall — the same two lines that I've seen many times above the portals of the All England Lawn Tennis Club at Wimbledon. I've even seen them in a pub in Bridport. But in India, these two lines from 'If' have taken on such power that they've become almost a national motto, and are to be seen in scores of schools up and down the country: 'If you can meet with triumph and disaster — and treat those two impostors just the same.'

They're two lines I've known all my life — known them so well that I've hardly bothered to think of their import. But of late, they've had a much greater resonance for me. I stare at the lines for hours on end and perhaps I have finally learned to treat those two impostors just the same: with, that is, the most complete indifference.

Sometimes I go out into the yard. What can I tell you about it? It's a dusty parade ground of a yard, surrounded by walls. I don't think there are any plants. Just the brown-red dust.

It sometimes squeaks under the wheels of my chair. Lots of dead people too — sepoys for the most part, sprawled dead around the compound. Sometimes there are the cannons, with the shattered limbs of the mutineers still strapped to the gun barrels. Nurses wandering around, tending the sick.

There's one nurse, the loveliest smile, who usually looks after me. She's called Priti, Priti by name, Priti by nature, and she changes my sheets, helps me with my food. I like it best when she takes me outside.

I only have the one visitor. He pops over intermittently. I never have any notice of his arrival. I wake up and he'll be sitting there by the bed, puffing on his cigar and playing with his piece of amber. He was here just this morning in fact.

We're like old friends now. There are many minutes of silence, but they are not uncomfortable.

'Hello Lucky,' he says as he notices my eyes flicker open.

'Hello Jimmy.'

'How are you feeling today?'

'Not too bad thanks.' I don't hold a grudge against Jimmy anymore. I see him as an instrument of divine justice, come down to pay me in kind for Sandra's death. Got me hooked on heroin; blew Karen out of the picture; did for my legs — oh, and the Aids too. Pretty comprehensive demolition job, when you think about it.

Jimmy leaned back against the wall, oblivious to all the other wretches in the room. He was dressed immaculately, cream suit and a light blue shirt that matched his eyes — it was all for me, I'm sure of that. Wearing his Old Etonian tie too, just for a change. With cigar in hand, he seems to find a certain tranquillity with me. He'd normally sit next to me, so that we were both looking out of the window towards the parade ground.

'Can I do anything for you Lucky?' he asks. 'Do you need anything?'

'No, I'm fine thanks, Jimmy.'

'You only have to ask.'

'Thank you.'

I don't know why it cropped up then — what made me say it. It had been an accepted part of my life for so long that it was just a given — like, say, having a disability since birth.

'Actually, you know Jimmy, there is one thing. What was it? What turned you against me?'

His face was so expressive at that moment, mouth turning down in a show of monumental distaste. 'How do you mean Lucky?'

I pulled myself up a little further on the pillow. I can see the slaughtered sepoys better from here.

'I don't fault you for it. I know that you were just doing what you had to do — the drugs, Karen, the rest of it. I know that now. But was there any special reason for it?'

'What *are* you on about?'

'I have it!' All of a sudden it came back to me. 'It was that race at Lewes when you won the triple. You were grandstanding to the crowds and I called you a vulgar bloody Jew. I can still recall the look of hatred that flashed over your face.'

'Are you mad?' He turned to me now. Getting a bit of a paunch in his old age. He'd always loved his food. 'Were you even at the Lewes races?'

'I was there.'

'Well — ' He exhaled cigar smoke in twin jets through his nostrils. 'I have absolutely no recollection of it.'

Suddenly I was becoming extremely agitated. 'Why did you do it then? Why did you put me through all this? Why?'

'Put you through what, exactly?'

I'd been nursing my grievances so long that they had become a catechism: 'There was the boat, first of all, that hell-hole boat when you and your man Hammel introduced me to heroin. Had me addicted for over 15 years. And then when I found a way out, when I found Karen, you had those drugs planted in her rooms and had her arrested.' I break off, wracked by a fit of coughing. I don't have the strength to wipe away the phlegm that showers onto the sheet. It calms. 'And even after I'd tried to get away from you, you had your men hunt me down. It was you who broke my knee-caps, infected me with Aids. All I want to know is why?'

'Mad. Quite mad.' Jimmy inspected the end of his cigar.

'You can't deny it. You can't possibly deny it.'

He inspected his cigar again, hitched up his trousers, and leaned on his knees, his face so close to mine that I could see the red veins creeping over the side of his nose. 'You won't believe me Lucky — in fact you'll probably forget it all in a few minutes. But this, for what it's worth, is my take on what's happened to you since Sandra's death. You were not, as you would like to imagine, introduced to heroin on your passage out of England — by me or by anyone else. As far as I know that all passed fairly uneventfully. And I don't know of any man called Hammel.'

'You lie.'

'I don't, as a matter of fact, but seeing as

my take is so very different from your own, I can see that it must be easier to think that. No, I think it was you yourself who got hooked on heroin when you joined that hippie commune adjacent to Anjuna beach. Became their number one dealer, by all accounts. Certainly made you a lot of money out of it — '

'But it was you who fixed me up on that farm with Neeraja and Jay.'

'Absolutely. You were nearly dead. So I fixed you up in a small place with Neeraja, tried to wean you off — '

My mouth was champing up and down, I so wanted to speak. 'Lies! Such damnable lies!'

Jimmy switched the cigar to the side of his mouth. 'Do you want to hear what you want to hear, or do you want me to tell you what I think? You were in such a bad way with Neeraja that eventually I hired Karen to look after you — '

'You hired Karen? But we met by accident in a café!'

'Indeed? Is that what you think? I'd guess she was with you for about three years or so — '

'Oh — how you lie!' I could feel the tears stinging at my eyes and slipping down my cheeks. 'How you lie! And you deny planting drugs in her rooms?'

'Lucky! My dear Lucky! Just try and control yourself. I don't know who planted those drugs in Karen's store-cupboard, but if I had to guess, I would say it was you, doubtless done in a fit of pique — '

'You are vile! How can you say that?' I would have smacked him in the face if I'd had the strength.

'It's unpalatable, but there it is. You may not remember it, but you don't remember anything, do you Lucky?'

I howled with rage. 'Now you're going to say it wasn't you who knee-capped me in the Humber? Who had me infected with Aids?'

'Mad,' he said, quite casual as he let his cigar fall to the floor and ground it underfoot. 'You're quite mad.'

'You don't deny it. You can't deny it.'

'Oh I do,' he said. 'From what the doctors tell me, I believe your legs were amputated after some drug-related infection. And Aids? You seriously think I had you infected with Aids? Don't be ridiculous. You probably picked it up in the same way that every other drug-user on earth contracts Aids — by sharing an infected needle.' He made to get up.

'But — ' It was as if he'd whipped away the foundations of my very existence.

'Look Lucky, I can't really be bothered with this. You'll probably have forgotten it all in an hour anyway.' He flicks at some ash on his leg.

'Really?' I say. 'Is this really true? It's not some new way to spite me? I just want to know the truth.'

Jimmy sucked as he bit on his lower lip. He was ready to go — but all of a sudden leaned back in his chair. 'It is as true as I sit here.'

Was it? Could it? Little glimmers of memory. Impossible to explain how, but it felt right. My hands flew up to my face, as one distinct memory seared out of the murk.

Karen and I had had a row, a furious row. It was soon after Jimmy had come over to see us. They'd had a drink together. So angry that I was determined to teach her a lesson. I leave my cache of drugs in her store-room and go to the post office. I call the police and simply tell them that Karen's a drug-dealer. Easy as that. Return home to my shack. By the time I arrive at Karen's, she's already been arrested. Had I really sat there, absent-mindedly scratching a dog's ear, as she'd been driven away in a police truck? But, like so much of my life, my vile behaviour has already been erased from my mind. Blame Jimmy instead. Always blame Jimmy. So much easier to blame Jimmy than to blame myself.

'Godfathers!' I say, digging the heels of my hands into my eye-sockets. Another shard of memory cuts through the gloom. I can see myself stabbing more heroin into an artery and the grotesque infections spreading up my legs, mottling the skin and turning it a swollen purple.

I gnaw at my fingernails, trying to blot out the horror of what I had done. Had there ever been a Hammel who'd got me hooked on heroin? Had there?

When I lifted my hands from my eyes, my face was numb and wet with tears. Goldsmith was still there. He was patiently smoking another cigar, glazed eyes staring out of the window.

'I'm sorry,' I said.

He puffs. He's learned to blow smoke rings now. 'That's all right. It's been difficult for you.'

'But — but you've been so kind to me. And I always thought the very worst of you.' I fumbled for his hand. 'I apologise.'

He patted my hand. 'That's all right Lucky.'

He puffed — and he puffed, and the light outside began to fade until the red tip of his cigar glowed in the darkness.

'Actually,' he said, 'I have an apology of my own to make.'

'You have? What do you need to apologise for?'

He squirmed in his chair. 'I feel . . . I have felt partially responsible for your predicament in the first place.'

'You? What have got to do with Sandra's death? You had nothing to do with it.'

'I didn't . . . and I did. After considerable reflection, I think it was the last resort of a truly desperate man. It was never just about Veronica. You were practically bankrupt. It was a last roll of the dice.'

'I — I don't understand.'

'It's like this.' Goldsmith stared dead ahead of him, for once unable to look me in the eye. 'We cheated. We cheated at cards.'

'We?'

'Aspers and I. He started up the Clermont with a view to stripping any rich young pullet who came along — and you were one of those young pullets. It was nothing personal. In fact by the end, you'd become one of Aspers' closest friends. But at the start, I'm afraid, we just wanted your money.'

'No — '

'I'm afraid yes. Most often we'd use a marked pack, usually the ones with flowers on, little lines at the side to indicate the card's suit and rank. Used them mostly for poker.

Anyone playing Texas Hold 'Em was going to get — '

'Crucified.'

'Yes.' He became almost chatty now. 'It was one of the great advantages of having such a select clientele. They were richer and they were thicker and they were certainly less suspicious; it wouldn't have occurred to them that the very owner of the casino would be playing with a marked deck. But let in one of those young spunks from America and they'd have spotted the marked cards in an instant.'

My arms slump at my sides. Of course. Of course. I'd known full well that Aspinall had cheated the bookies blind whenever he could. And so, by natural extension, he'd rook his club-members too. So many things started to make sense. I remembered the time we'd been playing Texas Hold 'Em, and how Aspinall had told me that I was beat even before the last card was drawn.

And how, after he'd sold the Clermont, he'd handed me over a sheaf of my uncashed cheques.

And kept me on at the Clermont as a hireling house-player, paying me pocket-money and using my peerage to lure in more of the suckers.

And — of course — the way that time and again Aspinall had staved off near-bankruptcy with yet another miraculous win at the card-tables. There was only one way on earth that he could ever have maintained that sort of winning streak at the poker-table.

And how, after squandering each fortune, he'd just create another casino for the suckers with, for good measure, a bust of the biggest sucker of them all, Lord Lucan, in pride of place in the dining room.

Such a deflating moment in my life to realise that even my Pole Star, my stalwart, was as much of a shyster as the rest of them.

But the more you knew of the man, the more believable it became. Right from the first, Aspinall had had nothing but contempt for the bulk of humanity. He certainly hadn't baulked at cheating the bookies — and if cheating the upper-classes at cards helped pay for the upkeep of his two vast menageries, then so be it.[16]

The clincher came as I recalled my last ride up to Felixstowe docks with Aspinall. I think he'd been on the verge of confessing then. But he didn't, and I'm not surprised as he'd behaved like a heel and he knew it.

I sighed and clicked my tongue. All the stuffing had gone out of me.

'Well — ' But there was nothing more to say. What do you say after something like that?

Goldsmith's cigar was out and he was playing with his amber. It ran over his knuckles and through his fingers, as obedient as a trained mouse. 'I'm sorry,' he said — and with that, he left. He never turns back and as I look after his receding figure, for the first time I do not feel hatred or bitterness, but just this overwhelming fatigue and a longing to be back in England.

It would be spring there now, the daffodils in full bloom. What I would give to be able to walk again on English soil.

But one thought troubles me. Would Sandra be able to come too? She is with me always now and I would miss her if she could not return with me to England.

The wounded sepoys are quieter tonight, though I think a few of them are actually dead. The smell of rotting flesh is rank and I can hear the odd crackle of gunfire from the mutineers outside. Yesterday we had a cannonball come clean through the window. It took a man's head off. I don't talk to many of the men. They're from the ranks, for the most part. Precious few of the officers are in a fit state for conversation. It rained this afternoon. The ward is deliciously cool.

Priti is doing the evening rounds, closing the shutters one by one. There is such a quiet harmony about this moment in the day. It is so ordered, so regular. You could time her almost to the minute. She closes the shutters along one wall and then does all the shutters on the other side. Each shutter makes an identical sound as it is closed. First there is the clap as the two wooden boards come together and five seconds later there is the click as Priti slots the bar into place. I don't know why I like the sound of the shutters so much. Perhaps I have now just come to associate the noise with Priti, moving efficiently down the ward in her trim white uniform.

She stands at my bedside, stretching up on tip-toes to reach the handle.

My eyes follow her. 'Hello Priti.'

She smiles at me. Did I mention she has a lovely smile?

I smile back. Not a very nice smile these days, I'm sure, not nearly as nice as it was when I once used to have all my teeth. 'Did you know I'm Lord Lucan?'

Priti does not reply, but instead lightly strokes the top of my head. Such an affectionate girl. But I do hope she hasn't messed up my hair. I like a short back and sides, with a knife-edge parting and a slight cow-lick tousling over my forehead.

'Could you call the British embassy, dear? I think I'm ready to go home now. Just tell them you've got Lord Lucan here. They'll know all about me, I'm sure they will. Yes — can you remember that? I used to sit in the House of Lords, you know. I am . . . ' I touch at the clipped moustache on my upper lip, my fingers luxuriating in the smoothness of my clean-shaven cheeks. 'I am the Seventh Earl of Lucan.'

Priti is still smiling. She looks all about her to check that the ward is in order. 'Of course you are,' she says, and with a wave of her fingers she is gone.

Notes

1. It was Lord Lucan's great-great-grandfather, George Charles, who was held responsible for that notorious military blunder the Charge of the Light Brigade. The Third Earl of Lucan was the commander of the Cavalry Division in 1854, and it was him who gave the order to attack the Russian Guns during the Battle of Balaclava. Undoubtedly there was some confusion as to what the Cavalry was supposed to be doing. The Earl of Lucan had received some scrawled orders from the Commander-in-Chief, Lord Raglan which did not make clear where the charge was to be directed. But ultimately it was Lucan who issued the order, 'Forward, the Light Brigade!' and in consequence it is him who has been blamed for the disaster. There have been many other fiascos in British military history, but thanks to the poetry of Lord Tennyson, the Charge of the Light Brigade remains one of the most infamous.

2. Sandra Rivett, 29, was a bubbly redhead who'd been working as Lady Lucan's nanny for just over two months. Estranged from her

husband Roger Rivett, Sandra was a one-time hairdresser who got her job with the Lucans through an agency. Although she had no nursing qualifications as such, Sandra was by all accounts a good-natured cheery worker who adored the children.

3. John Aspinall staged a memorable coup at Wincanton race-course in 1955 which netted a staggering six-figure win for him and his cronies. At the time, Aspinall's friend Gerry Albertini owned Simon de Montfort, which was a horse with a nationwide reputation as a long-distance hurdler. Simon had already won its first race by 15 lengths at odds of 6 to 1, and for its next outing, the bookies were much warier. But Aspinall had picked his course precisely, for Wincanton was one of the few tracks with no phone through to the starting price offices up in London.

On the day, Aspinall and Albertini arrived at the course in a chauffeur-driven Rolls Royce, with Aspinall decked out in all his finery complete with beaver-collar overcoat and a fabulous orchid. The uniformed chauffeur was instructed to have the car at the exit and with the engine running.

As the horses were led out for the third race, Simon de Montfort opened at the miserable odds of 13–8 on. But Aspinall and Albertini wagered hundreds of pounds on the second favourite. By the start of the race, Simon de Montfort was being quoted at 9-4 against. Simon duly romped home — and Aspinall and Albertini lost their bets on the second favourite. But unbeknownst to the bookies, a huge collection of friends from all over the UK had been backing Simon de Montfort at the course Starting Price. Aspinall himself had risked everything on the horse, pawning and borrowing money from wherever he could get it.

4. The Lucan crest was of two chained wolves on their hind legs guarding a shield and a coronet. The family motto is 'Spes Mea Christus', 'In Christ lies my hope'. Some believe that the wolves — snarling, with mouths open and tongues lolling out — uncannily reflect the notorious temper of several of the Earls Lucan.

5. Lord Lucan is, perhaps surprisingly, quoting from *Song of Myself* by Walt Whitman (1819–1892). One wonders at what stage in his life Lucan took to reading the works of one of America's great romantic poets. Is it too fanciful to believe that Lucan may have chanced upon Whitman during his sojourn in Aspinall's bunker?

6. Goldsmith had staked £10 on a three horse accumulator on Bartisan, Your Fancy and Merry Dance. All three came in to net the 16-year-old tycoon around £8,000. John Aspinall later gave Goldsmith a solid gold box with the names of the three winning horses etched inside.

7. Ginette Lery was Goldsmith's secretary when she was a pretty, blonde 18-year-old — three years his junior. She became his second wife after Isabel Patino.

8. Lucan spent his two years national service with the elite Coldstream Guards in Germany. His father George had been a distinguished Guards officer in World War II and had won the Military Cross. Lucan appears to have spent most of his army career on the slopes of the Swiss Alps or gambling with his fellow officers. The high-point of his military career came after he was selected for the Army bobsleigh team.

9. Charles James Fox (1749–1805) was a fat Falstaff of a man who gambled his way through two immense fortunes. The first time, when Fox was 25, his father Lord Holland paid off his colossal debts of £140,000. Some 20 years later, Fox had been

bankrupted by his gambling again — and this time was bailed out by his political friends.

He was a wonderful orator and is believed to have been a lover of Georgiana, the Duchess of Devonshire. He is buried in Westminster Abbey alongside his great political rival William Pitt.

A friend, Samuel Rogers, recalled: 'Fox (in his early days I mean . . .) led such a life! Lord Tankerville assured me that he has played cards at Brookes's from ten o'clock at night till near six o'clock the next afternoon, a waiter standing by to tell them whose deal it was, they being too sleepy to know.'

10.   Lieutenant Colonel Sir William Gordon-Cumming was in 1890 accused of cheating at cards with Bertie, the Prince of Wales. During a number of late-night baccarat sessions at Tranby Croft, near Doncaster, Sir William was spotted increasing the size of his bet after the play had already started. He was confronted by some of the other players and tried to hush things up by agreeing in writing never to play cards again — but within weeks, the scandal was the talk of London. Sir William subsequently issued a writ for slander and the Prince of Wales had the ignominy of

appearing in the witness box. Sir William lost the case and was never seen in London Society again.

11. Seringapatam had been a thorn in Britain's side for some years. Throughout the end of the 18th Century, Napoleon had been trying to get a toe-hold in Asia, and had been stirring up the Mahrattas in Southern India.

Wellington was the man who was despatched to India to bring the Mahrattas to heel. He had some memorable victories and one of the biggest was at Seringapatam. It was the last stronghold of the Tippoo Sultan of Mysore, who was one of the more colourful characters in Indian history. The Tippoo Sultan loved his tigers and had his thousands of troops decked out in special tiger-stripe uniforms.

His passion for tigers even extended to creating a life-size mechanical tiger that was in the very act of devouring a Redcoat. The tiger could not only champ down on the Sepoy's neck, but also emitted a very life-like roar from an organ inside its belly. The tiger was periodically brought out to entertain the troops. It was part of the many spoils of war that Wellington brought back home from India and can be seen today in London's Victoria and Albert museum.

12. As the Tippoo Sultan fled Seringapatam, he was wearing dozens of jewels. The largest of them all, in his turban, was a ruby the size of a pigeon's egg. When Wellington came to inspect the Tippoo Sultan's corpse, there was not a jewel left on him.

13. Gawilghur Fort lies at the top of a mountain that seems to jut straight out of the Deccan Plain. It gives every impression of being impregnable. The Mahrattas certainly thought so. It was so taken for granted that Gawilghur could never be captured that no-one had ever bothered to attack the fort.

But when Wellington came along in 1803, he set about besieging Gawilghur with all his customary zeal. Within the week the castle was captured, the Mahrattas beaten, and Wellington was finally fit to lead his troops on the Continent.

14. A breach was made by peppering a small section of the walls with 18-pound cannonballs until eventually it collapsed in a roar of dust and rubble. This fallen masonry then provided a ladder of sorts, and a group of hero Redcoats known as 'The Forlorn Hope' would be sent in to storm the breach. Almost all of these volunteers were destined to die in the

attack, but any Sergeant or Commissioned Officer who lived to tell the tale was rewarded with instant promotion.

15. The Gawilghur gates have long since rotted away, but the zig-zag entrance way to Gawilghur was a perfect-killing ground for the Mahrattas. The milling Redcoats were trapped between the two sheer walls, while from up above the Mahratta troops fired down a hail of bullets. Scores of troops died trying to storm the gates, including their leader Lieutenant-Colonel William Kenny.

Wellington's full-frontal assault had practically stalled, but the Redcoats were saved by a typical piece of British audacity. Captain Archibald Campbell, leading the Scotch Brigade, blind-sided the Mahratta troops by scaling near-vertical cliffs. Campbell had just enough men to hack his way through to the gatehouse and open up the fortress from the inside.

16. That John Aspinall was a cheat and a rogue became common knowledge after he died of cancer in 2000. Aspinall used his casinos and his top-notch connections to fleece many of Britain's leading aristocrats. Huge estates would be lost in a single evening — for, as Aspinall once remarked, 'It's very

easy to steal from your friends.'

Aspinall's card-sharping started off with a relatively simple trick. At the end of an evening's gambling, he would offer to go 'Doubles or Quits' on the single cut of a card — and would then immediately cut the Ace. The trick, which could be mastered in minutes, depended on having one card which had a slightly different shape to the rest.

From these small beginnings, Aspinall moved onto cheating on a grand scale, even going into league with a group of London mobsters. Aspinall provided the wealthy clientele, while the mobsters provided a coterie of highly skilled card-sharps.

One of Aspinall's most lucrative scams was 'The Big Edge', whereby cards were put through a small press that looked like a miniature clothes mangle. This card crimping enabled the house card-sharps to know the rough value of a card, and was invaluable in games such as chemin de fer.

All of these scams — and more — are detailed in Douglas Thompson's definitive book *The Hustlers*.